DARKNESS WATCHING

THE DARKWORLD SERIES: BOOK ONE

EMMA L. ADAMS

A dungeon horrible, on all sides round,
      As one great furnace flamed; yet from those flames
      No light; but rather darkness visible
      Served only to discover sights of woe…
   Milton, *Paradise Lost*, The First Book, 61-64

1

DOOMSDAY

The demons first appeared on the day everyone said the world would end. Maybe someone meant that to be ironic. Perhaps.

I never found out.

"Hey, Ash, you know there's supposed to be a zombie apocalypse today?" My best friend Cara gestured towards a clove of garlic she'd pinned to her jacket, hoping it would fend off potential supernatural threats. I decided not to mention it would only help with vampires, not zombies. Besides, I doubted a single clove of garlic would be much help in surviving the End of Days.

I had my own demons to contend with.

As people sloped into the assembly hall for the annual Careers Talk, I skimmed through my notes yet again, hoping in vain something would stick. For me, Doomsday was a more fitting title for the following day, the day of my interview at my top-choice university. *Hell would be a better fate.*

"Come on, Cara," I said. "How many times is the world supposed to have ended now?"

"I'm not taking any chances," said Cara, pointing at her headband that was threaded with garlic and perched on top of her purple-highlighted hair.

"You'll have a nightmare getting the smell out," I told her. "Aren't you supposed to be going out tonight?"

"Some guys like the smell of garlic," said Cara, although she looked doubtful. "Hmm. Maybe it's a bit much."

"Well, it better not be Armageddon, seeing as it's my interview tomorrow," I said. "Not to mention we're in a careers assembly."

Cara laughed. "I don't know why I bothered coming, anyway. I've heard all this before." She leaned back in her seat, hands clasped behind her head.

"Yeah," I said. "Besides, if we're going to die, I'd rather not be in this hellhole when it happens."

"You know, Ash," said Cara, squinting at me—the fluorescent lights in the hall gleamed far too bright for a Monday morning—"*you* look like a walking zombie. When did you last get a decent night's sleep?"

"Define 'decent?'" I said, a touch too flippantly.

"More than an hour. And not in the middle of school."

Guilty.

Her dark eyes—outlined in purple, in blatant defiance of the school's no-makeup rule—saw past my carefully constructed mask.

I blinked at her concerned face. "Um… a couple of days ago? I can't sleep, or I forget everything I know about Milton."

"Jesus, girl." Cara shook her head. "Who gives a crap about Milton, really? You're going way over the top about this."

"Hello?" I said, indicating the garlic-headband.

Cara swatted at me with a rolled-up brochure for Edinburgh University, *her* top university of choice—which had offered her a place that very morning.

"Very funny," she said. "Seriously, though. Sleep is more important. You don't want to be passing out in the interview."

Naturally, now she'd suggested it, I imagined doing exactly that. Groaning, I buried my head in my notes. "Not listening," I muttered.

Definitely mature enough to get a place at Oxford. Yep.

"Ash, you'll be fine. You're a genius."

I shook my head. "No, I'm not."

I felt more like an imposter. I might be able to memorise past papers, but that didn't make me an intellectual. I'd rather play Mario Kart than read Wordsworth. Not exactly something I wanted to bring up at the interview—but if scores of disastrous interviews for part-time jobs had proven anything, it was that I'd be lucky to remember my own name. But this time, I couldn't afford to screw up. *This has to be worth it. Somehow.*

Most of the time, I felt helpless, as if I teetered on the edge of a cliff and couldn't do a damn thing to stop myself from falling.

Mr. Darton, our ever-clueless head of sixth form, began his customary mutter into the microphone. Always the same speech: *We had only one chance. This would affect the rest of our lives.* Like any of us needed to hear that right now.

I tucked an errant dark brown curl behind my ear and tried to focus on the passage from *Paradise Lost* I wanted to memorise. *It'll serve them right if I drop out and run away to Australia.* And not for the first time, I imagined doing it. I felt like a cage surrounded me on all sides—a glass case no one could see but me.

Focus, for God's sake, snapped a voice in my head, jolting me back to reality.

The words jumped around the page, like they possessed a will of their own. How would I ever remember any of this when staring down at a table of distinguished literary professors? In the mock interview with my personal tutor, I'd lost my head and babbled about a book I'd never even read for a good ten minutes. Panic obliterated all intelligent thought.

At that moment, the lights in the hall went out, as did the projector, plunging us into dusty darkness.

Cara let out a shriek. "It's happening!" she wailed, clutching at her garlic clove, which, not being securely fastened to her jacket, fell to the floor. With another shriek, she dove underneath her seat to retrieve it.

"Calm down! It's just a power cut." I furrowed my brow, trying to read my notes. Everyone talked amongst themselves as Mr. Darton struggled to turn on the projector. I couldn't see any lights outside in the corridor, either. *A whole school power-cut. Great.* And why did I feel so cold?

A stream of faint winter sunlight shone through gaps in the blinds that covered the windows, lighting the myriad dust motes in the air. I sighed and tilted my head back, rubbing my temples to keep my eyes from closing. I could feel a headache building.

A pair of eyes appeared amongst the rafters and stared right into mine. They gleamed violet, with vertically slit pupils like a cat's. They blinked, looking down at the confusion below. Then they locked back onto me.

Once, when I'd cut my finger on a kitchen knife, I'd gone into shock and nearly passed out. My vision turned blue around the edges, and everything acquired an odd, blurred quality. Right now, looking into those sinister, alien eyes, I felt exactly the same.

I'm going mad. It's not real. Cara's superstitions have made me start seeing things. That, or the lack of sleep.

I'd stopped breathing. Sweat beaded on my forehead, but, at the same time, I felt cold all over, cold as the frigid December air outside. As if fresh snow covered me, slowly seeping into my skin through my hoodie and jeans. Like the kind of paralysing chill I associated with that moment in horror stories when someone saw a ghost.

Was it a ghost? I'd always thought ghosts would look... human. If I believed in them—which, up until now, I thought I didn't.

All around me, the other students chatted and laughed. No one screamed, cried, or ran for the doors. It was as though my own private bubble of horror enclosed me like the cage I'd envisioned earlier. Trapped.

I heard a faint whisper, almost like a breath: *"Ash."*

I would have screamed if I'd been capable of making a sound. I knew beyond doubt that those eyes and that voice belonged to something that wasn't human.

The eyes blinked again, becoming part of the shadow once more as the hall lights came back on. For a moment, a swathe of blackness remained in the rafters, like a single patch of mist left behind after a fog has lifted. Not a single speck of dust disturbed the area around it.

Then it vanished.

I still couldn't breathe. Those cold eyes remained

imprinted on the insides of my eyelids—light purple, glowing, and staring.

Staring at me.

My vision blurred. The world went hazy. When I came to, Mr. Darton's low mutter into the microphone had started up again—not that anyone listened. Whispers filled the air, ordinary conversations. People talked about their plans for the weekend, not about monsters with violet eyes or piercing, unnatural coldness. The more studious skimmed through revision notes. I looked down and saw mine scattered all over the floor. I didn't remember dropping them. I didn't remember anything but those awful eyes.

I've cracked. Did staring violet eyes fall under the category of stress-induced hallucinations?

Cara tried to laugh off her moment of panic.

"I didn't *really* think it was the end of the world," she insisted. "God, how lame."

The end of the world. Maybe that was what I'd seen. A sign.

Ridiculous.

The rest of the day passed in a blur. My parents tiptoed around me like I was a bomb about to go off, thinking I wanted to do my final interview preparations alone. Like I could concentrate.

My nerves over the interview seemed laughable by comparison to the lingering nausea in my stomach. This fear went bone-deep, like I'd tapped into some kind of primitive instinct against an unseen danger. The fear of a child lost in the woods, seeing monsters in every shadow. Fear of the unknown, not of muggers or rapists or murderers. Unlike Cara, I didn't have the slightest belief in the supernatural. At least, not until now.

the window behind my desk. *Cara has a point. I do look like a zombie.* Or a ghost, watching through shadowed eyes…

IT STARTED out as yet another exam dream. I sat in the school hall, looking at an unfamiliar paper as all the other students wrote with frantic enthusiasm, pens racing down the page.

I didn't revise this at all. Panic rose within me. I twisted in my seat, glancing from side to side. Everyone else scribbled away. The clock ticked, seconds passing. Minutes. *Shit.*

I felt a familiar surge of dizziness, the same chill as during the assembly. My breath stuck in my throat, and my heart pounded. I stared at the back of the seat in front of me, which wavered and shimmered before my eyes, turning to blackness.

From out of the darkness, a face grinned at me. Sharp teeth formed a malevolent smile. Violet eyes stared at me, unblinking. I could see nothing but the smoke, which obscured everything before my eyes.

My chair tipped of its own accord. In slow motion, it leaned back and teetered for a moment. The demon grinned as I sat there, powerless to move. The panic inside my chest spilled over, and I tried to cry out. But I couldn't move my jaw, couldn't open my mouth. I was frozen to the seat as it hit the floor with a soundless thud.

I couldn't move.

I couldn't feel anything.

And I couldn't speak, couldn't scream.

I lay on my back, and, around me, people continued to write, like robots programmed to scribble endless pages. No one spared a glance for me. I was trapped on the floor, and no one even knew.

The eyes blinked then vanished.

My heart restarted with a jolt, hammering in my ears. I fought to escape the trap. My eyes felt as though something heavy weighed them shut, but I managed to force my eyelids apart. The sight of my digital alarm clock greeted me, sideways. I'd fallen asleep at my desk, my head resting on my laptop, the cold edge digging into my face.

I tried to lift my head, but I couldn't. I tried to open my mouth, but my jaw remained locked.

Impossible. I'm awake.

Not a muscle in my body responded to my pleas. I couldn't feel my hands, but I knew my right one rested under my chin, where I'd used it as a pillow. I couldn't feel my face, either. I'd lost all feeling in my entire body, as if an invisible presence lay on top of me, pinning me down.

I tried to cry out, but not a sound escaped.

Move! I thought, the weight continuing to press on me. One of those web sites I'd browsed had mentioned poltergeists that sat on people in the middle of the night, leaving them unable to move. Terror washed over me, cold and merciless.

Every short breath hurt my chest. *Let me go. Please. Please! I'll do anything. Just let me move.*

"*Anything, Ashlyn?*"

That voice. *There's no one there,* logic screamed at me, but it went against all the evidence of my senses. A thousand invisible hands gripped me all over, numbing all sensation. At the edges of my vision, I thought I saw dark shapes, but there were no eyes, no mouth to match the voice.

What do you want from me?

It didn't respond.

Are you a demon?

"*Yes, Ashlyn.*"

Finally, the messages between my brain and nerves

seemed to hit home, and I managed to raise my head, to lift my arm an inch. Slowly, I regained feeling in my limbs. I shifted, twitched my hands, my feet.

There was nothing in the room. No demons, no staring eyes.

But even then, I knew they watched me.

That day, the fear began.

2

GROWING COLD

ne month later

"Ash! You've got something in the post!"

Groaning, I pulled the covers up over my head. *Not now. Any time but now.* I knew the rejection letter was coming, but that didn't make it any easier to deal with.

"Ash!"

I sighed and pushed the covers back. Thirty days to the day of that disastrous interview—and here was my future, signed and stamped in a shiny envelope. I went through the motions of pulling on clothes and getting ready for school, dragging it out as long as possible. When I stepped out of my room, Mum hovered near the door.

"Later," I told her when she showed me the *three* large envelopes, all addressed to Miss Ashlyn Temple. "Why three? Isn't one rejection letter enough?"

"It might not be a rejection," Mum said, trying to console me. "This one's from your Aunt Eve, anyway."

"But it's not my birthday," I said. "She's either five months too late or seven too early. Can I go to school now?"

"I'm not stopping you." Mum stepped back into the kitchen, a touch of reproach on her face.

"Right. Sorry."

I *was* sorry, but God, was it hard pretending to be a normal daughter when "normal" had disappeared down the rabbit hole over a month ago. Besides, I ranked today's exam next to the Oxford interview in the enjoyment factor category. At least I had Milton down now. *No light, only darkness visible.* How appropriate.

I saw another one on the way to school—a dark space, as I called them now. A square-ish patch, no more than half a metre either way but enough to block my path. And within, a pair of eyes glinted. Purple, as usual. Bigger than human eyes, narrowed, with vertical pupils like a cat's—and watching me.

Closing my eyes, I tried to ignore the prickling fear. I shivered, feeling the customary coldness intensify as it always did when I saw a dark space. Sometimes I felt like I could never get warm again. *Nothing's going to stop me from passing this exam. Not even evil manifestations of my subconscious.*

Drawing in a deep breath, I opened my eyes and veered across the road like I'd intended to walk that way all along. Ignoring them didn't help, but it made me feel a little better. Talking back to one would bring me to a whole new level of crazy.

A car horn beeped as I narrowly avoided walking right into it. The driver swore colourfully, jolting me back to reality. My feet hit the pavement on the other side. I resisted the urge to turn back and check if the dark space was still there. Maybe my luck would hold, and they'd stay out of the exam hall.

Yeah, right.

Mum and Dad wanted to send me to therapy. Like that would help. *I think I have a problem. Is this a demon I see before me?* Not that they knew about the demons, of course—they thought my nightmares and constant jumpiness were caused by stress.

If only it was that simple.

I didn't see anything else unusual on the last of the walk to school. I glanced at the clock as I entered the school building. One hour to fit in some last-minute revision in the library.

To my relief, the library was open. My phone buzzed as I made my way between the shelves. Cara had sent me a text saying she'd join me in a bit. "It's bad luck to revise on the day of an exam," she scolded me.

I like to think I've already used up my bad luck quota for today. First a rejection, then the demon. Now all I needed was—

I swore under my breath. There was a dark space in the library, too, right over the table where I'd intended to sit. A piece of reality cut away, and within it... those eyes.

"Hello, Ashlyn."

"What?" I dropped my revision notes. *Did that demon say hello?* I put my trembling hands behind my back.

Aside from that first dream, none of the demons had ever said a word to me. This one watched me with its sinister violet eyes. Coldness seeped into me, and my heart pounded against my ears.

Great. Now I've insulted it. Or something. I don't have time for this.

Fear warred with common sense, and common sense won. I scrambled to pick up my notes so I could get the hell out of there. Why did they have to keep watching me like that?

Thud. A book fell off the shelf, narrowly missing my foot.

"What the hell?"

Another book fell with a *thud*, a hefty volume of the Oxford English Dictionary. This time, I couldn't put it down to the library's old shelves falling apart.

Somehow, the demon could move things. Since when did they make threats?

I picked up the dictionary, weighing it in my hands. A reckless daring sprang up in me, and, before my nerve left, I lobbed the book at the demon. The dictionary sailed right through the dark space, as if it wasn't there.

I turned tail and ran, nearly colliding with a group of Year Eights, who all sidestepped sharpish without looking at me. *Don't look at the crazy girl.* Expecting missiles to crash into my head at any moment, I ran without paying much heed to where I was going and nearly collided with Cara. I skidded to a halt.

"Jesus, Ash!" A pair of exam invigilators glared at both of us. "What's the rush? You aren't late," she said. "You're ridiculously early, actually."

"Nothing," I said, glancing up and down the corridor. "No tables in there. Come on, let's wait by the hall."

I steered her away, again having to duck out of the way of a group of students. Why did people walk towards me as if I wasn't there? Sometimes, I felt like I was invisible to everyone except Cara. Even the teachers often forgot my name. *So much for being the amazing Oxford candidate.*

No dark spaces waited for us around the assembly hall this time. Mr. Darton stood, barring the door to make sure no one sneaked in to get a look at the exam papers. I raced through quotations in my head, praying to the gods of exams that the right question would come up so I could give a coherent answer. Avoiding a panic attack would be nice, too.

Breathe. I didn't want a repeat of the interview. The word *fiasco* came to mind when I thought of the day after the demons came, when I'd sat before the stereotypically grey-bearded, distinguished professor of literature and, intelligently, said, "I like, um, reading." Thirty minutes of nonsensical rambling later, I'd left the interview room and walked right through a dark space, densely black yet somehow transparent. I could see through to the other side where people walked along the corridor, talking, oblivious to the darkness.

Only I could see it. And before I could even gather my thoughts, a pair of violet eyes stared at me from the blackness. I'd cracked, screamed my head off, and ran.

"I think you made quite an impression," said Mum that day, after I'd calmed down. "Not everyone runs screaming out of their interview."

"Ha-freaking-ha," I said. Hardly the impression I'd hoped for——Ash the lunatic as opposed to Ash the knowledgeable literary critic.

I stared at my exam paper, unable to tear my mind away from that horrendous day. The fear never really went away. Everywhere—at school, in the street, at the shops—dark shapes would appear, and I'd be greeted by cold, violet eyes and a chill that went bone-deep. Slowly, I'd adjusted to their staring eyes, like people who went on those reality TV shows and adjusted to cameras being there all the time, and I'd learned to glare back. It was that or let them intimidate me into never leaving the house, never seeing Cara or going to school, or, well, *living.* They'd never tried to harm me. Hell, I didn't even know if they could. But if I'd learned anything from the few horror films I'd seen, there should be *some* way to get the demons to leave me alone. Until today they'd never really *done* anything. Just watched me, constantly.

I was so tired of jumping at shadows.

The clock's ticking brought me back to the present. *Shit, how do I have only five minutes left?* I pushed my hand to its limits, pen racing down the page, but the stubborn hand of the clock ticked on relentlessly. *I wish it would stop,* I thought, realising that I'd misjudged the timing and still hadn't written a conclusion.

The clock's hand stopped. *Holy shit. Did I do that? Impossible.*

I glanced at the other students scribbling away, the invigilators prowling between the desks.

The old school's clock broke down; that was all. People couldn't stop clocks.

People couldn't.

I looked around frantically, searching for any sign of a demon. Any shadow could be a dark space. This hall was where it had all started.

Don't be an idiot. Finish your answer! I turned my gaze back to the page and scribbled the end to my final paragraph, splattering ink everywhere. Hell, would anyone even be able to read this?

A minute later, Mr. Darton said to our deputy head, Mrs. Cathers, "I make it half past the hour. Do you?"

The two exchanged whispers. I heard the clock mentioned. *I can't have done that. There's only so much weird I can see in one day.*

But I still had to open my rejection letters.

∼

THE OLD NERVES tightened around me like a vice as I hurried home after dismissal, Cara rushing to keep up.

"Text me the news!" she panted, as we went our separate ways. The cold air blew my hair sideways, but it was refreshing after that stuffy exam hall. What would happen in summer, when I wanted to go out walking? Would I ever be able to do anything again without fearing the presence of a demon?

"Will do," I said to Cara, who waved goodbye.

No divine force intervened to stop me finding the three ominously thick envelopes on the kitchen table when I let myself into the house. I took in a breath, my heart fluttering, and picked the most official-looking one.

Come on, you threw a dictionary at a demon today. Just open it.

I slid the wad of paper out of the envelope. One word leapt out: *unfortunately*. It never meant good news. I threw it aside, tears stinging my eyes. *Dammit.* I slumped down on the living room sofa, feeling hollow inside.

Worst. Day. Ever.

And yet... what had I expected? Oxford didn't want lunatics who saw demons.

"Great," I muttered to myself. "Suppose I'll have to go with my backup plan and join the circus."

"Maybe if we plead for mitigating circumstances?" said Mum, coming into the room and retrieving the letter.

"For what?" I wiped my eyes. "Being hopeless at interviews? They'll never buy it."

I could plead insanity, I suppose. Or stress. I'd give a psychiatrist a field day if I told them about the dictionary incident.

"Some people get nervous at interviews. It isn't your fault." Mum came and put an arm around me. My parents weren't usually the affectionate sort, so I responded, curling up to her like a kid. Mum patted my head. Neither of my parents really knew how to deal with a highly-strung teenager—or any teenager at all, really. I mostly got to do my own thing, once I'd proven I could be trusted not to trash the house when my parents went away for the weekend.

It wasn't the independence I wanted, going away to university. It wasn't even academics. Just the thought that there might be something else out there. A different life.

Stop that. Thinking about what I'd lost my chance at made me even more depressed.

Ever since the demon, I'd never really believed that I'd have a shot at normality—sooner or later, I'd slip up and get carted away to a madhouse. But now my chance of going elsewhere had bit the dust. Staying at home for another year while Cara and everyone I knew went off to university would send what was left of my sanity spiralling within a week. Could I really handle reapplying? Did it matter, if the demons followed me wherever I went?

Dad came into the room.

"Sorry, kiddo," he said, when he saw my face. "You missed this one," he added, picking up one of the other envelopes, which I'd left on the coffee table. "I think it's from… Where else did you apply?"

"Good question." I took the paper from him and unfolded it. "Blackstone University… where's that?"

"Don't ask me. You're the one who applied there," said Mum, reading over my shoulder.

"I suppose I did," I said, uncertainly. It didn't seem right that I had no recollection.

Wait. Back when I'd been in Crazy Ash mode, pulling all-nighters for the Oxford admissions exam, I'd picked my alternatives at random in one energy-drink-fuelled overnight study session. Not my best idea. Funny how fear made you forget things. Even oh-so-slightly-important considerations like where I was going to spend the next three years of my life.

"What does the letter say?" said Dad.

My gaze travelled down the page. I blinked at the paper, convinced I'd misread it. "They've apparently offered me a place." *What?*

"But that's great news!" Mum swept us into a group hug as I blinked again, disbelieving. "Ash, you're freezing. Are you coming down with a cold?"

"Never mind that now," I said, staring at the page. "I'm going to uni?"

I looked over the page again, letting each word sink in. *Conditional offer.* It was real.

Except I had no clue where the place was, let alone if it was somewhere I'd actually like to live for the next three years.

"Their website was a bit dodgy," I remembered. Cara, insisting that Blackstone wasn't a real place, demanded to see it, only for the website—then the computer—to crash. This was typical in our school computer room, so I'd forgotten all about it until now.

I grabbed my phone to text Cara—maybe she remembered why the course had caught my eye.

"Ash, don't forget Aunt Eve's parcel," said Mum, pressing it into my hand.

I'd forgotten about the third envelope. A letter, in her illegible looped handwriting, came with a smaller package. I broke the Sellotape and found a pendant inset with a purple stone. Amethyst.

"What's this for?"

Mum read the letter, frowning. "Early eighteenth birthday present. Make sure you write back and thank her."

"I don't know her address," I said. "I thought she moved to Canada. Five years ago, wasn't it?"

"You're right." Mum's frown deepened. "I'm sure I must have it somewhere… put that somewhere safe, Ash. You don't want to lose it. Let's see how it looks on you." She pushed back my curly hair and lowered the necklace over my head. "Lovely."

The gleaming stone did look beautiful, though its purple glint reminded me a little too much of demon eyes. I picked up the letter, trying to decipher it. The first part told me that the pendant was a family heirloom, but the ink ran through the middle section, making it unreadable.

I made out two lines, which made little sense. "Your mind is your own. Guard your heart well." *She does have a weird way of putting things,* I thought, recalling her strange tales of monsters in the woods when I'd spent summers at her Windermere cottage, before she'd moved.

A shiver danced over my skin, and I turned back to the brochure that had come with my university offer. Blackstone. Small village, middle of nowhere. Sounded like my kind of place—as long as it had an internet connection, of course.

My phone buzzed with Cara's response. "Yes! Told you so. Do they have a visit day?"

"Yeah, on Saturday," I typed, checking the date on the brochure. *Good timing.* Almost spooky. But hey, I wasn't complaining. I had to at least give this a go.

"Awesome," came Cara's response. "I'm coming with you. And you, missy, are going to celebrate."

I smiled at my phone. I could always count on Cara. By the weekend, she'd probably know all Blackstone's local ghost legends.

I wished I could leave my own ghosts behind. Or, demons.

I always saw more demons where there were more people—crowded shopping centres were the worst. In the middle of nowhere, though, it might be different. I *needed* a new start. I needed it badly. Anything had to be better than monotony and constant fear, exams and eyes staring from the darkness.

Mum skimmed through the brochure. "This looks perfect! You'd have on-campus accommodation. Not too far from Preston, either."

"We have to celebrate! How about we go out for a meal tonight, Ash?" Dad asked.

"I have to pass my exams before we can really celebrate," I reminded him. "It's only a conditional offer. Besides, I've not even seen the place yet."

"I'm sure you'll have done fine," Mum said. "This course sounds up your alley. That Milton book you're always carrying?"

I groaned. "No more Milton," I said. "I'm going there on Saturday with Cara, anyway. Visit day."

"You are?" said Mum.

"Our little girl's all grown up," said Dad, grinning.

"Are you *sure* you don't have a cold?" said Mum, touching my forehead.

"I'm *fine*," I said, wriggling away.

It didn't seem worth explaining, again, that I'd stopped noticing it altogether. I always felt as though there was a constant draft against my skin, but on the inside, not outside.

There has to be a rational explanation. But I knew the demons made it cold. It always got worse around them.

Please. Don't let them ruin this.

～

EARLY SATURDAY MORNING, Cara and I took the train to Preston, where a bus service ran to the university.

"Bloody hell, it's freezing," she yelped as we jumped off the bus into a gale. The tour began at the student village, which was helpfully signposted.

"Pretty, though," I said, indicating the collection of sandy-coloured houses surrounded by patches of vivid green grass. A field doubled as a car park, with a path down the centre leading into the nearby woods to the other side—the village, also named Blackstone—and through the woodland that surrounded the campus on all sides.

Blackstone University was about as isolated as you could get, a small campus tucked away on a hillside. As Cara put it, "The only inhabitants are students and sheep." Several of the latter watched us from the field, woollen coats fluffed up against the wind.

The tour took us on a winding loop around campus, and I felt my smile growing bigger by the minute. *Perfect.* Cara shook her head when I grinned at the reading list.

"You're crazy, Ash."

"You know you love me for it."

"Damn straight. Enjoy your Milton. But"—she tapped me on the nose—"*no stressing*. Got it?"

"Yes, mother," I said with another grin. I could trust Cara to stand by me. She might be going to Edinburgh, but neither of us were about to let distance ruin thirteen years of friendship.

"And another thing," she added. "You have to actually go out there and talk to people. You know… *people* people? Not fictional ones?"

I stuck my tongue out at her.

"Come on, Ash, if you're staying in student halls, you can't hide in your room playing *World of Warcraft*."

"I'm not planning on going out and getting shitfaced every night, either."

"Me neither. Not like my sister. She tells me she woke up next to a new guy every week and has a collection of road signs mounted on her wall."

"Seriously?" I said. "Definitely not the life for me. Quiet literary discussions are more my thing."

"You're like an old woman, Ash. What about dating?"

Good question. *I see demons* wasn't exactly a good way to start a relationship.

"If I meet a guy who loves Milton, it's clearly meant to be," I said. "Well, I guess that'd be more like a threesome." Truthfully, I never wanted to read *Paradise Lost* again, but my comment made Cara shriek with laughter.

"You're a riot," she said.

"Don't forget about me," I half-joked. I'd never been Miss Popularity—less so since I'd ostracised myself—but I found it hard to ignore the way people sidestepped me in the corridors like I'd contracted leprosy or walked into me like I was invisible. Even Alice and Sammy, my friends from primary school, pretended I didn't exist. I knew I looked the same, outwardly at least. I kept the insanity all on the inside. People changed, I guessed.

Still, Cara and I had shared memories of the awkwardness of surviving seven years at an all-girls' school. Nothing could take that away, not even a two-hundred-mile separation.

"This place is like the set for a bad horror movie," said Cara later as we waited for the bus back, this time from Blackstone village itself. "You're asking for an encounter with a serial killer. Hannibal Lecter probably hangs out at the Coach and Horses." She referred to the local pub frequented by students. Personally, I thought it quite cosy.

"It'd be pretty handy living on a hill if there's a zombie invasion," I said.

"True. But that forest is damn creepy. When I come and visit, we should film our own version of *The Blair Witch Project.*"

I smiled at the memory of that time we'd taken her dad's camera when we were twelve and run around the wild part of the local park, looking for a scare. No ghosts or monsters had materialised, but we'd had to flee from irate neighbours after accidentally trespassing in someone's garden. Good times.

"I don't think it's creepy," I said. "At least, this is like the safest university campus, ever. No risk of serial killers here. There were people walking on the woodland path."

"Yeah, well, I wouldn't want to go in there at night. Honestly, Ash, you get freaked out over exams, and yet you look at that forest and don't think 'I'm going to get murdered?'"

"Pretty much." Hey, I never said I had my priorities in order.

"You're dead sure you want to come here?"

"I think so." I nodded, smiling. "Yeah."

One thing swayed it for me. All day, I didn't see a single demon.

3

FOLLOWED

Ten Months Later

"*Ashlyn.*"

I shuddered at the voice, which felt like cold breath on the back of my neck, and twisted around, even though I knew there was nothing behind me. There couldn't be, because I was hemmed into the back seat of the car by stacks of bags and boxes, and my feet were pinned to the floor. The claustrophobia didn't help.

Breathe. It can't hurt you.

But not knowing *where* the demon's voice had come from made the situation worse. My throat went tight; I couldn't swallow, much less speak. My heart drummed frantically, and blue began to inch around the edges of my vision. *For God's sake, not here.* It wouldn't be a shining start to my future if I passed out before I even reached the university.

Breathe. Concentrate on something else.

I kept my eyes on the car in front, which, like ours, sagged under the weight of bags and boxes. A girl sat in the back seat, pinned on either side by luggage. I could make out a cloud of dark red hair behind a pile of books, which looked in danger of spilling everywhere.

By the roadside, a patch of air shimmered, like a heat haze, a distortion in the world. Blink once, and it looked normal. Blink twice, and a black void appeared, a patch cut away from reality. And within it, a pair of eyes gleamed at me through the dark fog.

Even after almost a year, seeing one of those creatures still elicited the same physical response, teasing the hairs on my arms up, making my skin prickle all over. Everywhere I went – except inside my house, that is. Odd, because they had no physical substance, if the OED experiment proved anything. I assumed they could materialise anywhere at all. They appeared inside the school building all the time.

Sometimes I spoke to them, like a five-year-old conversing with imaginary friends. Insulting them brought no satisfaction. It was like swearing at my laptop when it stalled. But doing that now would push me over into crazy-land again.

Anger rose in me. I directed my thoughts at the creature, along with my fiercest glare: *Why do you bastards keep trying to ruin my life?*

The thing just grinned at me, impossibly white teeth gleaming in a half-invisible mouth.

But the girl in the car in front shifted in her seat. She pushed aside a pile of bags, twisting around in her seat. Looked in the direction of the void. Then she looked at me. Right at me. As if she *knew.*

The traffic started moving, and she was gone.

So was the black void.

Breathe.

The car rattled along the country road as we drove between rolling green hills, jolting me out of my seat every few seconds. My new iPhone—an unexpectedly extravagant birthday present from my parents—buzzed every few minutes with updates from Cara, who'd departed to Edinburgh the week before and seemed to have discovered every haunted establishment already.

I wished ghost stories were the worst of my problems.

Relax, I told myself sternly in Cara's voice.

On cue, Cara texted me, "Serial killers always target small towns! Don't get murdered!"

I rolled my eyes. I'd already survived eighteen years in the Manchester suburbs, where stabbings made the headlines every day; I highly doubted a serial killer would pick this insignificant little village as a target.

It was threats of the non-human variety that weighed on my mind.

By the time we began the slow climb through the hills towards the university, a fine drizzle surrounded the car in a cloud and turned the countryside into a blur of green. But then I spotted a familiar sign: *Blackstone University: Student Village.* I knew from my last visit that the village was a collection of fifty or so sandy-coloured houses, four stories each, containing two flats per floor, each for six students.

"Hi!" squeaked a voice. A pink face underneath an umbrella greeted us with a wide smile. "The car park's this way!"

The girl directed us to an expanse of grass behind the student halls. Dad parked the car next to a flashy-looking motorbike.

"I'm Danielle, your Student Rep. I'll show you to your new room," said the girl.

My hand shook as I opened the car door, but I managed to stumble out, ducking my head against the rain. My feet skidded in the wet grass as we crossed the field to the buildings. The air smelled clean here, untainted by urban life. I pushed the image of the demon from my mind. *New start. Got it.*

Danielle led me to my new home on the ground floor of House 12. I tried my best to remember the number. I'd rather avoid the embarrassment of walking into the wrong flat.

"Right, here are your keys." Danielle handed a bundle of them to me. "Here's your welcome pack, and if you have any questions, don't hesitate to ask!"

A fob attached to the bundle opened the door to the house. Blue carpets and beige-painted walls gave it a cosy feel. It all looked brand-new. I remembered then that student village had been built only ten years ago, quelling Cara's claim that an old university meant a troupe of ghosts would haunt my house. Mum, Dad, and I glanced around the entryway in silence. I think the moment hit us all at once: *I'm moving out.* A mixture of excitement and nervousness made my pulse race.

I entered Flat 1 to the left and nearly tripped over a pile of bags scattered throughout the hallway. A pile of motorcycle manuals wedged one door open; another wore a sign that said: *Abandon hope, all ye who enter here.* I smiled at that. A quote from Dante—surely that was a sign of another eccentric.

I unlocked Room 3. The smooth, polished, wooden door squeaked as I turned the key and let myself into my new room.

Two hours and many trips to the car later, I surveyed the room, pleased. With Mum and Dad's help, I'd arranged my books on the shelves—one shelf for course books, one for my favourites—and I'd set up my new printer on the large desk next to the television and my PlayStation. The blank notice board now bore a collage of photos: Cara and me throughout our teenage years, and a postcard from her trip to Australia. Mum and Dad had given me several pictures from our family photo albums, too. The wardrobe accommodated far more clothes than I owned. I tested the brand-new mattress. Not lumpy at all. Best of all, the window overlooked the field, with enough space to sit in the windowsill and read.

"Ash," said Mum, hugging me. "We're going to miss you. The house will be so quiet without you there."

"Are you saying I'm loud?" I said, with a smile. I wasn't great with goodbyes, and it was weird to think that I wouldn't come home to Mum's cooking every day or wake to Dad's classical music collection.

Dad pulled me into a one-armed hug. "Keep yourself safe, kiddo."

"I'll be fine," I said again, even though my new room and the five unknown flatmates made me feel like a four-year-old about to start school for the first time. "Honest."

If only I could convince myself.

Mum gave me a final hug. "Have fun! I'll call you soon!"

"Sure," I said. "See you in a few weeks."

"Bye!" my parents called to me as they left the flat, leaving me alone. I watched from the window as they walked to the car, a lump in my throat.

Right. I could handle this. At home, I tended to play up the "weird loner" angle, if just to avoid awkward questions when people my age found out I had nothing in common with them. But hey, maybe I'd luck out and find myself in a flat of closet nerds. It wasn't as though I didn't want to make friends.

Here, maybe, things might be different. It would be my first shot at living independently, but it comforted me to know that, in this aspect at least, everyone else started in the same position.

I changed out of my crumpled, damp clothes into a comfy hoodie and jeans, tugging a brush through my tangled dark-brown hair. I checked my jewellery box, where I'd tucked away Aunt Eve's pendant. It winked at me. I shivered again. Winter came early up here. I hated the cold almost as much as I hated demons. *They'd better stay away from here.* Things *would* be different. I was done being afraid, done hiding in fictional worlds, playing video games, and reading books. Cara was right. It was time to stop living anyone's life except mine. Time to start living my own.

Someone knocked on the door. I took a deep breath and opened it.

"Hi!" Danielle's smiling face appeared in the doorway. "We're having a meeting in the kitchen, to get to know each other."

"Sure." I followed her out into the corridor, where another girl had come out of her room. Her red hair was a splash of colour against the pale wallpaper, and she gave me a friendly smile, which I returned.

"That's five of you," said Danielle. "One more." She banged on the door bearing the Dante quotation, which opened a crack.

"Go away," said the occupant. Through the gap, I could see a pair of grey eyes narrowed at Danielle.

"Go. Away,' he repeated. "I'm not interested in getting to know any of you."

And his door shut with a *snap*.

That's friendly, I thought. *Now there's a lesson in how to alienate your flatmates on the first day.*

Danielle tossed her hair back, unperturbed. "Come on, then!" she said to me and the other girl.

"Jesus," said the redheaded girl. "What's his problem?"

"No idea," I said, following Danielle. "Guess he's our resident nutcase?"

"Unless he's pissed because he thought he was coming to Hogwarts."

I laughed, and, typically, almost tripped on the threshold to the kitchen. The three people sitting at the table looked up at that moment—two guys and a girl. I joined them in a vacant seat, hoping they'd think my flushed face was my natural colour. Like I'd be that lucky. Still, better to be known as the klutz than as the freak who saw demons.

The redheaded girl took a seat next to me. On her other side, a sandy-haired guy shorter than me sipped from a can of beer. The other girl sat opposite me, looking shyly at the rest of us from beneath her round glasses, whilst picking at her nails. The other guy had dark hair and wore an odd, stiff-looking shirt.

"Anyone want to break the ice?" said Danielle. "Tell me your name, where you're from, and one aim for this year. It can be anything you like. This is your chance to do something you've always wanted to do."

"Does sleeping with all the girls on the swim team count?" asked the sandy-haired guy, with a smirk at Danielle. The redheaded girl gave him a disgusted look and inched her chair away from him.

"If the swim team has a thing for trolls," she said.

The guy nearly dropped his beer can, while the rest of us tried and failed not to laugh.

"Um…back to the topic," said Danielle, after attempting to turn her giggling fit into a coughing fit. "Who wants to introduce themselves first?"

The red-haired girl grinned, and said, "Hey, I'm Alex. I'm from Kendal, and I'm studying English Literature. My goal for the year is to learn to shoot a bow and arrow. Oh, and to climb the highest mountain in England." She turned to the sandy-haired guy. "Your turn. Wow us."

"Huh." He glared at her, but Alex didn't look remotely intimidated. Shrugging, he tilted back in his seat. "I'm Pete, and I'm studying Mechanics. Oh, and for you lucky ladies' information, my number's 07936453751." He winked at Danielle.

Is he being serious?

Danielle giggled. "You can save that for later. You next." She pointed at me. I blinked, momentarily forgetting my own name. *Idiot.*

"I'm Ashlyn. Usually people call me Ash. I'm studying English Literature, too. Um, and my goal for the year is…" *To escape the demons. To have a normal life. A new start.* "Um, I guess I kind of wanted to figure out who I am."

Instantly, a flush crept up my face. Ugh. That had to be the lamest thing I'd ever said. I clamped my mouth shut before I embarrassed myself even more.

Alex nodded. "That sounds better than my goal."

"It's the point of university," said Danielle, smiling. "Self-discovery. What's your name?" She directed her question at the other girl.

"Um, hey. I'm Sarah. I'm doing English, too. And my goal is, um, well, I'd like to sing karaoke someday." She gave a nervous cough. Alex smiled at her.

"Hi, I'm David," said the boy in black. "I'm from Oxford, doing Literature and Politics. And, well, I want to join the debating club this year." He paused like he expected someone to laugh. Well, it was hardly lamer than what I'd come out with.

"Cool!" Danielle beamed at us. "Right. Now you have

your welcome talk in the Great Hall—I'll show you the way—then in the foyer, there'll be free drinks. Can't say no to that, can you?" She bounded to her feet.

We all got up in a scraping of chairs and followed her out into the hallway.

"So you're doing English, too?" Alex smiled at me. "Have you read any of the course books yet? Because I've been using mine as a doorstop."

"Well, I started," I said. "They only arrived last week." And had cost a small fortune. Still, it'd be worth it.

"The course sounds pretty good," said David, the Literature and Politics student.

"Uh-huh," said Alex. "Take it you're an intellectual?"

He shrugged. "Nothing wrong with that."

"Never said there was," said Alex. "You aren't going to go all crazy-psycho, are you?"

He blinked at her. "Huh?"

"The other guy," I explained, gesturing in the direction of his door. "Danielle tried to get him to come and introduce himself and he acted like she'd asked him to volunteer for human sacrifice."

Alex giggled. "Yeah, that's pretty much what happened."

"Lovely," said Sarah, joining us. "Just as long as I'm not the only person who hasn't been within fifty feet of a textbook since our exams. I'll have to buy them this week."

"Plenty of time," said Alex. "I for one am looking forward to studying *Dracula*."

"Well," I said, "I'm looking forward to studying more of Shakespeare's plays. Not that I usually admit that in general conversation," I added.

"Hey, you can pretty much say anything here," said Alex. "No one judges. Well, I won't."

"Nor me," said Sarah.

"Well, that's a relief," said David. "People who judge others are sad. University's supposed to be about finding out who you are, right?"

He was looking at me, and not in a derisive way, either.

"Didn't realise I was that inspiring," I said lightly.

"Hey, you put the rest of us to shame," said Alex. "I'd rather have that on my door than 'Abandon All Hope.'"

It was a start. I had three friendly flatmates, who, as an added bonus, were on my course, meaning I'd have someone I could walk with to lectures. And, even though I'd been here just a few hours, I felt an affinity with the place itself. It felt safe.

Which was a miracle in itself.

Finding out who I was. Figuring out my mess of a life. Here, maybe, I could do that.

4

WAKING NIGHTMARE

"Terrence," said Alex, "is a total dickweasel."

Sarah spat out a mouthful of cereal. "You what?"

"Who's Terrence?" I said, though I could hazard a guess.

"Our resident nutcase," she said, confirming my suspicion. "I only wanted to ask if he was coming out tonight. Figured it'd be nice to give him a second chance. But he told me to piss off." She made an aggressive gesture.

"Ignore him," I said. "Clearly, he isn't here to make friends."

"You're telling me."

After a day of introductory talks—and obligatory photographs at early-morning registration, which, thanks to the rain, made us look like drowned-rat-zombies—we were relaxing in the kitchen, anticipating our first night out of the term. Well, most of us were, the exception being our resident nutcase. At least Terrence made me look almost normal.

Actually, I'd struck gold with my flatmates. Sarah was

a quiet, bookish girl, and our personality types were pretty much an exact match. True, our reading tastes differed; she preferred romance novels, whereas outside of the classics I mostly went for fantasy and sci-fi. But Alex and I had already exchanged a ton of recommendations, seeing as she had an obsession with hefty, epic *Lord of the Rings*-style books. And David and I liked the same classics.

Right now, though, he was reading a politics textbook, earning raised eyebrows from Alex—even I couldn't claim that level of dedication.

"Did you see Terrence last night?" Sarah asked, setting her cereal bowl down. "I thought I saw someone walk past my window."

"I thought a giant bird flew into mine," said Alex.

I stared at her. "I thought I did, too."

I'd also thought it was one of my weird Ash-hallucinations, seeing as I'd been half-asleep at the time. Not that the giant bird's appearance had seemed threatening, but I wasn't about to rule anything out after almost a year seeing freaking *demons*. It unnerved me, if just because it was the first strange event that had happened since setting foot on campus.

"Weird," said Alex. "Unless we both had the same dream. I've heard of that happening when people live together."

"Where on earth did you hear that?" said Sarah. "I don't think mind-reading was on that list they gave us about what to expect from living in student housing."

"I read it on the Internet somewhere."

"Because that's the pinnacle of information?" said David. I could tell he'd meant it as a joke but it came out sharper than he'd intended.

"Wow, someone's grumpy," said Alex. "What did you

do after the talk last night, anyway? I saw you skulking around outside."

"Just checking on my bike," said David. "I know there are security cameras and everything, but you can't be too careful."

"Sure," said Alex. "Didn't know you had a motorbike."

"Can I have a go on it?" interrupted Pete. He smelled like a brewery, and, by the looks of things, hadn't bothered to change his clothes since last night. *Ew.*

"No," said David flatly.

Pete glared at him.

Possibly in an effort to diffuse the testosterone brewing in the air, Alex said, "Ash, are you sure you saw that giant bird? Maybe it was a waking dream."

A shiver ran through me as an unwelcome memory stirred.

"A waking dream?" I said. "You mean, you're awake but dreaming at the same time?"

"Kind of," said Sarah. "Have you ever had sleep paralysis? *That's* freaky. You're awake, but your muscles haven't woken up yet, so you can't move. Even with your eyes open."

"That happened to me!" I said, forgetting to disguise the intense relief in my voice that at least *one* of my weird events had a rational explanation. "It was horrible. Like I was paralysed."

"That's what it feels like," said Sarah, shuddering.

"Well, it wasn't that. Never mind," said Alex. "Unless Terrence has an army of murderous crows."

"You mean a murder *of* crows," said Sarah.

Alex waved a hand. "Technicalities. He has that weird quote on his door, right?"

"Dante," I said. "Kind of a weird thing for a physics student to have on his door."

"'Abandon hope, all ye who enter here,'" said Alex. "It'd be funny if Terrence didn't look so much like a serial killer. For all we know, maybe he *does* have a collection of torture instruments in there."

"That, *and* crows?" said Sarah, laughing.

"Maybe he's raising the devil," I joked.

David gave me a strange look. I shifted in my seat. *I was joking.*

"He's boring," said Pete. "Maybe he thinks being a dick will help him get laid."

"And downing ten cans of Strongbow will?" said Alex.

Pete shrugged, tipping his can back to catch the last drops. "You'll see."

Sarah jumped from her seat. "Alex! Your pan's on fire!"

"Oh—crap!" Alex pelted across the kitchen, where flames had sprung up in the frying pan she'd left unattended. She shrieked and dropped the pan into the sink, where, thankfully, the flames died down.

A shrill alarm blared overhead.

"Way to go," said Pete, staggering to his feet.

David said, "The whole block will hate us now."

Alex gave him an evil look. "Are you claiming responsibility?"

"Everyone out!" someone shouted outside.

"Back me up, guys!" said Alex. "Those alarms are way over-sensitive."

"Alex, weren't you paying attention at the fire safety talk?" said Sarah. "I—come on, it'll look more suspicious if we hang about inside."

And that was how we ended up spending our first afternoon of university huddled on the field in the rain, waiting for the cue to go back inside.

"What?" Alex grumbled, returning any glare from someone who'd figured out we were the culprits with a glare of her own. "It's not like I burned the flat down or anything."

"Almost," said Sarah. "We could have burned to a crisp."

"You'd have had to pay for all our funerals," I added.

"Very funny," she said.

Terrence stood a few feet away, hood pulled up against the rain. He did *not* look impressed.

I grinned at Alex. "You've made an enemy of him now."

"Oh, who gives a crap?"

"Your face when you saw the pan…" said Sarah, starting to laugh.

"I vote we go to the burger bar instead," said Alex.

And then all three of us were laughing, oblivious to the glares of people around us. It felt natural, like we'd known each other for years—not less than a day. But this was a kind of strange I could live with.

AFTER A TRIP TO BARGAIN BURGERS, the restaurant on campus, we came back to get ready for the big night out. A nightclub, appealingly called Satan's Pit, in Redthorne, the nearest town to Blackstone, would be our first adventure. My first time clubbing. I hoped the name wasn't an omen.

I phoned Mum and Dad to let them know I'd settled in okay, facing the predictable one hundred and one questions about my new flatmates. Then I rang Cara, who also wanted to know every detail—especially whether I'd met any cute guys.

"I'm not looking for a boyfriend," I reminded her semi-truthfully. It had crossed my mind once or twice that being at uni would give me far more opportunities to meet guys than seven years at an all-girls' school, but to get that close to someone without revealing everything about myself didn't feel right. Mentioning invisible demons would send any guy running a mile.

"I'm going clubbing tonight, anyway," I continued.

"Seriously? That's awesome! You'll love it. If you come visit me, you should totally come with me to Frisson. They've got this new DJ. He's *fit*."

"Does he like ghost stories?"

"Watch it, you."

"I'm terrified."

My phone's connection chose that moment to drop.

"Crap, I'm losing signal," I said. "I've got to get ready, anyway."

"Yes, you have! You can't go out in a hoodie and jeans."

She knew me too well. I rolled my eyes. "Talk later."

"Sure thing! Have fun—but not *too* much fun!"

After she hung up, I surveyed my wardrobe. New black dress—the only one I'd liked out of the hundreds Cara had insisted I try on: check. New plain, black flats—heels combined with alcohol and my less-than-reliable sense of balance didn't seem like the best idea: check. Basic makeup: check. Silver earrings: check. I hesitated before putting on my new amethyst pendant. *Might as well wear it.*

My hair was too plain to do much with, but I combed the tangles out of it, wondering if the others would think the dress was a bit too Goth. But I liked black. It was simple and didn't clash with anything. I wasn't big on heavy makeup either. Mascara emphasised the dark shadows under my eyes. Not a good look.

I decided to check on the others. David waited in the corridor, hands in his pockets. He wore the same plain T-shirt and jeans as earlier. Guys were lucky no one expected them to make an effort. "You look nice," he said.

I felt myself flush. "Thanks. Um, so do you." *Idiot.* But he didn't laugh at me, which was a surprise.

"Have you been into the town before?" he asked just before the silence drifted into awkwardness.

I shook my head. "Not yet."

"It's nice. We should go to the shopping centre there sometime this week. Might as well make the most of having no lectures."

His words bounced around my head as I tried to figure out whether he meant *we* as in *me and him* or the whole flat. *Stop that.* Of course he meant *all of us.* It was Cara's fault for talking about boyfriends.

Sarah spared me further embarrassment by coming out of her room. She wore a flowery green dress and matching flats. No heels. At least it wasn't only me. I sacrificed height in favour of keeping my balance.

"You both look awesome!" said Alex, joining us. She wore a cute, little black dress and butterfly slides in her vivid red hair. Her heels made her the same height as David.

"Wait a minute," said Sarah. "Isn't Pete coming with us? Where is he?"

"Probably still in the kitchen," said Alex.

She was right—Pete was passed out at the table surrounded by empty beer cans.

"So much for him getting laid," said Alex. "Let's leave him here."

We left Pete slumped in his chair, drooling, and set off for the bus stop.

By the time we reached Redthorne, the four of us felt as battered as if we'd ridden the Big Dipper seven times in a row, thanks to a journey down winding country roads which threw us into the air at each twist and turn.

"Ouch," said Alex, as we stepped off the bus. "I've got to hand it to the driver, at least he's efficient."

"Yeah, except buses back home usually arrive the right way up," I said, rubbing an egg-sized lump on the back of my head.

Satan's Pit was a plain, red brick building in a typical urban area, complete with dismal rain clouds. Inside, nothing suggested anything satanic, unless the red carpet in the entrance hall was made of human entrails.

"Seems a bit of a dump," Sarah whispered as we queued to pay. The guy behind the counter looked bored out of his mind, giving each of our IDs no more than a brief glance before stamping our hands.

"You never know," said Alex. "It *might* be full of fire and brimstone downstairs."

At those words, a chill tingled through me, and I felt a sudden desire to get the hell out of there. *Why did I leave the university?* I didn't know for certain, but I'd concluded there must be something about the place that stopped me from seeing demons. I'd never gone so long without spotting one of those sinister creatures peeking through a gap in the universe.

I told myself to stop being stupid. *I'm entitled to go out and have fun with my friends. I won't let the fear rule my life. Not at home, and not here, either.*

I paid the guy, got my hand stamped, and followed my flatmates through the black-painted double doors.

5

SATAN'S PIT

Appropriately enough, we found the dance floor in the basement. I wasn't sure if the thick swathes of cobwebs were an intentional feature, or no one could be bothered to do any dusting. Crooked candle-holders hung from the walls, holding red lights, which threw eerie shadows around us. The spindly, wooden stair-case looked like it belonged in a crumbling old house, not a nightclub.

"I heard they used to have real candles down here," David said, "but they stopped because of the fire regulations."

"Yeah, candles and drunken dancing aren't a good combination," said Alex.

"Can't say I see what all the fuss is about," Sarah said, fiddling with a fingernail.

Satan's Pit reminded me of a school disco when a handful of people turned up and everyone felt too awkward to dance. The few people here before midnight stood near the bar in groups, talking and drinking.

"Let's go get drinks," said Alex. "Oh, come on. Let's pretend we're enjoying it, just for tonight."

An hour and a couple of bottles of WKD later, the atmosphere in the club started to pick up. Clubhouse music pounded out of the speakers and sent a ripple through the crowd. Everyone swayed in time to the beat, arms aloft, feet thumping. The blazing strobe lights painted flame-like patterns across the floor. It was actually pretty cool.

"Hey, Ash, you never said your necklace glows in the dark!" said Alex. "Neat."

I looked down. The amethyst shone bright, rivalling the bright lights. For some reason, I had the urge to tuck it away. It felt a little conspicuous.

The DJ yelled, "Annnnnnnd... Satan has arrived!"

The music quieted, the clubhouse beat replaced by the sinister tones of an organ, like haunted-house music. A rope descended from the ceiling above the centre of the dance floor, and a tall, horned figure carrying a pitchfork spiralled down to the ground.

The club went crazy. Satan—a normal guy painted from head to toe in red paint, who'd probably performed this act a hundred times before—roared at the crowd, and, as everyone flocked to the dance floor, a sea of flailing limbs swallowed him whole.

"Let's dance," said Alex.

Usually, I wasn't a fan of dancing, but, perhaps due to the fiery strobe lights and the alcohol buzzing through my veins, my self-consciousness melted away. In fact, I started to enjoy myself. Everyone seemed possessed with endless energy. I didn't feel like one person but part of a laughing, dancing crowd.

My head buzzed after a while. I could sort of see the appeal in clubbing; it felt like being in a different universe, one with no responsibilities, where I could stop thinking and lose myself in the rhythm. At least until a drunken girl staggered through the crowd, crashed into me, and almost knocked me off my feet.

"Sorry!" the girl yelled over the music, trying to stand and stabbing me in the foot with her heel.

I yelped. *This is why heels are evil.*

"Sorry!" she said again. She looked kind of familiar. Had I met her before? Her long, curly, dark-red hair bounced around her shoulders, and thick mascara framed her brown eyes. Her off-the-shoulder black dress was of the sort I wished I had the confidence to wear.

Then it hit me. It was the girl I'd seen from the car, who'd looked at me when I'd seen the demon. I opened my mouth to say something then closed it again. I'd probably imagined it. Now was hardly the time or place, anyway. I watched her disappear back into the crowd.

I couldn't get back into the mood, and not because my foot throbbed like a bitch. My thoughts raced, and, try as I might, I couldn't keep them under control. Could she really see the demons? Was it possible there were other people like me out there somewhere?

Stop it. Even if there are *people like me, what are the odds I'd run into them here, at one of the country's smallest universities, in the middle of freaking nowhere?*

Alex tugged on my arm. I couldn't hear what she said over the music.

"Huh?" I asked.

"I said, I'm going upstairs! It's too hot in here."

"Good idea." The smell of sweat was almost overpowering. We fought through the crowd to the stairs and climbed them to the outside world, breathing in the fresh air with relief.

David turned to me. "You okay? I saw that girl stand on your foot."

"I'll live," I said, examining the ugly purple bruise already forming. "Ouch."

Then I saw something that chilled me. Not two feet away, one of those dark spaces hovered, a patch of nothingness, like a tear in the universe. I stared, waiting for the inevitable pair of malevolent purple eyes to meet mine. But there was nothing there. Just blackness.

"Ash? What're you looking at?" said Sarah.

"Nothing," I said, tearing my gaze away. "Thought I saw someone I knew."

Out of the corner of my eye, I continued to watch the dark space. *Don't come near us. Not now. Not here.* I couldn't flip out again, not now I'd just started my new life.

"I think clubbing's kind of overrated," said Alex. "I don't care how lame it sounds, I'd rather be watching a film or sitting in a pub."

"I'm up for that," said Sarah.

I shifted my gaze back to the dark space—and almost stopped breathing. Something *stepped out* of the darkness. The figure was a shadow, black as the gap itself, hunched and shapeless. But, as it moved, it seemed to solidify into an animalistic shape, crouched on all fours. Shadows blurred around it like a long shaggy coat. One step. Then another.

I could hear its soft footfalls on the pavement, actually *hear* them. Before, I'd always known the demons weren't part of the world as I knew it. But this creature was as solid as I was. *What in the hell is it?* I backed away, almost tripping over the front step of Satan's Pit. *No. Not here.*

"Ash? You okay?" said David, reaching out to stop me falling.

"Fine," I said, amazed at how steady my voice sounded, despite the tremors that made my heart rattle against my rib cage. "It's really cold out here. I think we should go back inside."

"You sure?" David squinted at me. "Okay, then."

But before I could follow Alex, Sarah, and David, someone grabbed my arm. "It's sensed you," a voice hissed. "You can't go back in there."

I turned. It was the girl who'd knocked into me earlier, the red-haired girl from the car. Swaying on her three-inch heels, she pointed at the creature, which crept closer, until its muzzle almost brushed my feet. It looked like a shadowy, oversized fox, but the eyes it fixed on me were crimson, like bloody gouges in its face. An icy claw gripped my heart, rooting me to the spot.

"Shit," I whispered. "What the hell is that?"

"A shadow-beast. It can't see you, but it can sense you," whispered the girl. "Move."

But I couldn't. I was backed against the door to Satan's Pit, and my feet had locked in place. Like in one of my dreams. The girl swore, stepping to stand beside me. Dark tendrils rippled across the pavement like a creeping plant. The creature edged forwards, raising its head to bare two rows of teeth. *Shit. It's really going to kill me.*

The girl cursed and moved in front of me, whipping something out of her bag. A plain, black Japanese-style fan, patterned with flames. She held it in her right hand, between us and the creature.

Confusion leaked through my terror. *What's she doing?*

A spark flickered down her arms to her fingertips, then flames appeared out of nowhere, igniting the fan. She made a threatening motion towards the creature, which let out a high-pitched squeal. Flames shot into the air like a match flung into darkness, and the fox jumped back, hissing, its eyes dilated with panic. Faster than I could blink, it leapt at the dark space, vanishing into nothingness.

The girl flicked the fan, and the flames receded, becoming a simple pattern once again. She snapped the fan into its case and stashed it in her bag.

I stared, fuzziness creeping at the edges of my vision. My heart beat louder than the music thumping from the clubhouse. *Oh, God. Oh. My. God.*

"That should scare it off," she said, "but there might be more. Bloody sorcerers. You'd better get back inside."

Before I knew what was happening, she'd ushered me into the club.

"What the hell happened?" I gasped. "You—how did you—what *was* that?"

"I'm sobering up," she said. "That's a bad sign. I'm off to get another drink. Find your friends."

"Wait!" I said. "At least tell me your name."

"Claudia," she said. "I'm sure I'll see you later."

Before I could say another word, she'd descended the stairs into Satan's Pit, tottering slightly.

Leaning on the wall for support, I followed, my mind whirling. It made no sense. *That can't have been a demon.* Shadowy creatures had stalked me for nearly a year now, but I knew from experience that if I threw something at a regular demon, the object would pass right through it. But the girl had thrown *fire* at it. Like a character from an anime show. I shook all over. *Did that even happen?* Logic said, *yes, it happened. You're not mad. There's someone else like you out there.*

Except she'd gone, along with all evidence that I wasn't crazy.

Breathe. In. Out. My trusty breathing technique. But the club seemed twice as crowded, and I couldn't see Alex or the others anywhere. I hovered at the bottom of the stairs, on the outskirts of the noisy, raving mass of human bodies, my breath coming in short bursts. What if something attacked my friends, too? There hadn't been any more of those creatures, had there? In a weird way, I felt somehow responsible for the creature's appearance. After all, no one else could see them.

"Ash! Where've you been?" Sarah yelled, waving at me from behind a nearby group.

Thank God.

"Um," I said, making my way towards her, "there was this girl. She was drunk and couldn't find her way to the bus stop. I helped her get there." That sounded plausible enough to my own ears, and, to my relief, Sarah nodded.

"Alex and David are by the bar. A creep tried to come onto Alex, so she punched him in the face. It was pretty funny."

"Damn it, I missed that?" I said, hoping I sounded annoyed. I still trembled all over, but I supposed I could always put it down to the effects of the alcohol. And the presence of my friends made my breath come a little easier.

We found Alex by the bar. "David met a friend and buggered off," she said, raising her voice so we could hear her over the music. "I think we should get the bus back."

"Good idea!" I said. Right now, I wanted out of Redthorne as quickly as possible.

I couldn't stop myself from looking around anxiously as we shivered by the bus stop, but I couldn't see the dark space anymore. Only ordinary shadows sat between the brightly lit clubs and bars, between the blazing strobe lights spilling out onto the pavement. This looked like the least likely place for monsters to appear. But I'd learnt by now that fear walked out in the open, unseen.

I knew the creature I'd seen tonight had been different from the others. Although I'd been scared witless, it had been more, *holy shit, this creature's going to kill me,* than the cold terror brought on by the sight of a true demon, the primal fear of the unknown.

A thousand questions chased each other around my head, and an irrational surge of anger boiled at the girl for not explaining anything. She'd saved my life and vanished.

"You're pretty quiet, Ash," Alex commented, as we took the back row of seats on the bus.

"I'm just tired," I said and didn't have to fake a yawn.

"You enjoy your first clubbing experience?" Alex asked me. "Apart from the foot injury. See, this is why I avoid spiky heels, unless I'm planning to murder someone."

I smiled—or tried to. "Yeah, they're pretty lethal. But I'm not sure I'll be coming back here for a while."

"Yeah," said Sarah. "I definitely won't be going out every night. I need my beauty sleep. But I suppose it was fun—ish."

Fun, until the freakish monsters from my subconscious decided to make an appearance.

But I'd never expected it to happen in that way.

6

BLACKSTONE

That night, I dreamt I was encased in ice.

At first, I floated on the surface of a lake, enjoying the warm sunlight that stroked my skin. The lake water washed across my face, deliciously cool, and I could *feel* it, warmth and coolness, like before the demons. No more numbness. Normal.

Then coldness pierced my foot. The water around my feet rippled as the surface froze, covering it in a glassy sheen. Before I could move, the ice gripped me like a thousand icy pins, digging into my skin all over, making me cry out in pain. I struggled, but numbness paralysed my arms and legs. I could only watch in horror as the ice inched up my neck, spread over my face. A final cry escaped my mouth before ice flowed in, stapling my lips shut.

A voice whispered, *"Did you think you could escape it by coming here?"* Cold. So cold. Piercing. Deadly.

But at the same time, I was aware of a quiet, angry presence somewhere nearby, a voice hissing in my ear, telling me not to give in. *Fight it.*

I couldn't move...

You're asleep. Wake up!

I forced my eyes to peel open and found myself lying on my bed with my covers strewn around me. When I tried to lift my head, nothing happened. *Shit. Not again.*

I forced myself to stay calm. *This isn't supernatural. It's just sleep paralysis.*

It still seemed to take forever for me to regain feeling in my limbs and sit up. My watch told me it was almost six in the morning. I groaned. I'd been asleep for only three hours. But the memory of the dream hovered over me, making me reluctant to go back to sleep. I shuddered as I felt cold sweat along my back and neck and decided to take a quick shower. Somewhat refreshed, I came out of my en suite bathroom and attempted to remake my bed. I pulled back the tangled sheets and noticed a handful of tiny, white shards scattered on my pillow.

Like slivers of ice.

Brushing them away, I rearranged my covers and opened my curtains to see a thick, light mist pressing against my window. Today, I remembered, we had the morning free, presumably to allow everyone to recover from the first big night out, but we'd be picking course modules this afternoon. *You have to hand it to the student union for being thoughtful.*

I decided to go to the kitchen and get something to eat. There, to my surprise, I found David eating cornflakes.

"Hey!" he said. "Another early bird."

"I couldn't sleep," I said. I shook Frosties into a bowl. "Did you have fun last night?"

"Yeah, it was a laugh. Where did you disappear to?"

"I was, uh, helping this girl find her way to the bus stop." I sat down, noting David's eyes were shadowed, like he hadn't slept.

"Ah, good call."

We munched cereal in silence for a bit. I felt self-conscious that all I was wearing was a hoodie and a pair of pyjama bottoms, but I supposed this came with being a student.

"Hey, Ash," said David. "Want to walk to Blackstone? I was headed there, and it'd be nice to have company."

"Sure," I said.

In my room, I pulled on some jeans, wondering when I'd get used to this bizarre arrangement of living with other people my age. So far, my suspicions that living in a student flat would give me less opportunity to be an antisocial hermit proved true—probably a good thing. I'd planned to spend the morning playing *World of Warcraft* and maybe reading a book. It would be nice to get out of the flat and see the town.

And forget about last night.

"Nice day," David commented as we stepped outside. I breathed in, savouring the fresh, cool morning air, and shook off the remnants of the dream. The mist swirling around as we walked through the student village us left drops of moisture on my face. Dew clung to the grass, making the lawns glitter.

Forget about monsters, I told myself as we approached the forest. Blackstone lay on the opposite side of the valley at the bottom of the hill, on the other side of the woods. The path went in a relatively straight line, as Cara and I had discovered on the visit day.

"We could get the bus if you'd rather," said David. "I normally take my bike."

I'd completely forgotten he owned a motorbike. He didn't look the type, but what did I know?

"Walking's fine with me," I said. "I never got the chance to visit the countryside much at home. I don't miss the lunatic drivers or exhaust fumes."

"Nah, instead you get weird intellectuals asking you to walk through the woods." He smiled.

"I don't think you're weird," I said.

"You don't really know me," he said.

I guessed he had a point. University kind of threw a bunch of people together and hoped they'd get along. I'd been lucky so far.

"Well, help me get to know you," I said. "What do you like doing in your spare time? Apart from reading?"

"I travel all over, go on trips. Camping. That's why I'm joining the hiking club."

"I'm not sure about camping," I said. "I've heard too many horror stories from my Aunt Eve. She used to travel all before she moved to Windermere. Flooded tents and that kind of thing. No thanks."

"Hey, it's all part of the fun. Windermere's a nice place."

"Yeah, I used to go there every summer. But I haven't been there for a while now—not since my aunt moved to Canada."

We talked as we followed the woodland trail. The conversation turned to university applications, and it turned out Oxford rejected David, too.

"Yeah, they didn't want me. I thought the interview went okay, but I guess there were a lot of applicants. No biggie."

"I hate interviews," I said. "I can't speak on the spot, least of all when I'm supposed to convince people I'm amazing."

David laughed. "Hey, to be honest, it's about bullshitting. But it's not worth getting stressed over."

I nodded and almost slipped. "Ah… crap." I grabbed for the nearest thing, which turned out to be David's arm, and steadied myself.

"You okay?" His eyes were wide, like I'd done something more serious than stumbling in the mud.

"Sure! Sorry." I let out a nervous laugh. "Damn. I should have worn better shoes."

"You should have mentioned you were so cold. That coat doesn't look very warm."

"Eh?" I blinked at him, puzzled. Then it sank in. Crap. I *was* freezing cold—all the time, now. Apparently, if I touched other people, they could feel it too. Just great. "I'm fine. Bad circulation." I hitched an unconvincing smile into place and started walking again.

By now, the mist had cleared to the point where we could make out the well-trodden path into the woods, marked with fallen leaves, dull brown and yellow. A river flowed alongside the path silently, as if unwilling to disturb the quiet. A blackbird sang softly from up in the horse chestnut branches, pecking at the spiny green conker shells. I liked that we could hear no traffic on the woodland trail, no human noise, only birdsong and a rustling in the undergrowth that might have been a hedgehog or rabbit.

"You've been to Blackstone before?" said David.

"I got the bus from there on the visit day," I said, "but I didn't really have the time to look around."

"You should see the art gallery. It's free to get into. We can have a look if you like."

"Sure," I said. It surprised me that a village as small as Blackstone had its own art gallery. "You've been there a lot? I didn't think many people knew about this place. It seems like it's off everyone's radar."

"My brother went to uni here a couple of years ago. I used to visit."

"Ah, right." That explained why he seemed to know the town so well.

I asked him about his motorbike—a good move, as it

kept him talking all the way to Blackstone. When he went into detail about mechanics, I stopped trying to understand and zoned out, focusing instead on not slipping on the muddy path.

Once out of the woods, we found ourselves on a dirt track that curved through the valley. Fields full of sheep and cows lay on either side. We passed the remains of a crumbling old manor house, surrounded by a swathe of ground bare of grass or life.

"That place was destroyed in a fire, about two centuries ago," said David.

The house resembled no more than a charred skeleton, most of the insides burned away so I couldn't tell what had originally been there. Soot-blackened bricks divided rooms of yawning emptiness like a giant rib cage. I saw a sudden, vivid mental image of flames ripping the house apart, scorching the area around it so no grass would ever grow again, and shivered.

"Who lived there?" I asked.

"The Blackstone family. The town's named after them, as a monument to their memory."

"Why? Were they important?"

"They were a really rich, influential family, and every one of them died in the fire."

"That's horrible." I shuddered. "How did it start?"

"Who knows? It was a long time ago, and, back then, few people cared about investigating a freak accident in the middle of nowhere."

"Doesn't seem like good karma, naming a town after a family who all suffered horrific deaths." My morbid thought came out before I could stop it.

David gave me a crooked smile. "Well, it hasn't hurt it."

Blackstone was a network of cobbled streets and old-fashioned houses, with the town square the main focal point. A pedestal sat in the centre, on which there was a carved statue of an angel. Though its stone face wore a benevolent smile, the raindrops gathering in the corners of its eyes made it look as though it were crying. The Art Gallery sat nestled in the shadow of an enormous Gothic cathedral.

The oak doors creaked as we entered, and our footsteps echoed off the wooden floor. No one else was here this early, and the quietness made me acutely aware of David's presence at my side. He seemed content to meander through the rooms, talking like one of those guided audio tours, but my traitorous imagination kept straying back to last night. The shadow-thing, and the girl. The reminder that I wasn't fooling the darkness, playing the role of Ash-the-intellectual and listening to David's commentary on the various paintings we passed. If my quietness bothered him, he didn't say so.

The display ended with a wall devoted to depictions of Dante-esque visions of Hell. The signs told me they were imitations of Bosch paintings of the damned falling into the deep, of sinners on their deathbeds tempted by denizens of the underworld.

"Creepy," I said, gesturing towards a painting of one unfortunate soul, surrounded by insect-like creatures which, for reasons unknown to me, wore human heads.

"Yeah, Melivia was an odd one."

"Melivia?"

"Melivia Blackstone. She painted most of these."

"Blackstone? Was she——?"

"Yeah. She was their eldest daughter. These paintings survived the fire, somehow. I think they must have been kept somewhere else."

My eyes jumped to the one on the end—the only

portrait. It showed a girl with delicate features, gazing into the distance. Her black hair curled to her shoulders, and she wore a long, black, Victorian-style dress. Around her neck hung a silver chain, on which gleamed a purple crystal, an amethyst. For some reason, my hand jumped to my own neck, before I realised I'd left my necklace in my room. An odd shiver went through me. I couldn't tear my eyes away from her pensive stare.

I jumped as the church bells rang out, echoing through the building. When I turned back, I saw two other people inside the high-ceilinged room, though I hadn't heard them come in. Both wore odd navy blue uniforms. Policemen? No—they didn't have badges. Both looked right at me.

"Want to go?" asked David, suddenly close behind me.

I nodded, turning away from the two guys. A shiver raced over the back of my neck, though the two of them had already forgotten me and headed for the door into the next room. David glanced at them, and I caught a strange expression on his face. Fear?

He all but steered me out the door, something I'd have otherwise objected to. As it was, I couldn't get out of there fast enough. The hellish paintings didn't help.

"We can walk to the coast from here if you like. It's just that way." He pointed at an alleyway between the Art Gallery and the cathedral.

"Sure!" I said, a touch too enthusiastically. "I haven't seen the sea in forever. We were going to go to France this summer, but my parents needed to pay for all my stuff for uni. Like those six-hundred-page textbooks."

"Yeah, I know what you mean. It's expensive, moving out. You don't realise how much you take for granted until you're on your own. This is the quickest way," he added, climbing over a stone wall.

I followed. The hairs on my arms rose as I realised we were in a graveyard, around the back of the cathedral. We walked swiftly, not speaking. A presence seemed to press on us like a heavy blanket of fog. I didn't believe in ghosts—not the traditional ones, anyway—but, if ever a place appeared haunted, that place did. Like the inhabitants sat all around us, watching. The image of those two guys standing in the shadowed corner kept coming back.

As we climbed over a stile into a field, David said, "That place is abandoned, but it still creeps the hell out of me. I think it's because that's where the Blackstones are buried."

I nodded. No one could escape that family here. The ruined house, the paintings, the cemetery—even the name. I wondered why I hadn't heard about it when I'd first visited. It seemed like the sort of thing Cara would have picked up on. She could find the creepy in the most mundane situations.

We walked through a small copse, large oak trees forming a canopy that blotted out the sky. The salty tang of the sea breeze mingled with the scents of decay. Crows nested in the branches above, looking down at us with distrustful eyes. Once or twice, I thought the shadow of a larger bird passed overhead, but, whenever I looked up, I saw nothing there.

We emerged from the trees to find ourselves at the top of a rugged cliff overlooking a pebbly beach. Waves crashed against the jagged rocks below.

"People have barbecues down there in summer, when the weather's nice," David said.

"*Is* the weather ever nice here?"

He grinned at me. "You'd be surprised."

I suddenly felt awkward. We were alone together. Cara's words echoed in my head: "If a guy asks you out alone, it means he likes you." I rarely took notice when she said things like that, but, then again, maybe that was because no one had ever been interested in me.

"It's nice here," I said. *That was lame.* Score one for the conversational queen.

He looked away from me, out across the rippling sea. "Yeah, it's nice. A bit isolated, but I guess you knew what you were getting into when you applied, right?" He said this with a strange kind of emphasis, but I couldn't put my finger on it.

"Sure," I said. "No one from my sixth form was coming here. It was perfect."

"You wanted a fresh start?"

"Yeah, I guess so."

"A lot of people do. You're lucky to have had the chance."

Lucky. Now I thought about it, I guessed I *was* lucky to be here, even though part of me worried it was a deception, that I'd not quite escaped the fear. I hesitated, on the brink of confessing what had really happened last night. *Stop.* No, I couldn't tell him. What would he think of me?

But the girl. *She* was proof I wasn't the only one who could see the demons. She was a student at the university; it wasn't unreasonable to assume we'd meet again. And, next time, I'd get some answers.

7

THE FORTUNE-TELLER

T he following day, Alex, Sarah, David, and I headed to the Great Hall to sign up to student societies. Maybe there was a secret society for people who saw demons. You never knew.

Rain surrounded us in a constant haze of drizzle. In the fog, it gave me a start of surprise when a troop of people dressed as medieval warriors walked past. For a second, I was half-convinced we'd jumped back to the fifteenth century.

"That'd be the RPG Society," said Alex.

"What—they walk around campus like that?" said Sarah. "With the swords and everything?"

"So I've heard," said David. "You get all sorts here. They're not the weirdest."

"They're not doing any harm," said Alex. "I think it's pretty cool, actually. Y'know, in a nerdy way."

You've got to admire their nerve. Although using cardboard as the basis for their props might have been a mistake, given the weather.

"Not sure I'll be joining," said Sarah.

"Might be a laugh," said Alex. "I'm joining hiking. And maybe climbing and badminton. And——"

"Isn't that a bit much?" I said. "You do have course-work, as well. Don't forget."

"We have only three years here," said Alex. "I want to make the most of every second!"

Apparently, nothing could dampen Alex's spirit——not even the torrential rain that hit us when we neared the centre of campus. I half-expected her to start singing. Sarah groaned and ran for shelter. I didn't mind the rain so much, but the wind kept me awake at night, rattling the windows and making me dream of shadowy figures trying to break in.

The Great Hall, as we'd discovered at the welcome talk, was at the far end of campus, a large, grey brick building, more like part of a ruined castle than a university. Moss covered the aged bricks, and the oak doors wore a furry green coat. It gave me the odd feeling of stepping back in time as we passed through the doors, but the inside was a riot of bright colours. Banners advertising the various societies adorned the walls, accompanied by demonstrations.

Alex ran in the direction of the Mountaineers' climbing wall and was soon swinging towards the ceiling. David queued next to a serious-looking group that advertised itself as the Politics Society. Nearby, the Cheerleading Club formed a human pyramid, and the Gaming Society demonstrated their various consoles. They looked more interested in kicking ass on *Resident Evil* than signing people up, though.

I signed up for Hiking, though I declined the Mountain Biking Club's offer of a discounted membership. I also sidestepped freestyle dancing, recalling the traumatic time my parents had signed me up for classes when I was younger. Definitely not for me. But I did sign up to the Literature Society and the student newspaper. Alex joined no fewer than seven different societies, insisting she'd easily make time for hiking, climbing, backpacking, tae kwon do, swimming, kayaking, and badminton. Somehow, she also managed to talk Sarah and me into putting our names down for the first hike of the year, a day trip to Borrowdale in the Lake District.

"You're a fan of the great outdoors, aren't you?" I said as we left the hall, laden down with freebies.

"Hell, yeah. Speaking of, are you guys up for a walk down to Blackstone? I've heard they have some neat little shops there."

"Sure," I said. "I didn't get to look at the shops when I went there with David."

"Funny, that," said Alex. "He doesn't really speak to either of us, but he asked you to go with him to Blackstone. I think there's something there." She gave me a Look, like Cara's *don't you try bullshitting me* expression.

I blinked. "I don't know. We were both up early, and he was going to go anyway. Nothing happened." I hadn't mentioned our little outing to Cara, either, to avoid this exact conversation.

"*Sure*. Oi, can I have a few more of those condoms?" She snatched another bag from the guy at the Safe Sex stand outside the hall. "I'm planning a wild night."

"Alex, you're terrible!" I said, laughing. "I think he thought you were being serious!"

"How d'you know I'm not?"

We'd established already that none of us was at university for the one-night-stands. Sarah had a boyfriend back home, where he was studying at the local college, and Alex was more interested in climbing mountains and joining every student society imaginable. As for me… well, I didn't yet know what I wanted.

"I heard the person above me going at it last night," said Sarah. "The walls in the flat are stupidly thin. You could hear *everything.* It was traumatising."

"Fun," said Alex. "I heard some weird-ass music coming from Terrence's room."

"Me, too," I said. "Sounded like screaming. At first I thought he was torturing a small animal."

"You never know," said Alex. "That guy's seriously weird. If we see him carrying a body bag out, then we'll know for certain."

"My best friend back home would say he's planning to poison us all," I said.

"Hope not," said Alex.

"I think he's given me the plague," said Sarah, shivering. "I keep losing my voice."

"That'd be Freshers' Flu," said Alex. "Keep your germs away from me!"

Today was the day of the weekly market in Blackstone. Stalls selling everything from cupcakes to jewellery, dog collars, and DVDs sprung up overnight along the street under white marquees. The cobblestones were slick with rainwater.

"Neat," said Alex, examining a collection of precious stones.

"Lucky charm for you, love?" said the stall owner, a middle-aged woman adorned with layers of coloured shawls. "This amethyst here'll ward off all evil." She held up a stone like the one Aunt Eve had sent me.

"Um, no thanks," said Alex, raising her eyebrows at the price tag. "We're just looking."

The stone winked at me as she put it back down, and I felt the hairs rise on my arms.

The strange feeling grew more pronounced as we moved farther into the market, nearing the town square. We hovered around a stall, that sold old books, for a while, and I gave into temptation and purchased one of Victorian vampire stories along with a second-hand version of the poems of Lord Byron. After all, I reasoned, I'd probably need them at some point.

Last time I'd seen the town square, it was deserted. Bare cobblestones had circled the stone statue of the angel, and the wooden benches had been empty. Now, stalls and crowds of chattering people filled every inch of space, and a large, black tent obscured the entrance to the cathedral. My skin prickled with uneasiness. I walked towards the black tent to take a look, the tingling intensifying as I neared it.

My heart dropped. All around the tent were dark spaces, tears in the universe, overlapping with reality like patches in a quilt. The untouched gaps between the dark spaces looked unreal, as flimsy as the fabric of the tent, like the world could collapse around us and send us spinning into a black void. I closed my eyes, trembling all over.

Someone stepped up behind me. "A fortune-teller?" said Alex.

I opened my eyes and saw the sign above the tent: *Madam Persephone: Fortune-Teller*.

"Not sure I want to waste my money on that," said Alex. "Those things are usually hoaxes."

"I think some are genuine," said Sarah. "It's just there are a lot of fakes out there."

Once, I'd have agreed with Alex, but now, who was I to judge? "Might as well get a free Tarot reading," I found myself saying.

"Huh? Didn't think you were into that stuff," said Alex.

"I'm not. I'm kind of interested to see what she says."

Right now, I'd take any chance to find out the truth about me, why I saw the dark spaces, and what the hell happened the other night. Questions bounced against my skull as I joined the line of people waiting outside the tent. Blackstone was supposed to be safe, and I couldn't see any demons, but the dark spaces remained.

The queue inched forwards. I couldn't focus on anything except the dark gaps, scared that, if I looked away, a huge, black, and menacing shape would appear behind me.

"Hey, we'll meet you later, okay?" said Alex as I reached the front of the queue. I nodded and ducked under the tent flap, emerging into what resembled the interior of a small shop.

It was very dark, lit by a few candles in bright holders on the table. The strong smell of incense filled the air. The table, draped in black cloth, showed an assortment of objects: glinting crystals; a deck of battered-looking cards; and, in the centre, a large crystal ball. A placard read: *Madam Persephone.* Charms hung from the ceiling, glittering moons and stars, and behind the table sat a beautiful woman. A cascade of silver-fair hair fell past her shoulders, and she wore a long, black coat that covered her from head to toe. I couldn't tell her age; she could've been as young as twenty-five, but her eyes assessed me with the sharp look of experience.

"Well, now," said the woman. "This is a surprise. I had no idea you'd come and find me of your own accord."

I stood and gaped at her, all questions forgotten, as if my thoughts had been sucked into one of the black spaces. Her sharp, silver-grey eyes pinned me to the spot, as though looking for symptoms of guilt over some crime I hadn't committed.

"Are you incapable of speech?" she enquired.

"Um, no. No, I was just—I mean—have we met before?"

"Who knows? People meet in all kinds of extraordinary circumstances."

Great. She's going to screw with my head.

"Look, I came to ask—"

"I know you came to ask me to read your fortune. Forgive me, but I don't think that will be necessary."

"Huh?" The questions came flooding back. "I don't understand. If you aren't going to read my fortune, then why are you here?"

"I think you could do with advice that's a little more direct than cryptic messages in tea leaves and lines on the palm of your hand."

Something in her tone made me feel defensive. "Why? How do you know who I am?"

"Nobody knows who you *are,* save you yourself."

I could about wrap my mind around that, but it wasn't particularly helpful. "Fine. How do you know I need advice?" I asked.

"Let's just say that I see things the way they really are. My first piece of advice is to avoid the Venantium."

"The what?"

She gave me that assessing look again. I found myself unable to look away from her eyes.

"You haven't spoken to Miss Delaney, yet?" she asked.

"Who?"

"Claudia Delaney and her companions have taken to finding people like you and making sure you know not to do anything that attracts unwelcome attention."

"Claudia," I said. "I met her at Satan's Pit, she fought off the—" I hesitated. Could I really trust this strange woman? What if she'd somehow lured me inside and manipulated me in some way?

"Look," I said. "Not to be rude, but who are you, anyway?"

"I'm known as Madam Persephone for the purposes of maintaining my position here in Blackstone. You do not need to know any more than that. Just trust that I can help you. I have your interests in mind, far more than the Venantium do."

"Who are the Venantium?" I struggled to pronounce the word. It sounded like Latin to me.

"You haven't met anyone else of your kind yet?"

"Kind?"

"Magic-users. Sorcerers. Those with a connection to the Darkworld."

My breath caught in my throat. "Magic-users?"

"What do you know about the Darkworld?"

I paused whilst my thoughts tumbled, as if in freefall.

"Nothing," I said. "I don't know a damn thing. Except I can see things that aren't there."

"Like what?"

"Dark spaces. They're everywhere outside." I gestured at the tent around us.

"The spaces hide nothing more dangerous than spirits. People like us attract a lot of attention from the Darkworld, some more than others. They're harmless."

"But… those creatures. The purple-eyed ones…"

"You've seen demons?"

I nodded. "They stare at me, all the time. Like—like they're after me." My voice dropped to a whisper.

"They can't harm you," said the fortune-teller. "Not from that side of the Barrier. They reside in the Darkworld."

"What *is* the Darkworld?"

It was her turn to gesture around us. "The world beneath. The domain of spirits. Most are harmless, but demons… well, you'd be better to remain ignorant, for the sake of your mental health."

A wry grin stole onto my face.

"Try me," I said. "I dream about them anyway."

"Demons are the ruling league of spirits and are more dangerous than anything in the physical world. Some would say that, given access to our world, they could rise from beneath to take possession of the entire human race. They're immortal, cunning—and utterly inhuman. Are you frightened yet?"

Yes, I wanted to say. The thought of the world dissolving into a black void like the Darkworld turned my legs to jelly, but my voice sounded surprisingly steady. "So, what are they—devils? Are there angels as well?"

The fortune-teller gave me a pitying look. "Are you religious at all?"

I blinked. "Me? No, not at all. I just thought it was logical. If there's something as evil as that out there, doesn't it stand to reason there's something good out there, as well?"

"Not necessarily. That would depend on your definition of good and evil. Things are rarely so clear-cut. Spirits can be benevolent as often as deceitful. And, as much as many of the Venantium might protest that what *they* do is in the way of good, so far as we can prove, there are no angels."

"Great," I said. "I don't suppose there's a way to turn off my second sight, or whatever the hell it is?"

"No, I'm afraid you're stuck with this." She glanced her watch. "Sorry, but I have other customers, and I know it'll take time to adjust to what you know already."

"I don't know anything!" Frustration made my voice rise. "I can see things that aren't there. I can't get warm. And last night, I got *attacked* by a monster. Now, you're saying I'm a magic-user or whatever—that I'm not even human!"

"Oh, you're human. I can assure you of that. Being a sorceress doesn't take away your humanity. If it did, we'd all be hypocrites." She gave a heavy sigh, and, for an instant, her composure seemed to waver, as if she were struggling to shoulder something heavy.

Then she snapped her attention to me so fast I thought I'd imagined it. "And you're not mad, either. You're just one of the unfortunate souls doomed to suffer a connection to the Darkworld. You'll always be able to see what others cannot. You'll always be able to see the darkness beneath. But, in other ways, you're quite lucky."

I raised my eyebrows at her mock-cheerful tone. "How's that?"

"You can see what's *really* there." She waved her hand in a gesture of dismissal. "Go. I've said enough for now, and I've fortunes to read."

"Please," I said, wincing at the obvious plea in my voice. "This is driving me mental. I just want to know."

"Talk to Miss Delaney. She and her little group are always on the lookout for people like you."

"But… I don't understand. How can you tell I'm a—that I have this connection?" I couldn't use the word *sorceress*. It sounded too absurd to my ears.

"There are ways of telling. I saw the way the spirits reacted to you."

I snorted; I couldn't help it. Cara and I had been accosted in town once by a woman who'd claimed she could talk to spirits. She'd insisted her dead husband was standing right beside her and tried to convince us *the system* was stifling her powers. When we'd backed away, she'd returned to conversing with a stray dog.

"I can see you'll take some convincing, Ashlyn. Do you doubt everything you can't see with your own eyes?"

"Sometimes," I said. "I mean, the demons... I can see them. The Darkworld, too. But magic?"

"Real magic isn't like what you read about in fiction, nor is it the kind performed by stage magicians. It has its roots in ancient alchemy, the manipulation of fire and water. One can make subtle changes to the elements that make up our world but cannot achieve total control. The strongest sorcerers can bend the laws of nature to their will, but few can achieve that without demonic assistance. And that never ends well."

She gave me a stern look, as though she thought I planned to go and cast a spell there and then. "I usually specialise in advice, not warnings, Miss Temple, but I think you ought to know that it is magic that attracts demons."

A chill settled on the base of my spine. "Is that... is that why they keep following me? Because I'm——" *What? A sorceress?* It still sounded absurd. I might play RPGs and read a lot of fiction, but apart from the demons, I was ordinary. I couldn't start a fire from nowhere, like that girl, Claudia. It felt like reality was shifting, breaking beneath my feet. My head spun.

"Yes." The fortune-teller's voice was steady and, oddly enough, made my feet feel less like they were about to fall through the ground. "Spirits are generally drawn to magic, but it is demons that crave it most of all. It is pure energy to them. Most sorcerers who form a contract with a demon do so by exchanging magical energy for enhanced abilities. But demons have a will of their own, and it rarely works in a sorcerer's favour."

"Well, I didn't plan on summoning one," I said, my voice shaky. "I wouldn't know where to start. Where can I learn about magic, then? Is there a guidebook?" Images of *Harry Potter*-style textbooks sprang to mind.

"Not as such. It isn't a widespread skill, and the Venantium work to keep it hidden. I have made it my goal to learn as much as possible, and the main lesson I have learned is that few know the true potential of magic. Even divination, and reading these——" She flipped over a Tarot card: The Magician——"are not true magic. I can tell you now that no one can see the future, not even those who have contact with spirits. This is merely a disguise. Though it has its advantages. You certainly get to meet some interesting people…"

She looked at a timepiece on her table. "You have distracted me, Miss Temple. But I have other customers to provide assistance to."

"Is that what you really do?" I said. "Help people like me?"

"If you need my help, I am here. Even when I'm not open for business, so to speak, my tent is always in the corner of the square. You'll be able to find it if you look hard enough. Well, goodbye for now, Miss Temple."

Her face set, and I knew it would do no good to ask any more questions. Thinking about it, I'd never told her my name. *Did the spirits tell her?* I wanted to laugh at myself. It had to be some kind of joke. Spirits, sorceresses, a place called the Darkworld… It was totally ridiculous. And yet, in a weird way, it made sense. Everything I'd seen, the demons, the Darkworld, the fire… Reality was breaking, crumbling into a void.

"Wow, you were ages!" said Alex. She and Sarah waited for me on a bench nearby. "What did she say?"

I shrugged. "Load of bollocks," I lied. "Told me I'd marry at thirty and have three kids. And I'd meet a tall, dark, handsome stranger next month."

Alex burst out laughing. Then she frowned, looking over my shoulder. "Speak of the devil," she said.

David approached, hands in his pockets and a deep frown on his face.

"Hi," I said, smiling, though I felt like I was playing a part, like this real-world conversation was less real than the bizarre, surreal interaction I'd had with the fortune-teller.

He didn't smile back. "Were you in that fortune-teller's tent?" he asked.

"Um, yeah."

"Well, it's a hoax. A lot of people have been complaining."

"Oh, I know," I said. "Just thought I'd give it a go, seeing as it was free."

"Apparently, Ash is going to meet a tall, dark, handsome stranger," said Alex.

David didn't laugh. "Well, I'd be careful before I trusted the words of a *fortune-teller*."

"Huh?" said Alex. "Who are you, her mother?"

David shook his head. "I didn't mean it like that. Just... don't go back to that fortune-teller again."

Anger surged within me, without warning. "Excuse me? I think I can make up my own mind." I didn't know where the words came from—probably from my ever-growing frustration that had been bubbling away beneath the surface ever since I had heard the fortune-teller's first cryptic words.

David looked startled. "Sorry, Ash. I didn't mean to sound patronising. I'd better be going anyway. Sorry I upset you. See you later."

And he went, leaving me feeling like an idiot.

8

DARKNESS HAS A NAME

I tried my best to forget about everything I'd found out that day and enjoy the rest of the week. Unfortunately, the dreaded Freshers' Flu had invaded the flat. I spent two days in bed with a cool flannel over my face, half-dreaming, half-awake. Vivid dreams exploded before my vision—demons ripping their way out of the dark spaces, the world around me shattering like a mirror; fire searing a path of destruction through a manor house. I dreamt of being frozen, a living ice sculpture, whilst crowds of people gawped at me. I saw the faces of people I knew in the crowd. Cara. My parents. Alex, Sarah, David. The girl from the club. All turned their backs, oblivious to my shouts, until one remained—the fortune-teller, who regarded me with a pitying stare.

"Such a shame I couldn't save you," she murmured, her breath fogging the ice surrounding me. "But even the best of us can succumb to demons…"

In my rare lucid moments, I lay awake, my mind reeling, not with the fever but with the fortune-teller's words. Demons, I was used to by now, but magic was a whole other problem. The fortune-teller had said that magic was more subtle than flashing lights and explosions, but if I was supposedly a magic-user, then you'd think there'd have been some kind of clue before all the craziness had started.

Maybe I should forget about it. If magic attracted demons, then I'd be tempting fate. As attractive as I found the idea of trying a *Harry Potter*-style summoning charm, I didn't want to bring a horde of demons down on me. *But they follow me anyway.*

I hated when people refused to give me a direct answer, and the fortune-teller had left me with more questions than she'd answered. I considered going back to talk to her again, once I'd recovered from flu, but I suspected I wouldn't get answers this time, either. She'd only talked so much because… well, I didn't know. *Was she just trying to warn me off?*

But she'd made one thing quite clear: I'd have to face up to this now. I couldn't hide any more.

Still, I refused to let it take over my life. Once I felt less like death, I returned to the real world—which, in my new life, meant going on a fancy-dress pub crawl in Blackstone covered in blue paint.

"Brilliant plan, Alex," said Sarah, as we trudged uphill back to campus in the rain, rivulets of blue paint attractively streaking our skin. "Smurfs? Really?"

"Hey, you went along with it," said Alex, sniggering. "You both look ridiculous."

"Cheers," I said, wiping my forehead, and making the paint-smudge even worse.

At least our flat was in sight now. Loud music pounded from the building, which would likely mean a sleepless night.

"Is that Terrence playing that music?" said Sarah.

"Probably," I said.

I'd thought I was becoming nocturnal, but, judging from the noise coming from his room, Terrence didn't seem to sleep at all. At all hours of the day and night, we could hear raised voices, opera music, and the occasional scream.

"Who was he yelling at this morning?" I said.

"I think he was on Skype," said Sarah. "I pity the poor person on the other end."

"Ah." That explained it.

"Or he's not right in the head." Alex skipped off uphill, leaving a trail of blue behind her. Why did it have to be glow-in-the-dark?

"I think someone had too much red wine," said Sarah.

"Glad I'm not the only sober one," I said. "I'm too much of a lightweight to risk more than alcopops." I'd never been drunk, mostly because I didn't trust Crazy Ash not to make an appearance and start freaking out about demons. Even though Blackstone was, mercifully, a demon-free zone.

We caught up to Alex, who'd run right into the glass door.

"Are you okay?" I asked, alarmed.

She giggled, rubbing her head. "It's a beautiful night," she declared. "Let's go star-gazing."

"No, it's time for bed," I said, grabbing her arm.

"You're cold," she whimpered.

Between us, Sarah and I steered Alex back into the flat, in time to see Terrence come out of his room.

"Where're you off to?" I said in surprise—I hadn't seen him leave his room all week.

"The lab," said Terrence and stalked off as if I'd insulted him.

"Lab?" I said. "Are we living with Frankenstein?"

"I think he means the physics lab." Alex giggled.

As soon as Sarah and I had managed to convince a tipsy Alex to go back to her room, I made for my own room—and shower. Too late. Trails of blue paint covered our floor and dripped down my door when I opened it.

I groaned. We'd be getting a lecture from the cleaners about this.

What with having to scrub paint out of the carpet, and the music pounding from the floor above—someone having a party, I guessed—I gave up on sleep before dawn.

The stuffy air in my room made it hard to breathe, so I went to open the window—then jumped away, biting back a scream. A white shape lay outside.

I stood frozen for a minute, thinking of demons, ghosts, and God knows what else, before I forced myself to pull back the curtains again. *What the hell?* It was a sheep. It had wandered up to the flat from the fields and dozed off right underneath my window. *Good job no one saw me.*

Then a voice spoke. "I've been looking for you all night, but I guess I can't blame you for not going into Redthorne again." The owner of the voice walked into view.

My heart jolted. It was the girl from the other night—Claudia. Her reddish-brown hair was plastered to her face with rainwater, and her red mini-dress was sodden. Just come back from a night out, I guessed.

"Wha—what're you doing out there?"

"I locked myself out of my flat."

"What, you live in here?"

"First floor, yeah."

"Wait there, I'll let you in."

I pulled a hoodie over my head and shoved my feet into my slippers, just remembering to snatch up my keys as I went out the room and walked smack into Terrence.

"Oops!" I said, steadying myself. "Sorry!" *What's he doing outside my room? When did he get back?*

Terrence gave me a hostile look.

"Sorry," I said again, feebly. "What're you doing?"

He narrowed his eyes at me and stalked into his room, the door slamming behind him. The words "Abandon Hope, All Ye Who Enter Here" swung back at me. *Oh…kay.*

I found the girl still standing in the field.

"Aren't you cold?" she asked, through blue-tinged lips.

"Me? I haven't been standing out here all night! Come inside."

She shook her head. "I don't particularly want to go back to my flat right now. I had an argument with Berenice this evening. It wasn't pretty. You never told me your name," she added.

"I'm Ashlyn. People usually call me Ash. Why haven't I seen you in the flat?"

"Oh, I haven't been to any of the Freshers events this year. You're first year, right?"

I nodded.

"Thought so. I'm second year, so are Howard and Berenice. You're doing English, right?"

"Yeah. How'd you know?"

"Hey, don't give me that look. I was curious, so I asked around. Anyway, first year's a piss-take. You only need a pass mark. So, go wild when you can!"

"Right," I said, blinking at the abrupt change of topic. *Oh no. I'm not having someone dance around all my questions again.* I took a deep breath and plunged in. "Look, I spoke to this fortune-teller the other day, and she told me—"

"Oh, you've spoken to Madam Persephone? Isn't she the most exasperating person you've ever met?"

"Well," I said, glancing up at the flat. It didn't look like anyone was awake, but she probably knew better than I did. "I guess. She didn't really answer my questions. She said—look, can we go and talk inside? It's wet out here and anyone could be listening from in there."

"They'll be more likely to hear us if we're inside, trust me. Want to walk in the forest?"

I hesitated, on the brink of pointing out I was hardly dressed for the weather, but the rain had slowed to a drizzle, and I decided to just roll with it. "All right, then."

The predawn sky was grey as paving stones. As we approached the forest, the trees seemed to glow with an eerie, silvery light. My feet skidded on the rain-soaked carpet of leaves. I probably should have put on some shoes. Slippers weren't the best choice of footwear.

I spoke only when we were deep under the leafy canopy. "The fortune-teller said you'd be able to help me. She said I have a connection to the... Darkworld. Look, I barely know a thing about any of this."

She regarded me, wearing a thoughtful expression. "You're unregistered?"

"Huh?"

"Are your parents sorcerers?"

"No." I shook my head. "No way. They're totally ordinary." The idea of Mum and Dad casting spells was so absurd I wanted to laugh. Mum worked part-time in a charity shop; Dad was an electrician. Normal. How had they come up with an anomaly like me?

"Then you must have sorcerer ancestry somewhere. It's rare that the Venantium don't pick up on these things, though. They have every potential magic-user registered. They put it down to keeping neat records, but everyone knows it's because they're afraid."

"Who—who are the Venantium? The fortune-teller mentioned them, too, but I've no idea what the hell's going on. She seemed to take it for granted that I knew already, but, until I came here, I didn't know a thing. I can see dark spaces and demons, but I still don't know *why*."

"So, you've never used magic?"

Magic. Here, surrounded by ghostly mist and silence, it felt less like a joke and more like something that... fit. Even though it *shouldn't* make sense. It went against all reason and logic. But there it was.

"No. I don't think so," I said, although there was one particular experience I'd put down to coincidence. "How does magic work? And what does it have to do with the Darkworld?"

"The Darkworld's the source of all magic, the home of all non-corporeal species," Claudia recited. "Well, that's the textbook definition, anyway. We can use magic because we have a strong enough connection to the Darkworld that we're able to take on its power ourselves, to control it."

"So, is the Darkworld a place?"

"Kind of, but not one we can get to. As I said, only spirits live there. Some sorcerers have tried to travel into the Darkworld. Theoretically, they say it can be done, but it's a bad idea. People separate from their bodies, and then they can never come back. The demons claim them."

"So, where do demons fit into this?"

"Demons are evil spirits. Evil because they can possess and kill humans."

I shuddered. "The fortune-teller said they're attracted to magic. Does that mean they'll come after us?"

"Nah, we aren't important enough. But it's true that they're magical parasites. The Barrier stops them from getting through to our world, but, if a sorcerer summons one, it causes havoc. The first thing it does is drain your power away and use it to add to their own. Then it uses your body as a vessel. The demon can possess you and make you do whatever it wants. Even experienced sorcerers are no match for one, and there's no way of blocking possession."

I shuddered again, cold tendrils wrapping around me. I thought of those staring, violet eyes. What did the demons want from me? The word *possession* put me in mind of horror films such as *Paranormal Activity* and *The Exorcist*. It didn't match up with the real world I thought I knew. Even as nightmares stared me in the face, part of me still clung to the old notion of reality.

I shook my head. "It makes no sense. I mean, the Darkworld? Possession? It sounds——"

"Like a bad horror movie, I know. I said the same thing. My parents decided to wait 'til I was eighteen to tell me. It didn't go over well."

"At least you knew. My parents…" No. There was no chance they knew what really preyed on my mind. They knew nothing about this Darkworld. I didn't think either of them had ever picked up a fantasy book in their lives.

"Well, you'll never look at *The Exorcist* the same way. Pretty sure the guy who wrote it wasn't actually a magic-user; most of it's dead wrong. No ectoplasm, for one thing."

"How in the world do you know all of this?"

"I've lived in the crazy for a year." She laughed. "Honestly, once you accept that what you thought was reality is really a fucked-up illusion, it gets easier."

"The fortune-teller said something like that. Well, she said I could see what's really there."

"And there you have it." Claudia still grinned at me, like I was in on a secret. "Hey, it's not all bad."

I wasn't inclined to agree. "Why am I different?" I said. "Why do the demons look at me like that?"

"It's like I said—they're drawn to magic."

"But isn't there a way to make them go away?"

"Not from here. You saw me fight off that shadow-fox, but it was on this side of the Barrier. The Barrier's like a force field around our world. It's invisible. You can't see it or touch it, but it's there. Shadow-beasts can only get through if a sorcerer summons them. If that happens, we can fight them. There are kinds of magic demons are afraid of. According to the Venantium, that's what we're obliged to do. Like me sending off that shadow-fox. Though I've no idea who actually summoned the damn thing. They don't get here of their own accord."

"Who exactly *are* the Venantium?"

"They're the ones who maintain the Barrier, the people who keep our world safe from demons. They call the shots. Officially, all magic-users should be registered under the Venantium."

"So why aren't I?" This got weirder and weirder.

"If there aren't any other magic-users in your family, then they have no way of knowing about it. It's quite unusual, but it happens."

"So, do I have to register, or what?" *Please no.* I just wanted to get on with my life—not fall further and further into the *crazy*.

"No, you don't have to. They like to keep tabs on all magic-users. The unofficial reason is so they can keep an eye on all potential demonic summonings. Only sorcerers can summon demons."

"But why would anyone even do that, if demons can possess you?"

"Because a demon, like any other spirit, is temporarily under the power of the person who summoned it. A sorcerer can use a demon's magic to enhance their own. The risk of the demon turning on its summoner is a small price to pay, in their eyes."

"And if you're possessed? What then? Can you break free?"

Claudia gave me a pitying look reminiscent of the fortune-teller. "No. The demon has to choose to let you go. But in nearly all cases, the demon kills the victim before the Venantium can set them free then flees back to the Darkworld."

My breath caught, and the old fear clawed at me—the fear of the otherworldly. "But they're spirits, aren't they?" I said. "How do they kill you?" My morbid streak took over again, before I could ask myself if I *really* wanted to know that.

"They call it the touch of instant death. Once a demon's in your mind, it's a small matter of reaching out to the part of your mind that tells your heart to keep beating, and, as casually as you might flick a light switch, turning off your life."

Coldness flooded me, as if every drop of blood in my veins had turned to ice.

I said, in a whisper, "How do you fight them? You scared off that shadow-fox, right?"

"Fire," said Claudia. "Demons thrive in darkness, in coldness. Their deepest fear is fire." She paused. "Sorry. It's been a while since I had to explain this to someone. Figured it'd be better to get the scary part over with, first. Plus, it's a rehearsal for when you get to meet Berenice." She laughed. "Okay, now it's time for the fun part. Magic."

9

THE DARKNESS BENEATH

"Hold out your hands," Claudia said, extending her own palms. I did the same, observing that her nails were perfectly manicured—unlike mine, which were bitten down to stumps. "I've not gone through this for a while, but apparently it works. Right. This might sound weird, but trust me on this: the Darkworld's all around us. You're tuned into it, anyway. Just concentrate. You'll feel it."

Feel what? I wasn't sure what I was supposed to focus on. I was aware of the sun peeking over the horizon, faint rays seeping through the trees and turning the leaves below us into a golden carpet. The strong smell of bark hung in the air, and birdsong echoed in a tuneful melody. I knew I shouldn't be focusing on my surroundings but on the Darkworld. That dark place; the world behind the gaps.

I called to mind the feeling that always came when a demon lurked nearby, the prickling sensation of a presence being there which shouldn't be. Instantly, a familiar coldness shot up my arms.

"Now… I don't know how else to put this, but imagine you're holding something hot."

"Huh?"

"To create fire, you need to be in the right mind-set. That's the quickest way. Maybe imagine you have fire under your skin, that's what I do. Watch." She looked down at her hands, forehead wrinkled in concentration for a second. Then sparks ran down her arms, and her hands were suddenly aflame.

I jumped back in shock as the fire danced from one palm to another, smokeless but alive. I stepped farther away. Even from a distance, the fire felt uncomfortable against my skin. "Shit!" I said. "How in hell did you——"

"You try it."

I looked sceptically at my hands. They felt like they could easier turn to ice than fire. Maybe I wasn't cut out for this. All the same, I tried. "Fire," I whispered, imagining flames leaping into life. Nothing happened.

"It takes practice," said Claudia. "But you know how to do it if you get attacked again. I'm sorry I can't be more help. I've never taught a complete beginner before. I only learned myself a year ago. My mum and dad taught me to defend myself using fire, even though they don't really use magic themselves. Because, you know, demons."

"It's all right. I'm just glad I found you. I was totally clueless on my own."

"You should come to one of our meetings. Give me your number. I'll text you."

"Meetings?"

"A bunch of us meet up every week—well, we did last year. You know, people like us."

"I get it. Like a secret circle." I fought back an unexpected giggle.

"Not quite." She grinned. "There used to be four of us.

Cyrus started it. He's in third year now. Then there's Howard, Berenice, and me—and Leo, he's a Fresher, like you."

"So, what do you do, then? Save mankind from the evil demons?" I couldn't restrain another giggle. What was the matter with me?

"No, we just talk. It helps to talk to other people like you. Your number?"

I recited my new number, glad I'd memorised it, since my phone was in my room, and she added my name to her contacts on her mobile.

"It's dawn," said Claudia, glancing upward at the gleaming sun, which by now shone above the treetops. "I should probably head back. I think Berenice'll be ready to apologise now."

"Wait," I said. "There's something else I want to know. Why can't I see demons here? Or in Blackstone?"

"I'd have thought you'd have guessed," said Claudia. "The Venantium's headquarters operate not far from here. They have this whole area under their protection to prevent any demons from coming within a ten-kilometre radius. And before you ask if it's a coincidence, us being in the same area as them, it isn't. Did you think you picked this university by accident? This place attracts people sensitive to the Darkworld. You must have felt it when you visited, a sense of belonging."

My heart dropped. "So, it's fake, then? I feel like I belong here because of that?"

"No, but it does have more of an influence on people like us. I'm not sure of the percentage, but I'd say a good tenth of the students here have some kind of connection to the Darkworld."

"Really?" I said, thinking of my flatmates. Alex, Sarah, and David hadn't reacted at all to the appearance of the shadow-fox outside Satan's Pit. No one could be that good an actor, to be able to ignore a freaking monster. Unless, of course, they were used to it.

"Not my friends," I said. "They don't know about any of this."

"I wouldn't know," said Claudia. "Well, I might have seen that guy take a look at the shadow-fox, but I can't be sure. I was a bit drunk."

"You mean David?"

"The guy who looked like he was totally into you? Yeah."

What?

Claudia glanced up at the sky. "Anyway, I really need to get back to my flat. Come to our next meeting."

"When will that be?"

"Wednesday afternoon, at three-thirty. Last year, we met in the little games room above the common room. It'll probably be the same this year."

"I'll be there," I said. "Tell me one thing, though. That shadow-fox last night. It wasn't supposed to be there, was it? I mean, is it safe to go off-campus?"

I realised how stupid it sounded the instant the words came out of my mouth.

"'Is it safe?'" Claudia laughed. "Is anywhere safe? I don't know about you, but I come from a big city. People got stabbed down the road from where I lived. I didn't feel safe *before* I started seeing demons, Ash. Did you?"

Fair point. I shook my head. "Guess not. Just wondered, is all."

"Look," said Claudia. "There are weirdos wherever you go. It's a fact of life, unfortunately. But about the shadow-fox—well, there are people on the lookout for that kind of thing. I'll tell you more about it at the meeting, but the Venantium are on patrol through Redthorne. It's a problem area, because it's right outside of their barrier zone around Blackstone. But they've never attacked an ordinary person. No point in doing that. We're the lucky buggers they go for."

I breathed out, some of the tension releasing. They wouldn't attack my friends.

"Hell, I go out there nearly every night," said Claudia. "Freaky stuff's happened maybe a half-dozen times in the last year, and that was mostly because I'm friends with idiots who like to pick fights with monsters."

"Who?"

"You'll meet Howard soon." She smirked. "He's a handful, but you'll get used to it."

"Right."

"Anyway. I'm off. Try practising a bit, 'kay?"

"Sure thing," I said.

Watching her retreat, I tried once again to summon fire. There had to be some kind of trick I was missing. Now that I'd contacted the Darkworld, I could feel the frozen emptiness hovering at the edge of my awareness. But *heat* was the last thing on my mind. I closed my eyes— like that would help—and my hands curled into fists. *Fire.* I tried to give the thought the same confidence Claudia had.

Nothing.

I opened my eyes. Maybe I was going about it the wrong way. I hadn't known what I was doing when that shadow-fox attacked, but maybe now, it would work like a fight-or-flight response. My eyes closed again, and I imagined I stood outside Satan's Pit, cornered by a red-eyed creature of shadows. This time, I wouldn't freeze up.

Fire! I splayed out my hands, and *cold* rushed down my arms. My eyes flew open in time to see a handful of ice shards scatter onto the ground. I stared. *Did I do that?* Ice, not fire. Not helpful against the Darkworld, given that it was such a cold place itself.

Still, it was better than nothing. But I couldn't shake the uneasy feeling.

WHEN I RETURNED to my room and kicked off my muddied slippers, I didn't go back to bed. Knowing I'd never be able to focus on course reading, I switched on the television, only to be greeted by static. Flicking through the channels, I concluded there was no television signal out here in the middle of nowhere. It made sense. Half the time I didn't have a phone signal, and it always cut out during phone calls.

My concentration wasn't up to playing on my PlayStation, so I switched off the TV and started rereading Shakespeare's *Hamlet*. No progress later, I went to the kitchen to make some breakfast. I walked right past David, who stood in the middle of the corridor. My hand froze on the kitchen door, and I turned around.

"What're you doing?"

"Nothing." He moved in the direction of his room as though that was where he'd intended to go all along.

I stared. He'd been hovering between my door and Terrence's. "What, you just felt like standing out here?"

"I thought I heard something coming from there." He indicated Terrence's room, shifting from one foot to the other like he was nervous.

"Ah. Yeah, I've heard weird noises from there, too. Alex said she heard him yelling at someone. I think he must be using Skype. That's what my friend Cara and I are doing now, 'cause there's no signal."

"Hmm." He frowned. Then he gave me an unconvincing smile. "Sorry I was a bit of a dick the other day."

"Sorry I overreacted." I forced a smile of my own. "Don't worry about it. Are you doing anything today?"

"I was thinking of going to Redthorne. I need to get some hiking boots."

"Oh yeah," I said, remembering. "I do, too. My old trainers are in no shape to scale mountains."

David's smile became genuine. "We can go in an hour or so," he said. "Knock on my door when you're ready, okay?"

"Sure," I said.

I'D HOPED to push all thoughts of demons and magic from my head, but the first thing I saw when we got off the bus in Redthorne was a dark space, like someone had sliced through the air with a giant knife. A pair of violet eyes gleamed from its depths. Dread clutched at me. Claudia's words echoed in my mind: *They call it the touch of instant death. Once a demon's in your mind, it's a small matter of reaching out to the part that tells your heart to keep beating and, as casually as you might flick a light switch, turning off your life.*

I clenched my fists, nails biting into my palms. So I could see it. Big deal. It couldn't hurt me. I didn't care that I was naïve to think like that. I couldn't spend the rest of my life wondering if the next demon I saw would be my last. I wouldn't live in fear. Not anymore.

I walked right through the dark space as if it wasn't there. Or as if I had the normal sight of a regular person, someone who couldn't see the darkness. *The darkness beneath.*

David gave me an odd look. "You feeling okay, Ash?"

"Sure," I said with a smile. Stepping through that dark space felt like a triumph, in a way.

But I couldn't help noticing David walked slightly to the left of the dark space as I walked through it. *Can he see it, too? Is he like me?* Or had I imagined it?

Doubts crowded my mind, but I turned my thoughts back to the present. I couldn't keep suspecting everyone I knew of having a connection to the Darkworld. It would drive me mad.

Perhaps I was being paranoid, but the dark spaces stood out more than usual. Before now, they'd become part of the background, irritating but not threatening. Now, however, my spine coiled with tension whenever one caught my eye.

Relax. Claudia said it's safe. People are patrolling. And nothing's going to attack you as long as you're with David.

David seemed subdued, too, however. At least shopping with him was straightforward. It took only an hour for David and me to get everything we needed from the outdoors shop, and we still had time left for a visit to Waterstones.

"Cara always says I need someone to restrain me when I come into a bookshop," I said.

He didn't respond. I shot him a glance. He'd picked up a book, some dry-looking politics volume.

"That's for your course?"

"Um, yeah." Another forced smile. Strange. He hadn't acted shy before, but now the awkwardness was almost palpable. Still, I made for the classics section to see if there was anything I needed. Or that was my excuse, anyway. As always, it took extreme restraint for me not to buy everything on the shelves. Even so, I caved into temptation and bought a couple of books that Alex and Sarah had recommended to me. But definitely nothing involving magic or monsters.

David took a little longer, wandering through the politics aisle as though he didn't know what he was looking for. I was starting to feel I needed to check into the section that stocked books with advice on how to make general conversation.

And now my brain had successfully wrangled itself into a knot. Great. *Demons* were easier to figure out than guys.

"Want to go to Starbucks?" said David as we left the bookshop.

"Sure," I said. Maybe that would break the tension. I started to feel a little annoyed with David for not trying to initiate conversation. Not that I was one to talk, but still. Perhaps, like me, he'd made an effort to talk to people in the first day or two, but now things were starting to settle into a routine, he'd reverted to whatever he'd been like before. Yet another reminder that I didn't really know him.

As we sat over coffee in the middle of the noisy café, I asked about hobbies, but we'd already covered that topic, and what little information I could get out of him was kind of a conversation-stopper. Even the books he'd bought.

"I know, I know," he said. "They look boring."

I shrugged. "Well, I can recite *Paradise Lost* pretty much from beginning to end. Not that it helped much, but you know. Might come in handy one day."

"Hey, don't knock yourself like that. You're really intel-ligent, Ash. You shouldn't let other people put you off doing what you want."

"I don't." My face burned. "I came here because I wanted to."

"Yeah, same here. There's something about it, you know?"

What did his tone imply? Had he simply liked the

university, or, like Claudia said, was it some kind of psychic influence? Now I didn't know how much of what I thought I heard was coloured by the words of Claudia and the fortune-teller. Intentionally or not, together they'd completely fragmented my peace of mind.

Did David like me? Was I reading the signs all wrong? I had no previous experience to draw on. I'd never dated before. Going to an all-girls' school and having an eccentric best friend probably hadn't helped, but the truth was, I couldn't be bothered with the drama. Now, though, I wished I'd paid more attention. I hadn't a clue whether I *liked* him, or if I'd just been embarrassed by the compliment. Plus it was pretty clear we were on different wavelengths with a lot of things.

I sighed. *This is ridiculous.* I'd Skype Cara to ask her advice.

I sipped my coffee to fill the silence, gasping as it scalded the back of my throat.

"You okay…" He broke off, his face hardening into a different expression entirely. Eyes watering, I followed his gaze.

Two guys had come upstairs—two figures dressed in navy blue uniforms. They sidled through the door, almost knocking into a woman who was leaving. She stumbled aside, a puzzled expression on her face.

"You done, Ash? We should go," David said.

I frowned. The back of my throat smarted, but I was more spooked by those two guys. Something about them looked *off*.

They sat at a table near the front door. I squinted in their direction. It was like trying to peer through distorted glass, which made it hard to focus on anything. And I was conscious of David's agitated expression.

He hovered over me, shoulders taut with tension. "There's a back staircase over there."

David was right; there was another door at the room's other side. He was already crossing towards it. I set the half-empty coffee cup down on the table and hurried after him.

"What's up?" I asked as he pushed open the door onto the stairwell. "Who were those guys?"

"What guys?"

I raised my eyebrows. "The ones who just came in? Who made you jump like you sat on a hedgehog?"

David let out an unconvincing laugh. "Sorry about that," he said. "They just—they're not very nice. I knew them at school. I didn't want them to start on you."

"Bullies?"

"Something like that."

They'd looked older than students, but I hadn't really got a close look at them.

David didn't say a word as we descended to the ground floor of the coffee shop. The bustling noise drove away the weird feeling those two guys had given me, but suspicion nagged at me. I couldn't think of a way to push for more information without feeling intrusive. Sometimes I wished I was as bold as Alex—she'd have just asked straight out.

But as soon as we left the coffee shop, David started up a never-ending commentary on a group of motorbikes idling down the street, and I couldn't get a word in edge-ways. I tuned him out as we got on the bus back to campus, and I groaned as he started commenting on cars, too.

"Sorry," he said. "I forgot you probably aren't inter-ested. I tend to ramble when I've not had enough sleep."

"You can't sleep, either?" I said, in a last-ditch attempt to steer the conversation to common ground. I was no good at reading people at all. And the part when he'd called me *intelligent*?

"It's just hard being somewhere new, you know?"

I nodded, but my thoughts were elsewhere.

Was I overreacting? Those guys might have been part of a student group. Like the role-players. I hadn't seen dark spaces nearby, no evidence to connect them to the Darkworld.

But it was plain David was hiding *something*. And I wasn't sure I needed another mystery in a life which was already teetering over the edge of crazy.

One thing at a time. First, I had a degree to start next week. Then I'd see what Claudia had to say at the meeting on Wednesday.

10

THE CIRCLE OF SINNERS

Two days into my degree, and I'd managed not to mess up yet. Whatever psychic influence had led me to this course, I was grateful—even if I already had an essay to write. Not that I could focus. Claudia texted me the night before the meeting, asking if I was still coming. I replied in the affirmative. Even though I was half-tempted to let it slide and pretend this part of my life didn't exist, the fact remained that a monster had tried to attack me outside the club. What if it happened again? And, whether I admitted it to myself or not, I wanted to know more. I still needed answers.

When I finally got to sleep that night, I revisited an old childhood nightmare, one from the days when I used to stay at Aunt Eve's Windermere cottage every summer. As a young child, I'd loved to play in the woods behind the house, despite Mum nagging me to stay out of there, telling me I'd get lost. I loved the way the trees were so dense that they cut out the sunlight even on the sunniest day, making it seem like I wandered through a twilight-lit fairyland. I loved the atmosphere, the absence of human noise. Yet, it was so easy to lose track of time. Sometimes when the sun was going down, I'd lose my way, and darkness would steal in, making it unrecognisable. Then I'd panic. Fear would rise within me, and I'd run, feet pounding on the path, not knowing why but being unable to stop. Like I was running from an invisible threat. Maybe even then I sensed the presence of demons.

In my dreams, the monsters that chased me were real, solid creatures, and tonight they looked like shadow-foxes. Their teeth snapped at my heels. I put on a burst of speed, almost as if I'd grown wings, feet skimming the ground as I flew between dark, twisted trees. But the shadows kept pace alongside me, and, as one brushed against my leg, a familiar paralysing chill swept through me. My feet froze in position. My legs locked. Teeth sank into my ankle, and the searing pain jolted me awake.

I forced my eyes open to find myself half-in, half-out of my bed. My ankle burned with sharp pain, but I couldn't twist my head to look because, once again, I couldn't move. *This is effing ridiculous!* I put in every bit of strength I could muster, coaxing my body to roll towards the edge of the bed, and tumbled over, hitting the floor with a jarring crash.

The impact jolted me out of paralysis. Clambering to my feet, I examined the injury, expecting to see a line of teeth marks on my ankle. But, stranger than that, a pinkish line, like a burn, marked my skin. It itched like crazy. *Carpet burn? Weird.*

I felt a cold draft from the open window—also odd, because I never left it open overnight. Not after the sheep incident. I didn't want the local wildlife paying a visit to my room. Maybe I'd woken up in the night to open it and forgotten.

I sat in the window seat with a book, watching the sun

rise over the distant hills. Peaceful. But I knew all too well that, whilst this place might be free from darkness, it waited out there. And today I'd take my first step towards facing the nightmares.

Today was my free day, so I had no lectures or seminars to attend. I buried myself in reading for a few hours, preparing for my classes later in the week. But I was distracted—my mind kept skipping to the meeting. Glancing at the clock, I left the flat minutes before I was to meet Claudia and walked across the student village to the common room.

The only person inside was a disinterested bartender who didn't give me a second glance. It took me a while to find the Games Room upstairs; the staircase was tucked away out of sight in a corner. I walked past it at least six times before I noticed it. Heart beating fast, I pushed open the door and climbed the cramped, narrow stairs. I heard the buzz of a television and several voices behind the red-painted door at the top, and, before I could lose my nerve, I went in.

For a second, I thought I'd wandered into the wrong room. I counted four people grouped around a large flat-screen television. As I edged closer, I saw the two guys were playing some Xbox game whilst the two girls watched. One guy was large and muscular with fair hair; the other was smaller, with unruly dark hair and a T-shirt with the slogan "Why so serious?" scrawled underneath a picture of the Joker. The second guy seemed to be winning the game.

Claudia turned around as I entered. She wore a plain black skirt and a red shirt today, her hair tied back in a ponytail.

"There you are!" she said. "Guys, this is Ash. She's our newest recruit."

The other girl cast me a disinterested look then

turned her eyes back to the screen. She was striking, with glossy black hair, multiple piercings, and a butterfly tattooed on the arm she'd draped around the back of the sofa. There was no response at all from the guys, who appeared to be locked in an intense wrestling match on-screen.

"Come on, man!" said the blond guy. "Give me a chance! That wasn't fair!"

"Life's not fair, Howard," said the other guy.

"You're an asshole."

"That was totally legit, and you know it. You just can't take losing."

"Shut up!"

To my complete and utter astonishment, Howard stood up—he must have been at least six and a half feet tall—and hurled the wireless Xbox controller at the other guy's head. The other guy ducked out of the way just in time, and the controller hit the floor with such force the batteries shot out in all directions.

"I'm sick of this bullshit!" Howard roared and stormed out the room.

"Jesus," said the dark-haired guy, shaking his head. "Who pissed him off this time?"

"Some *venator* came knocking on his door this morning," said the girl on the sofa. "Said he wanted him to come and register. Again. Howard nearly tore his head off."

"You might have warned me." He put the controller down and started groping under the sofa for the missing batteries.

"God," said Claudia. "Did they give him another warning?"

"I don't think so. It was some new kid who did it. I think Howard scared him enough that he won't tell."

"At least there's that," said Claudia. "Sorry about that, Ash. Howard's a little… volatile."

"So I see," I said, a lot more composed than I felt. I was beginning to regret ever agreeing to come.

"Anyway, you've not met Berenice or Leo yet, have you?"

"Um, no." Feeling I might as well make the best of the situation, I said, "Hi, I'm Ashlyn, but I prefer being called Ash. Nice to meet you."

"Hey." The dark-haired guy emerged from underneath the sofa with two of the missing batteries in hand. "I'm Leo. You're a Fresher, too?"

"Yeah," I said. "What course are you doing?"

"Same as you. English Literature. I saw you at the lecture yesterday. Decided to show up for once."

"I guess I didn't see you," I said. "I've had a lot of new faces to learn."

"I joined up with this crew a couple of weeks ago," said Leo. "But my brother, Cyrus, is the one who started this little group of misfits a year ago."

Berenice snorted. "Well, Cyrus isn't here, he's *working*. I guess we won't be able to teach the newbie any of our tricks."

"I can teach her," said Claudia. "I told you, she doesn't know——"

"Anything." Berenice snorted again. "A fine little circle of sinners we are. Demons the world over should tremble in fear."

What had I done to rattle her chain? I'd only just walked in. "What exactly do you do, then?" I said. "What do you mean by 'circle of sinners?'"

"I picked the name," said Leo, sprawling on the sofa in the space where Howard had been sitting. "There are people——even in the Venantium itself——who think all magic-users are servants of Satan. Which is kind of ironic, really. You have questions, then?"

"I don't really get who the Venantium are," I said, ignoring Berenice's derisive snort. I wanted to learn everything I could. "What do they actually do?"

"The original Venantium was a group of sorcerers dedicated to protecting our world against demons," said Leo. "That's the reason for their name. *Venantium* means 'hunters' in Latin, and each member is known as a *venator*. Sounds more impressive than it is, trust me. Most *venators* I've met are total dickwads."

"Why?" I said. "Claudia told me they help protect everyone from demons. How can that be a bad thing?"

"They're blackmailers," said Leo. "The underhanded shit they get up to, you wouldn't believe. Howard knows it, and he won't forgive them for it. They arrested his parents for experimenting with magic when he was a kid—don't ask me what they were doing; I've no idea—and he hasn't seen them since. He tried to break into their Headquarters for answers about five years ago, and they blocked his magic for breaking the laws."

"That's horrible," I said. "Can they arrest anyone for using magic without their permission?"

"In theory, they can, but they often don't know about it. Simple protective spells will keep most sorcerers from detecting magic-users if they're done right. We'd never get any peace otherwise." He turned to Claudia. "I take it you want me to do it to her?"

She nodded.

"Right." Then he said to me, "Don't freak out, but I'm going to put a spell on you. A shield. It'll stop anyone from knowing if you've used magic. Even a Venantium member wouldn't be able to tell, unless they broke cover and used a spell on you."

I don't know what expression he saw on my face, but he seemed to interpret it as nervousness.

"Don't worry. It definitely works. Only me and my brother can do it, but we learned from an expert—someone in the Venantium itself. Seriously, don't panic. Just relax." He spoke in soothing tones, and, for some reason, this grated on my nerves.

"You think I'm going to freak out? I've seen demons. Trust me—it'll take more than a little magic to scare me off."

He laughed. "Okay. Well, Berenice freaked out when I did it to her. Nearly clawed my eyes out."

"No danger of that happening," I said, holding up my bitten nails.

He laughed again. The expression on Berenice's face would have sent anyone else running for cover, but Leo didn't look particularly fazed.

"Right," he continued. "The shield isn't totally fool-proof, but, even if you run smack into a *venator*, they won't know you from an ordinary person."

"And demons?" I said. "Will they stop staring at me?"

"They stare at you?" Leo gave me a curious look. "That's a new one."

"Everywhere I go. Well, except here and in Blackstone."

"Hmm," said Leo. "Must be fun, that. All the time? Do they stare at you when you're in the shower?"

"*Leo!*" said Claudia.

"Just curious," said Leo, shrugging.

"They don't come into my house, so no," I said, but I was pretty sure my face was on fire all the same.

"That's weird." Claudia frowned. "Do your parents have a protective shield put on the house?"

"No. No, I don't think so. They don't know anything about demons."

"That's not possible. Someone must have put a shield up there."

"Huh? I've lived there all my life, and… wouldn't I have noticed?"

"Could've been the previous owners," said Leo. "Strange. I've never heard of the demons taking an interest in one person before. When did it first happen?"

"Nearly a year ago. The first time I saw one was in the middle of a school assembly, before Christmas last year." But it felt like a long time ago. Life before the demons… it seemed more and more like a dream.

"Really?" said Leo.

"Yeah. It was on the day people said the world was going to end."

"Same day the Venantium went apeshit," said Leo, giving Claudia a significant look.

"Huh?" I said.

"There was a demon attack in Manchester on that day," said Claudia. "It almost made the news, but the Venantium worked their subliminal magic and managed to cover it up. Some smartass sorcerer decided to summon a demon, and it escaped. It took a day for the Venantium to catch it. Found the sorcerer in his secret lair, where he'd been up to all kinds of crazy shit. They killed the demon, but it was too late for the sorcerer."

"Manchester?" I swallowed. *They call it the touch of instant death…* "I live there. Is that why I started to see demons on that day?"

"I don't know, but I'm guessing it's because there was more demonic activity than usual," said Claudia.

"There's a theory that loads of people have the connection but don't realise it," said Leo. "If you grow up with it, like the kids of people in the Venantium, then you know how to use magic from an early age. But, if no one in your family's a magic-user, you'd have no idea."

"What about you guys, then? How did you find out?"

"My parents used to be in the Venantium," said Claudia. "They both quit when I was born, said it was too risky. They'd made too many enemies of rogue sorcerers. They told me about the connection, but said that I could make my own mind up whether to use it or not. I know the *venators* are keeping an eye on me in case I decide to go rogue."

"Sounds like paranoia," I said.

"It's ridiculous," she said. "They're watching Berenice, too, and Leo. Leo and Cyrus' father is really high up in the Venantium."

"Really?" I said.

Leo shrugged. "Haven't seen the tosser in years. He left me when my mother died, said he was going to devote his life to ridding the world of all demons—or some overblown claim. Moron."

"What? Your dad left you?" I said.

"It's not uncommon for higher *venators* to totally denounce their families," said Claudia. "They claim it's for safety reasons, but it's really the power that attracts them. They think they'll be the one to find a way to cut this world off from the Darkworld for good."

"Which is impossible," said Leo. "Our world can't exist without the Darkworld. They might put up Barriers, but the Venantium are afraid that demons will find a way to break through anyway. It's their biggest fear—the monsters will overrun their defence systems."

"Is that possible?" I said.

"No, not unless someone undid the work of a hundred generations of sorcerers," said Claudia. "The Barrier's a tightly wound net of spells, strengthened over the years. No magic can touch it, human or demon."

"So what are they worried about?"

"Losing their powers? Who knows? Anyway, you never told me whether anything happened that day, any reason your connection might have awakened."

"Just a power-cut," I said. "All the lights went out, and I saw it. Then they kept appearing."

"That's… bizarre," said Leo.

"I thought she must have sorcerer blood," said Claudia.

Leo nodded. "Could be. Have you ever seen your family tree? What's your surname?"

"My surname's Temple. No, I haven't seen a family tree. But, even if I had, how would I know if my ancestors were sorcerers or not? No one in my family's ever been famous enough to make it into the history books."

"There's a way of finding out." A smirk settled on Leo's face. "Howard'll love it. Oi, Berenice!"

No answer. Berenice appeared to be asleep.

"Berenice, you're not fooling anyone."

"Oh, so I exist again now, do I?" She sat up, flicking her hair back over her shoulder, and glared at me.

"Stop being a drama queen," said Claudia. "You could have joined in the conversation."

"I'm not interested in babysitting the newbie."

I bristled at that. "I never asked you to, so there's no reason to be a bitch."

"*What* did you call me?"

"Berenice! Stop trying to start an argument," Claudia said. "And stop laughing, Leo."

"Yeah, it's not funny," snapped Berenice.

"Course it isn't," said Leo, snickering. "Well, this'll liven things up."

"'This' meaning me?" I interjected.

"Now I remember why we need Cyrus here," said Claudia. "Someone has to keep the children in order."

"Excuse me, Miss Maturity," said Leo.

I rolled my eyes. "Is someone going to tell me what this big idea is?"

"Breaking and entering," said Leo. "You up for that, Berenice?"

"Count me out," said Berenice, glaring at me. "I've got other stuff I'd rather be doing. Like sleeping. Or getting pissed."

"Breaking and entering?" I said. "Why?"

"The Venantium's library has records of every sorcerer who ever walked the Earth," said Leo. "If there's anything on your ancestors, it'll be in there."

"And we have to break in… why?"

"Technically, I'm allowed in, but you won't be," said Claudia. "It's only for use by registered sorcerers. Howard's banned, too."

"That doesn't surprise me," I said. "Wait a minute—"

"I'm not convinced one night will cover it," said Leo.

"Well, we'll see what we find. We'll do it next week, after the meeting," Claudia replied.

What the hell have I gotten myself into? "Don't I get a say in this?" I asked. "I mean, it is *my* ancestors we're talking about."

"Exactly," said Leo. "If it were me, I'd want to know which naughty sorcerer in my family decided to hide him or herself from the Venantium. It's not a light decision."

"You're jumping to conclusions!" I threw up my hands. "I keep telling you—no one in my family can use magic. If you'd met my parents, you'd know. I'm just an anomaly, a freak of nature."

"We're all freaks of nature," said Leo. "But the demons

want something from you. If you come with us, we could help you find out what it is."

He was right, of course. I did want to know.

"And the likelihood of us getting caught?" I asked.

"Practically nothing," said Leo. "For a bunch of dusty old cretins, the *venators* rarely go into the library. Plus, I can put a shield on you to stop them seeing you're a magic-user."

I bit my lip. Saying yes would commit me to this life, one I wasn't yet sure I wanted.

And yet, a tugging sensation inside nagged at me. *I can always back out if I change my mind, right?*

"All right," I said. "Count me in."

11

LET THERE BE LIGHT

Once Leo put the shield spell on me—which took less than a second and felt like slipping underneath a large, feather-light coat—Claudia tried to get me to conjure fire again.

"I never asked you before—have you ever accidentally used magic before? I mean, done something you never intended to do?"

"I don't think so," I said, but one incident stole to the front of my mind, unbidden. "But… well, I don't know if I did it or not. It could have been a coincidence, but in the middle of an exam, the clocks stopped, with five minutes left of the exam. I don't know whether it was me, but I was thinking about how I needed to finish my essay in time, and…" I trailed off.

They both stared at me like I'd announced I could walk on water.

"It's probably nothing, just coincidence," I said.

"You think you can stop time?" said Berenice, whose eyebrows had disappeared into her curled fringe.

"No, of course not. Just the clock. Anyway, it was probably broken."

"Or you could have used subliminal magic by accident," said Claudia. "That's tricky to work, that is, but it could have been. I mean, it's not like you'd have known you were doing it."

"Subliminal?"

"Influence," said Claudia. "Generally, it works only on people, not objects, but that's what it sounds like. You want something to happen, so you make it so, sometimes without even realising it. I sometimes use it accidentally if I want to be left alone when I'm hungover. It can make you... not invisible, but unnoticeable. People avoid you, but they don't know they're being manipulated subconsciously."

I remembered with clarity the way people had avoided me in the corridors at school, even people I didn't know. Had I caused that myself without even realising it? All the times I'd been depressed, in a bad mood, and it was like people looked straight through me. Even the teachers didn't seem to notice me in their lessons half the time.

"Well, if it was, we know one thing," said Leo.

"What's that?" asked Claudia.

"Ash'll be in trouble if it ever gets out she cheated in her exam."

"It wasn't *cheating*," I protested, flushing. "It doesn't count as cheating if you don't do it on purpose."

"Tell it to the examiners!" Leo seemed highly amused by this. "'I didn't mean to subconsciously give myself an extra five minutes!'"

"Stop laughing at me!" I said. "It hardly matters now, anyway. I'm here." I turned to Claudia. "So, anyway, do you have any tips for conjuring fire?"

"Just keep your concentration. And it helps if you

really *want* it to happen——like stopping that clock."

So I tried. I concentrated so hard on fire that the room should have burst into flames. But nothing happened. Reluctantly, I let Leo take over the lesson. I got the distinct impression he'd got involved so he'd have the chance to show off to the newbie. His arrogance annoyed me; I wasn't sure if I liked him or not.

"The first thing you should know is that magic isn't a trick," said Leo. "And it isn't doing the impossible as much as manipulating the laws of nature to do as you tell them. You can't conjure or create anything, but you can meddle with what's already there. There's always the potential for fire. All it takes is a little persuasion. Look."

Sparks danced down his arms to his fingertips and flames sprang into being. He held the small fire in one hand then tipped it gently, and it fell. He caught the blaze on one foot and kicked it into the air like a football. As I watched, mesmerised, he rolled the ball of flames from one shoulder to another. It split in two, then four, spreading in a faint line until shimmering flames outlined his entire body.

"I'm the man on fire." He grinned.

I was too stunned to roll my eyes at his theatrical performance. "Wow," I said. "Doesn't it hurt you at all? Or at least burn your clothes?"

"Not if I don't want it to. You try."

I didn't even know where to start. And, although I was new to this, it still unsettled me that everything I did went against some unwritten rules. What if the Venantium caught me?

Leo seemed to read my mind. "Look," he sai, "if the worst happens and you do get caught by the Venantium, you can claim innocence and blame it on us. We've all been in trouble before."

His would-be casual tone suggested, however, that the consequences for breaking into the Venantium's library would be more severe than he was letting on.

"I don't want to drag you guys into this," I said.

"Honestly, it doesn't matter," said Claudia. "Half the crap Howard gets up to, it's a miracle we aren't locked in the cells. Try the fire, again."

I tried. But I could no sooner summon a flame than leap out the window and fly.

"This really isn't working. Look," I said hesitantly, "there's something else you should know about me."

"What's that?" said Leo.

"Ever since I first saw the demons, I haven't been able to get warm. And I don't feel the cold any more. I used to. I used to be cold all the time, but now I don't feel it at all. I don't know if that's what might be stopping me from conjuring fire." *And I summoned ice.*

Claudia looked at Leo. "Have you ever heard of that happening?"

"No." He shook his head. "I've heard of a lot of strange things—kind of inevitable when you grow up around sorcerers—but this is a new one."

"Great," I said. "And I thought I was a regular person, just a magic-user who can see demons."

Leo laughed. "Well, you're certainly full of surprises. All right. Forget about the fire for now. It's the Venantium's library we're breaking into. There's no place you're less likely to encounter a demon. But there's something else you might find useful."

"Like what?"

"This."

The lights in the room suddenly went out.

"What—?"

I jumped back as he blazed all over with dazzling,

white light. The brightness faded slightly, but his skin continued to glow an eerie shade of white. Then the light condensed into a point in the centre of his right palm, a glowing white ball, pulsing like a heartbeat.

"Better than a torch?" he said.

I blinked. The initial glare was still imprinted on my eyes, and I saw blurred shapes everywhere.

"Leo, stop showing off," said Claudia.

"What, it's not every day I get to dazzle someone."

The world came back into focus. "How'd you do that?"

"You can feel your connection to the Darkworld, right? Use that and imagine you're holding a bright light. Focus on the palm of one hand and tap into the magic at the same time. It's as easy as that."

It didn't sound easy to me, but I held out my right hand and focused all my attention on it, at the same time thinking of the Darkworld. *Light.* And, this time, a chill shivered down my arms, and the tiniest globe of light sprang into existence in the centre of my hand.

I stared at it, shocked speechless.

"Nice!" said Leo.

"Good job," said Claudia.

At that moment, the spark went out. "Oh."

"It takes practice and concentration," said Leo. "Not everyone gets it the first time. Keep at it. You'll get there."

"Where on earth have you been?" asked Alex, as I came into the kitchen that evening to find Alex and Sarah sitting around the table, with their laptops and a stack of books. The strong aroma of disinfectant almost masked the stench of what I assumed was another failed attempt at cooking—

sure enough, the blackened remains of an omelette lay in the sink.

"At the Gaming Society induction meeting," I said. That was a reasonable excuse, given I was the only one of us remotely interested in gaming. Not that I'd even had the chance to log into my *World of Warcraft* account since coming here.

"Oh, right. We thought you were dead," said Alex.

"Sorry to disappoint." I said with a smile. "Why does it small of bleach in here?"

"Terrence," said Alex. "We want to get him kicked out of our flat."

"Why?" I pulled out a chair.

"Because he left raw meat all over the place, I've been cleaning for the past hour. If we all get salmonella, it's his fault."

"Raw meat?"

"Yeah, dripping blood everywhere. For all I know he's harvesting human organs or something."

"Highly unlikely." I said. "But that's kind of out of order. We all live here, and we'll get charged if he leaves the flat in a mess, right?"

"Exactly," said Alex. "I don't want to get eaten by a gigantic cockroach infestation."

"I don't think that's going to happen, Alex," said Sarah. "I think this essay is more likely to kill me."

"Oh, don't remind me." Alex groaned, glaring at her textbook.

"Oh, crap," I said. "I need to finish that."

"You've not finished?" said Alex. "Thought you did that on Monday, right after we got the assignment."

"I decided to rewrite my conclusion."

"Well, I need to *write* mine." She buried her head in the textbook with another dramatic groan.

I fetched my own notes and my laptop from my room, but I suspected I'd have trouble concentrating. My fingers still tingled. Magic. I'd freaking used *magic*. More than once. I wanted to know more, wanted it more than I probably should have. Considering *magic* and *demons* went hand in hand.

No. One thing at a time. And this assignment was due tomorrow.

Sarah closed her laptop. "I'm done," she said. "A thousand words."

"Can I borrow some?" asked Alex.

"Less talking, more writing," I said, squinting at my laptop screen.

"You can talk. I thought you were done."

"She was, until she deleted half of it," said Sarah, poking my laptop. "You're such a perfectionist."

"True," I admitted, rearranging yet another sentence. "It's my fatal flaw."

"Like Hamlet's indecisiveness," said Alex. "I wish he'd jumped off a bloody cliff in the first act, then we wouldn't have to write an essay on him."

I laughed. Okay, maybe I should leave the damn essay alone now.

"Finished," I said, closing my laptop with a snap.

Alex promptly snatched it from the table.

"Hey!"

"It's mine now," she said, and, laptop tucked under her arm, took off into the hallway.

"Oh no you don't!"

Shockingly, Alex didn't finish her essay until past ten o'clock. Claudia had invited me to join her and her friends at Satan's Pit that night, but I'd declined. I didn't want another late night with lectures the next day. Whatever she'd said about first year not counting towards my final grade, the party lifestyle didn't appeal to me, however much Claudia and Leo had tried to persuade me that it'd be fun. In truth, the memory of the shadow-fox was enough to quash any desire I might have had to return to Satan's Pit.

"I declare tonight a Disney night," said Alex, when she'd finally typed her conclusion.

"Hell, yes," I said.

"Just as long as Sir Asshat doesn't interrupt with his creepy music," she said. "And put that book away," she added. I'd brought out next week's reading, figuring it was best to get ahead.

"But," I protested, earning me a swat with her rolled-up essay.

Shouts rang out from Terrence's room.

"Oh, he's at it again," said Sarah.

Alex shook her head. "This flat, seriously. I mean, there's good-weird, like you two——"

"Speak for yourself," I said.

"——and there's bad-weird. Like Terrence. You know, the guys in the flat upstairs are nice, normal guys, and we had to get saddled with the weirdos. Pete's almost as bad."

"Got your eye on someone, Alex?" said Sarah, as we went into Alex's room for the movie night.

"No, I'm just saying!" But she couldn't disguise the flush that spread across her face.

"Ha! Is it Rex?" I said. Rex was one of the guys from the Literature Society. He seemed nice enough, if a little too obsessed with *Lord of the Rings*. "Didn't he ask if you wanted to come and watch a film sometime?"

"He wasn't asking me out!" said Alex.

"Well, if you watch all three *Lord of the Rings* films, it'd be a pretty long date!" I laughed.

"Speaking of dates, what about you and David?" she

said.

I should have seen that one coming.

"We're just *friends,*" I said.

"He's always looking at you." Alex grinned at Sarah, like it was a private joke.

"Really?"

"Oh, so you *do* like him!"

"That's not what I said!"

Even with them teasing me, it was nice to have a *normal* conversation, nice to have a night in without worry. And without the feeling of demon eyes on my back.

WHEN I RETURNED to my room, I found the light still on, to my surprise. I almost never forgot to turn it off. Feeling a chill creep up my arms, I looked around. The window was open a crack, as if someone had hastily shut it, and I could smell... burning? I looked closer and found a line of black marks on the sill, like fingerprints.

I opened the window farther and ran my finger lightly over the marks. It came away black, imprinted by an odd, tar-like substance. *Who's been in my room?* I couldn't see anything out of place, but I double-checked that my valuables were still safe. I'd been given the impression when I'd applied for on-campus accommodation that the rooms were impossible to break into from the outside; all the bolts fastened on the inside. If someone had actually been in my room, why would there be marks on the windowsill? Either way, it unsettled me.

I tried to put it out of mind. I had other things to worry about—like breaking into a hidden library. Never expected that to be on my list of university experiences. Guess there was a first time for everything.

12

THE HIKE

Before the library, though, I had to survive climbing a mountain with a hyperactive Alex and a rather unenthusiastic Sarah. Thanks to the fingerprints incident, I wasn't sleeping well, and at the crack of dawn on Saturday, only Alex was remotely awake.

"This better be worth it," said Sarah, rubbing her eyes, as we boarded the minibus, wrapped in thick layers.

"Sure it will." Alex's eyes gleamed with enthusiasm. "We're climbing the highest peak in England!"

I ended up sitting next to David on the bus. He dozed off on my shoulder once or twice. As he told me, someone had sabotaged his motorbike the other day, so he'd been up half the night fixing it.

"That's why I've got oil all over my hands," he said, showing me his blackened palms and fingertips. "It's been stuck to me for days."

A jolt shot through me as I remembered the marks on my windowsill the other night. *Surely not*—No, that was stupid. What reason would David have to break into my room? Couldn't I even trust my friends? *Just ask.*

"Did you see anyone come into my room the other day? My light was on, and the window was open when I came back. I know I didn't do it. I'd have remembered."

"Huh? You think someone broke into your room? I didn't see anyone." His brow furrowed.

"Someone broke into your room?" said Alex.

I explained about the fingerprints on my windowsill.

"Terrence," she said. "Was that after we went to complain about him?"

"Nah, it was the night before," I said. Our attempt to get Terrence to take responsibility for the mess in the kitchen had been ineffectual. He never answered to the cleaner's knocks, and, in the end, the college secretary told us to talk to him ourselves. Alex had yelled after her, "If he murders us, I'm holding you responsible!"

We were in the Lake District now. Snow-capped mountains dominated the skyline. We drove past lakes of crystal-clear water that reflected the peaks above. Puffy, white clouds dotted the blue sky, and the sun shone brightly, belying the freezing temperature. Even wearing three layers, waterproof trousers, and a thick hiking jacket each, Sarah and Alex were still shivering. Though I couldn't feel the cold, I couldn't fathom why the hiking leaders were wearing *shorts*.

There were about thirty of us in total, ranging from us newbies to the seasoned hikers. Apart from my flatmates, I didn't recognise anyone else. The leaders consulted maps and planned routes, whilst Alex bounced on the balls of her feet.

"Calm down, Alex!" I said. "Save your energy for the hike."

We divided into groups, the hard-core hikers trekking off first, while the newbies and Alex, who said she wanted to keep us company, waited for the signal. Finally, one of the leaders shouted, "Let's go!"

I discovered in less than ten minutes that I was about as unprepared for this as I could have been. The ascent was not only steep but uneven. We had to clamber up stones jutting out of the cliff's side, clinging to whatever we could to prevent ourselves from falling. We crossed foaming rivers via precarious stepping stones—all the more tricky when wielding a camera, determined to catch every stunning view of the sprawling valleys and towering peaks.

I tried to keep pace with David, even though I barely had enough breath to talk. Or to think of a non-intrusive way to ask about those guys in blue. David, however, was more concerned with whoever had messed with his bike.

"Why'd you bring it to uni?" I asked. "Aren't you worried it'll get stolen?"

"The security around the village is pretty tight. Stuff rarely gets nicked here. Haven't you noticed?"

"No," I said. "I haven't seen any hidden cameras or anything."

"They're pretty well-concealed. They're one of the reasons I wanted to live on campus."

"It's convenient, too," I said. "Did you say your brother came here?"

"Yeah, he graduated last year."

I remembered what Claudia had said about this place attracting people with a connection to the Darkworld, but it didn't mean David's family had anything to do with the Venantium. I found myself thinking about our conversations last week, before I'd found myself suspecting everyone. This was university, for crying out loud. Some people were open; others put on a front. Could I really judge people based on a few misleading observations? I tried to put it out of mind.

"To be honest, this course is harder than I expected," said David. "I can't believe they set us an essay already."

"Come on, it wasn't that bad," I said. "*Hamlet's* pretty transparent, as far as Shakespeare goes."

"Are you in the Literature Society, by any chance?"

"You've got it," I said. "You're not?"

"Nah. I need more of a study group, really."

"I suppose…" Damn, why did I have to get nervous now? *Just say it!* "We could start one?"

"That's a thought."

His intent look almost made me miss my step. Talking and climbing a vertical cliff probably wasn't a good combination for someone with my level of coordination.

Before long the ascent steepened even further and it was all I could do to keep on climbing, feet slipping on pebbles, muscles screaming. For several minutes, we walked through clouds so thick; we could barely make out the path, having to wedge our feet into gaps between rocks we couldn't see. I kept my eyes on the ground to make sure I didn't slip, knowing the slightest mistake could send me plunging to my death. Then the clouds thinned out, revealing an unrecognisable world.

Snow coated everything, deeper than any I'd ever seen —at least two feet, judging by the depth of the footprints in it. The scene was a winter wasteland, paper-white with stones jutting out like tombstones. Even I began to shiver, forcing my numbing feet to keep walking. But I heard our leader's voice from above, muffled by the wind, shouting that we'd reached the summit.

"Victory!" Alex crowed, leaping on top of a rock and pumping her fists. God only knew where her energy came from. It was a struggle even to drag myself up the final stretch and collapse next to my friends. I'd wanted to get a photograph of the view but couldn't see anything below the thick, white clouds. It was like we were suspended in an alien, rocky landscape in the sky.

"Snowball fight!" A hunk of snow hit the back of my head.

Yeah, relaxing around Alex was impossible.

I grabbed a handful of snow. "You asked for it!"

At least it warmed us up for a bit. The sky had started to darken, and this made it even harder to see the path downhill. As we descended, I fell behind, not knowing who was behind or in front of me, or if I was still on the path. I was totally alone.

And then there was a dark space in front of me, gaping like an open wound. I froze as a large, shadowy monster crawled out of it.

The wind snatched away my scream as I half-fell down an incline. A colossal black shape pulled itself out of the darkness, bearing down on me. Slavering jaws snapped inches from where my head had been seconds before. I rolled through the snow, sliding downhill, screaming.

Snow crashed over my head as the creature stomped a huge foot, sending me sinking further into the cold.

Nowhere to run. The dark yet white wilderness seemed to go on forever, and one wrong step could send me plummeting over the edge. I had no weapons of any kind, no way to defend myself. I couldn't even conjure fire, the only way to kill a demon.

So cold…

The creature towered over me, its red eyes gleaming, and prepared to pounce.

No. It's not a dream this time. I could still move. And I could fight it. The idea filled me with a fierce will to survive, and, as the creature lunged at me, I reached out to the Darkworld with everything I had.

As I held out my hands to shield my face, the cold

burned me like fire. The Darkworld answered my call, and I felt icy numbness pierce even deeper into my skin. I gasped as ice flowed from my fingertips like water, spreading across my palms. The beast crashed into my outstretched hands—and simply glanced off, as if encountering an invisible barrier.

My hands wore gloves of ice, rock hard, impenetrable. As I watched, astonished, the ice became fluid and transparent, like blue fire, burning cold and hot. Streams of icy fire flared from my palms, striking the creature between the eyes.

The beast roared, shaking its head violently. Cracks appeared in its shadowy form, spider-webbing across its face. Its roar turned to a piteous whine, then it turned away from me and ran through the gap in the universe, leaving shards of darkness behind like flaking skin.

The world blurred before my eyes, and I drifted into a blackness as profound as the Darkworld itself.

∾

"Ash! Ash!"

The world swam into focus. I could see concerned faces peering down at me. The hiking leaders. Sarah and Alex.

"Are you okay? Are you hurt?" The leader of the hike hovered over me.

I tried to open my mouth to reply, then let out an involuntary moan as my lips cracked. "I'm fine," I mumbled, tasting blood. I managed to pull myself into a sitting position and stared at my hands. My knuckles had split open, blood seeping through the cracks.

"Can you get up?"

I was so tired. My legs felt like dead weights, but I was

unhurt. By sheer force of will, I managed to pull myself out of the snowdrift.

"You must be freezing," said the hiking leader.

"Can you walk? There's a blizzard forecast. We have to get down as fast as possible," said someone else.

I nodded, forcing my legs into motion. I barely heard the voices around me as I walked, stumbling on rocks. My brain seemed to have frozen along with my body. It wasn't until I was back in the minibus, clutching a blanket someone had given me, that I allowed the most pressing thought to enter my mind: *I won.* I'd beaten the shadow-beast. How, I wouldn't think about. I'd save that for next week's meeting. For now, I was just going to concentrate on the victory.

However, I couldn't help noticing David was avoiding eye contact. When the others had come back to me, David had been nowhere in sight. Had he known about the monster? Or was I overthinking things again? Was I afraid to think he might have been involved?

The creature being there couldn't be coincidence. But who had summoned it?

13

THE PLAN

Needless to say, I was less than attentive in lectures following week. Alex and Sarah kept giving me knowing looks, the former talking about how I was clearly distracted by *someone*—but I brushed it off. At least they were none the wiser about where I'd spend Wednesday afternoon. How long I could keep them in the dark, I didn't know, but I had no intention of alienating myself from my friends——or worse, putting them in danger.

I arrived at Wednesday's meeting ten minutes early. When I pushed open the door to the Games Room, at first I thought there was no one there. Then I spotted someone sitting on the sofa reading a book, a guy I didn't recognise. I stood there awkwardly, not knowing whether he was part of the group or not.

He looked up and saw me. "Hi, are you Ashlyn?"

"Yeah, I'm Ash."

"Nice to meet you. I'm Cyrus, Leo's brother." I saw the resemblance, even though Cyrus was sandy-haired and freckled, and at least a head taller than Leo.

"The others should be here soon," he said. "I take it you've met the whole crowd?"

I nodded.

"Total lunatics, aren't they?"

"Er…" I wasn't sure whether he was being serious or not.

"Well, my guardian always said it takes a special kind of crazy to be able to see demons. He used to work for the Venantium," he added. "So he knows a thing or two about crazy."

"Okay," I said, unsure why he was looking at me like he expected some kind of reaction out of me.

"I'm not saying *you're* crazy," he said. "You're not. Leo told me about you, said you're the sanest person who ever walked in here."

"Really?"

"It's a compliment. Doesn't sound like you got the best first impression. Well, not that there *is* a best impression as far as Howard's concerned… magic-users are generally not the most stable of people," he added. "I'm not sure how much Claudia told you, but being close to the Darkworld can mess people up. Demons can get in your head and play on what you're most scared of, and if someone spends a lot of time around them—like Berenice and Howard both did; they discovered their Darkworld connections when they were pretty young—then, well, there are side effects. You get paranoid." He paused. "Sound familiar?"

I rubbed my arms, feeling cold. Not Darkworld-cold, just… cold. Was this why I had bad dreams? Why I couldn't quite place myself in a normal life?

"I don't want to be a freak," I said, because I had to say *something.* "I wanted to be normal, but I guess that's not on the cards." As the words left my mouth, the image of the fortune-teller's Tarot deck flashed through my mind. Was it fate messing with me, or was something else?

At that moment the door opened, and Howard barrelled in, followed by Leo and Berenice. Leo gave his brother an affectionate punch on the shoulder, which Cyrus returned in kind. Howard switched on the Xbox without so much as acknowledging me. Berenice joined him, draping her arm around the back of his head and playing with a lock of his fair hair.

"Hey, Ash," said Leo, who'd commandeered the sofa, sprawling across it. His T-shirt today depicted an ice cream in the shape of a human head with brains oozing out. I drew in a quick breath, trying to push aside the uneasy feeling talking to his brother had given me.

"Hi," I said. "Nice shirt."

"Cheers," he said. "What's the latest? You still being stalked by demons?"

Berenice snorted. Seeing that Leo was sprawled across the sofa, she perched on the edge of an armchair and began filing her nails.

"I got attacked by a shadow-creature on Saturday, actually," I said.

"Seriously?" said Leo, sitting up.

"Seriously what?" said Claudia. She closed the door with a snap, which made me aware of the silence in the room. Everyone looked at me.

Cyrus said, "You kept *that* quiet! Ash got attacked," he added, for the others' benefit. "God… I'm sorry."

I told them the story in one breath, relieved to finally have the chance to talk to someone about it. Keeping quiet had been driving me mad.

"Who else was on the hike?" Claudia's first question caught me off guard. "If there's a rogue sorcerer running loose, there's trouble."

"Um, me and my flatmates, and a bunch of people I didn't know," I said. "I couldn't tell you all their names."

"It's too big a coincidence," said Leo, shaking his head. "No way there wasn't another magic-user involved."

Cyrus nodded. "I'd say the beast had to be waiting to ambush you. We can't rule out the possibility it was meant for someone else, of course, but——"

"Was anyone acting suspicious?" asked Claudia.

"Not that I saw. I wasn't really paying attention. I——" I broke off. "Actually, something else weird happened last week. I think someone broke into my room, the day of the first meeting."

"Someone broke into your room?" said Leo.

"Yeah, when I came back that night, my window was open, and there were black fingerprints on the windowsill. But nothing was missing. I checked."

"That seems suspect," said Claudia. "Whoever they were, they clearly didn't care whether you noticed they'd broken in or not. Can you think of anyone it could have been?"

"No," I said. "I don't understand why someone would, if not to steal anything. And I thought the windows were burglar-proof."

"They are," said Claudia. "Someone must have broken in using magic."

"Which means there *is* another magic-user around," said Cyrus. "And I'm taking a wild guess that they're not connected to the Venantium. Are you sure you have no ideas? What about your other flatmates?"

"Alex and Sarah wouldn't have," I said immediately. "They've nothing to do with this. And David, well, his bike got trashed by the person who broke into my room. There were fingerprints on the windowsill," I added.

"Unless he tried to divert attention?" suggested Claudia. "Hmm."

I shifted from one foot to the other, uncomfortable with where this conversation was headed.

"He won't have wrecked his own bike," I said. "Pete asked to ride it on the first day, but David said no. Pete's a total pervert, but I can't see him as a magic-user. He spends all his time stalking Danielle and drinking himself into an early grave, anyway. And Terrence... well, he's a weirdo. I don't know that much about him. He's really rude, stays in his room most of the time. He wasn't on the hike."

"I'll investigate them," said Claudia.

"I don't think——"

She cut me off. "So, what's the plan for tonight, then?"

"Tonight?" said Cyrus, looking blank.

"We're planning another trip to the library," said Claudia. "This time we're going to find out more about Ash's ancestors. You in?"

Cyrus rolled his eyes. "You might have mentioned it to me before."

"None of us have seen you all week. We figured you were up to something top-secret."

"I've been working on my dissertation."

Claudia rolled her eyes back at him. "God forbid we keep Cyrus from his First."

"You lot might want to think about actually doing some work this year," said Cyrus. "Second year's a bitch. Just saying." But he said this in a light tone. "Anyway, I guess I'm obliged to come along tonight, to keep you lot in line. Howard, we don't want any more accidents, do we?"

"It slipped out of my hand," said Howard defensively. In the middle of the conversation, he'd started playing a racing game, whilst Berenice finished filing her nails and joined him. I doubted that they had heard a word I'd said. I couldn't decide if it was because being attacked by shadow-beasts was too commonplace in their book to warrant attention, or if they just didn't like me.

On cue, Berenice rolled her eyes. "Why are we even bothering with this? If the demons are after Ash, and we get involved, it'll put us all in danger, too. What's she to us?"

Yeah, they just didn't like me.

"If the Venantium get involved, it could affect us anyway," said Cyrus. "To have a connection to the Dark-world and be unaware of it is almost unheard of. She must have sorcerer blood, and it's better for her sake that we find out how before the Venantium do."

"Yeah," said Leo. "Ash is one of us. She deserves to know the truth, and she needs our help to get to it. If you don't want to come, no one's forcing you."

I blinked, both surprised and bolstered by this show of support.

"Howard," said Berenice, "are you getting involved with this ridiculous break-in?"

"Sure, why not?" said Howard. "I've wanted to get my hands on that book for a while, anyway."

"Seriously? Why?"

"That's my business."

Berenice looked affronted, but she tossed her hair. "You're all idiots. I'm surprised at you, Cyrus."

"I'm not surprised Miss Princess doesn't want to coop-erate," said Leo.

"What're *you* getting out of it?" said Berenice.

Leo shrugged. "I dunno. It's just something to do."

"Seriously?" Berenice turned her laser glare on me, like she blamed me for everything.

"Well, anyway," said Cyrus. "If we're going to do this, then we need a plan."

The plan was simple. We were all going to go to Blackstone at different times in order to avoid drawing any kind of attention, and then meet up at the Coach and Horses at around eight. Then it was a small matter of breaking into an out-of-bounds magical library. *So much for simplicity.* I couldn't help feeling I'd be responsible if anything went wrong. Everyone was taking the risk for my sake, after all. But I had the feeling that certain members of the group would have gone ahead with it with or without me. They seemed glad of an excuse to make trouble for the Venantium.

JUST AFTER SEVEN, I grabbed my coat and, steeling myself, left my room.

"Ash? Where're you going?" David asked.

Shit. Why did it have to be him? "Um, Gaming Society social. In town."

"Ah, right. I was wondering if you wanted to come to the bar with some of my mates, but if you're busy, then that's cool."

"I won't be out late. I'll come join you then," I said, even though I didn't know when we'd be back.

"Well, have fun." His smile looked forced, again.

"Bye," I said. I felt a tad guilty. We hadn't really talked in a while, not after our less-than-impressive trip to Redthorne. But I had to do this. *This had better be worth it.*

I waited for Claudia outside. Once again, rain poured down, forming puddles around the student village and dripping from roofs. I was beginning to think a dark rain cloud hovered permanently over the university, underneath the demon-proof shield.

"Hey." Claudia snuck up beside me without my noticing. "You ready?"

"Not really," I admitted.

"Well, you'd better get used to it. We rarely plan ahead. I don't think Howard has any notion of what a *plan* is."

I thought of his temper tantrum the week before. "Is he likely to make trouble?"

"Cyrus'll keep him under control. Besides, he won't hurt anyone with Berenice there."

"Berenice? I thought she wasn't coming."

"She can't stay out of stuff like this. Plus, she won't let Howard go on his own."

"Are those two like, together, then?" I said, thinking of her flirtatious behaviour earlier.

"Howard and Berenice? No, but they did have a one-night stand a few months ago, and she hasn't been able to leave him alone since. He doesn't seem that arsed about her, unless he's pissed. Then they're all over each other, and it's revolting. But I don't think the guy's capable of understanding the meaning of a relationship. He's kind of self-absorbed. Mind you, so's she. So, in theory, they're the perfect match."

I thought of what Cyrus had said about magic-users being unstable. "Why do you hang out with him? I mean, he threw an Xbox controller at Leo's head!"

"Howard gets into fights at least once a week. We're used to it."

"Jesus. You'd think he'd have been arrested by now." I hesitated. "*Has* he?"

"No," said Claudia. "Well, there have been a couple of close calls. He's made a lot of enemies in the Venantium, but he's learnt his lesson about picking fights with the *vena-tors*, thankfully. Most of the time."

"Good to know," I said. "Is there any reason Berenice seems to hate me so much?"

"She hates everyone apart from Howard. Sorry she was such a bitch to you. I'll get Howard to have a word. Maybe she'll listen."

"So she comes to meetings because of him?"

"Basically, yeah. But she hates the Venantium, too, even more than she hates demons. Sometimes I think she hates everything."

"And have the shadow-beasts ever gone after her?" I thought of her pristine make-up and carefully straightened hair. I couldn't picture her getting into fights with shadow-beasts. Though her acid tongue was enough of a weapon in itself.

"Yeah. She's not really a fighter, but she can throw a punch if she's pissed. But she's had a worse time of it than any of the rest of us have. I think—" She hesitated. "I think someone she knew was killed by a demon. Something like that. Obviously, she won't talk about it."

"R-really?" I swallowed. *That,* I hadn't expected. "Like, a sorcerer?"

"I don't know. It's just a theory, I mean, I've known her a year, and she's never told me. I inferred it from the way she reacts to new sorcerers. It's taken her the past year to get used to us being a group, and then we get two new members within a couple of weeks. She's not the type to admit to being uncomfortable."

I guessed I kind of got that. Didn't mean she had to be a bitch.

The woods were eerie after dark, the moonlight breaking through the trees and throwing menacing shadows on the ground. Even following the path, it was difficult to tell if we were going the right way. Tree trunks loomed up out of the shadows, and roots snaked underfoot to trip us up. I concentrated on the Darkworld, trying to summon a small light to my hand, but the feeble spark kept going out. Clearly, this was something else I needed to work at.

Blackstone, at night, turned into a maze of dark streets winding between shadowy buildings. I began to see Cara's point when she had said it looked like a horror movie set. One of those strange, giant, black birds swooped overhead as we approached the Coach and Horses.

"What are those?" I asked Claudia. "I keep seeing them everywhere."

"They're the Venantium's harpies." She pushed open the door, and we stepped over the threshold into warmth. "They send one as a warning before they turn up somewhere."

"Harpies?"

"They're the one thing we really don't want to run into tonight."

"There you are," said a snide voice. "Took you long enough." Berenice waited for us inside the Coach and Horses.

"Nice to see you, too," I said. I couldn't look her in the eye after what Claudia had told me.

"Whatever," said Berenice. "Let's get this over with. Oi, Howard! Get over here."

"Draw attention to yourself, why don't you?" said Howard, as he came stomping up behind us. I could picture *him* making mincemeat of shadow-beasts. Volatile temper aside, he was built like a tank and had to duck to fit under the roof beams. "C'mon, Leo."

Leo downed the rest of his pint in one and hurried to us, Cyrus on his heels. "Let's go."

"Why're you so eager all of a sudden?" muttered Berenice. "You've been saying for the last hour you'd rather stay in the pub."

"That guy over there's looking at us," he whispered.

I turned around, and my heart somehow sank and flipped at the same time. It was David.

"That's my flatmate," I whispered. "I told him I was at the Gaming Society social. Crap, we'd better leave before he comes over."

"Good thinking," said Claudia.

We raced out of the pub before David could meet my eyes.

14

THE LIBRARY

I couldn't stop looking around as we made our way through the dark streets, Cyrus leading the way. I didn't see any of the strange birds swooping overhead, but somehow that made me more nervous, as though we were being watched by unseen eyes. We crossed the town square in silence, like thieves, and slipped into the alleyway between the art gallery and the cathedral.

"Where are we going?" I whispered to Claudia.

"The library entrance is hidden in the cemetery," she replied. Sure enough, Cyrus jumped over the stone wall onto the damp grass that surrounded the gravestones.

"Really?" I said, following him over the wall. "Seems a weird place to hide a library."

It was even creepier at night. The sense that the dead were present all around us was almost suffocating. An almost-full moon was caught between two spires reaching from the cathedral into the indigo sky, surrounded by a halo of ghostly light. Black shapes flitted overhead. Knowing they were sinister messenger birds, belonging to the Venantium, did nothing to ease my apprehension.

"The Venantium seem to have a thing for creepy places," said Claudia. "This place has been around as long as the library itself—about five hundred years. I'm guessing they figured no one would go snooping around a graveyard at night, right under their noses."

"They thought wrong," said Howard. "I've sneaked in there a dozen times, at least."

Cyrus stopped in front of a pedestal, on which stood a large statue of a weather-beaten gargoyle. The rough stone was covered in so much moss; it was impossible to make out any of its features. The foot of the statue was on a level with Howard's head and towered over the rest of us.

Cyrus rummaged in the pockets of his jeans and pulled out a silver key.

"I didn't steal it," he told me, before I could ask where he got it. "Leo borrowed it from our guardian, who used to work for the Venantium."

I wanted to ask more, but he'd already inserted the key into a hole on the side of the pedestal and turned it once, clockwise. With a grating sound, the front of the stone pedestal swung open, revealing the top of a dark staircase.

"Lights," whispered Cyrus, and five small white lights flared up in the others' hands. I concentrated hard on the connection to the Darkworld, and it responded, my hand igniting like the others'. I hoped it wouldn't go out.

Down we went into the darkness. At once, the sense of claustrophobia hit me, but I forced back my panic and concentrated on keeping up with the others. The staircase gradually grew steeper, and the walls became narrower until Howard's shoulders brushed them on either side.

Just as I thought we must be a hundred feet under-ground—or more—the stairs opened into a wide passage-way. I saw several tunnels branching off it, but Howard led us in a straight line. Candles cast an eerie, blue light from old-fashioned brackets either side, each clasped in the claws of a crudely carved, stone bird.

"Who lights those?" I said.

"Lucky *venators,*" said Leo. "Some poor sod has the joy of checking that they're still burning every few hours. It's magic fire. It doesn't go out easily."

The tunnel was obviously manmade. The walls so even, it was as if they'd been expertly dug out then smoothed by some sort of machine. *Magic.* Claudia had said the tunnels were hundreds of years old. It couldn't have been anything else. Strange, how fast my life had gone out of control. Magic was real. The old laws that governed the universe no longer applied. Now it was rational to take a night-time stroll through a tunnel, hidden beneath an old graveyard, to find answers.

Our footsteps echoed behind us, as if our own shadows pursued us. A musty smell hung in the air, the sort of aroma I associated with old books. One final pair of candles marked the end of the tunnel. The last two statues were so horrible; I stopped for a second to stare. They looked like grotesque hybrid creatures, old crones crossed with birds of prey. Each was the size of a small child, with cruel, hooked talons. As we passed, I could have sworn one of them moved, a sunken eye flickering in our direction. But when I saw the library, I forgot all about it.

For a good minute, all I could do was gape. The circular room appeared, at first glance, like a giant maze——a maze formed of bookshelves that seemed to grow out of the tunnel walls. Books beyond counting lined the shelves, towering up to a ceiling so high it was lost in darkness.

"Impressive, huh?" whispered Claudia.

"Yeah." I had to exercise extreme self-control to stop my quivering hands from picking up some of those enticing volumes. I breathed in the scent of old tomes and felt a smile creep onto my face. "It's awesome." Then I remembered why we were there, and my smile faded. "How on earth are we supposed to find what we're looking for in here?"

"That's why we have Howard," said Claudia.

Howard said, from somewhere amongst the shelves, "The *Sorcerer's Almanac* isn't here."

"Seriously?" said Leo. "I thought no one could remove it."

"Only senior Venantium members," said Cyrus. "Maybe they're investigating someone?"

"Right," said Leo. "Well, that makes things tricky. The *Almanac* has the details of every magic-user known to the Venantium."

"We can still look in the records," said Claudia.

"If they've repaired the damage," said Leo. "Remember last time?"

"I told you that was an accident," said Howard, through gritted teeth.

"Why, what happened?" I said.

"There was an incident involving a candle and a shelf of priceless manuscripts," said Leo.

"Ah."

"Okay. Let's just look around for a bit. You might find something."

I walked amongst the shelves, moving my gaze along the rows of books, scanning titles as if I were merely browsing in a bookshop. A large, leather-bound volume caught my eye, and a strange shiver passed through me. I pulled the book from the shelf: *The Seven Princes of the Dark-world: A General Guide to Demons.*

"Not exactly what I had in mind," I said as I opened it

to be greeted by the grinning face of a demon. Shuddering, I closed it.

"Neat, I've been looking for something like this," said Claudia, peeking over my shoulder. "It'll help you understand demons, too."

In the end, I had a small stack of books piled at the entrance, and we each took one—except Berenice, who played Angry Birds on her mobile instead. *Why did she even come in the first place?* It wasn't as if Howard was paying her the slightest attention.

None of the books I'd chosen contained a single mention of the name Temple or my mum's maiden name, Francis. I realised too late that I didn't know the surnames of my grandparents. If my parents had ever told me, I didn't remember.

"I'm bored," Berenice announced.

"Then go," said Cyrus.

"We can't check every book," said Berenice, without moving. "We'll be here all night."

Cyrus put down his book. "I suppose we could wait a couple of weeks then come back and see if the *Almanac*'s here."

"And what if it isn't?" said Howard.

"It doesn't matter," I said. "We're clearly not going to find any—" There was a noise above, somewhere in the gloom of the ceiling. "What was that?"

"Shit," said Howard.

I heard another noise, a ringing shriek—and one of the crone-bird-creatures dived at me, talons outstretched. I flung my arms in front of my face to shield myself, crying out as the claws sliced into my skin. For a moment, I stood frozen in shock and pain.

"Run!" shouted Cyrus, and, in a flurry of dropped books, we fled the library.

The instant we ran into the corridor, all the candles were extinguished, plunging the tunnels into an absolute darkness that even our conjured lights could barely penetrate. Horrible, shrieking cries echoed around us, and, every time the rush of wings sounded overhead, I ducked farther down, until I almost ran at a crouch.

"They're blind, but they can hear us!" shouted Howard.

"Shut the hell up, then!" said Leo.

But it was impossible to run without making a sound. The echo of our footsteps pursued us, as though we were followed by a ghost army. Terror gripped me as I dodged the swipe of another creature's claws. I wasn't imagining it. They were targeting me.

Then my light went out.

"No," I whispered. *Light!*

Nothing happened. I could make out Claudia's outline ahead of me, pelting down the tunnel, but I wasn't fast enough. I was falling behind.

Talons grazed my scalp as the creature flew at me yet again. I ducked and sprinted flat out, faster than I'd ever run before. I could have sworn my feet hardly touched the ground. Each breath tore at my throat, but fear kept my feet moving in tandem with my thudding heart. I heard an exclamation up ahead and skidded to a halt, narrowly avoiding a collision with Claudia.

"The stairs have gone," she whispered. "Someone must have raised the alarm."

"But, then we can't get out, right?" Panic squeezed my heart once again.

"Don't worry, Howard knows another way."

"Come *on*," said Berenice from somewhere up ahead. "I'd quite like to get out of here alive."

"Shut up, I'm trying to think," Howard said with a

snarl. "I don't plan on any of us dying down here, you clear?" After a moment, he said, "All right, it's this way."

He took one of the other tunnels that branched off the main one. No sound of the bird-creatures followed us. That struck me as suspicious. Had we lost them? The others slowed to a hurried walk, and I took advantage of this to catch my breath.

"Claudia?" I whispered. "Wha——what were those?"

"Harpies. I used a spell to put them off our scent, but it took a while to aim. Did they get you?"

"Yeah," I whispered. Blood dripped down my arms, and my skin burned as though it was aflame.

I lost track of time as we walked through the darkness. My arms felt heavy and numb. It took me a moment to realise we'd reached the ladder, and the others were hauling themselves upward. I grasped the rungs with sweaty, shaking hands and pulled myself up after Claudia.

The night air had never smelt as sweet as it did in that moment. I inhaled, purging the stuffy air of the tunnel from my lungs. We were back in the cemetery, but at a different part. The ladder came up in a ditch behind a large, memorial statue. Howard slumped against it, cursing.

"Please tell me none of you used magic," said Cyrus.

"Only to throw the creatures off the scent," said Claudia.

"And the lights," said Leo. "Shit, I forgot."

"Lights'll be okay," said Howard. "The Venantium will know someone trespassed, but not who it was. As long as none of you did anything that'll leave a trace." He gave me a hostile glare. "Did you use magic?"

I shook my head, regretting the movement when dizziness swept through me.

"Good. Then we're safe."

"I hardly think that matters," said Berenice, tossing her hair. "We shouldn't have taken the risk. It wasn't worth it. Not for her."

"Well, I vote we get the hell out of here," said Howard.

"Yeah, you're right," said Berenice. "I'm going back to my flat. You coming?"

"Sure, why not? You lot all take alternate routes," he said to the rest of us.

"We know," said Leo.

I dropped to my knees as a deeper wave of dizziness engulfed me. I looked down at my arms. They were stained with blood, which glowed in the disorienting, white moonlight.

"Ash!" Leo shouted.

Howard turned back to face me, and the others moved closer.

"Shit," said Claudia. "We have to get her to Madam Persephone!"

White-hot pain burned both arms, and my head pounded. Spots danced before my eyes, and everything blurred into a dark mass interspersed with dazzling lights. I tried to speak but could only groan.

"Shit. She's marked. It'll bring the Venantium right to our doorstep!" I heard Berenice say. "Someone'll have to fix that glowing. I'm not getting arrested."

"Spoken like a true philanthropist," said Leo.

"Don't start arguing now!" said Claudia.

"Madam Persephone will be in her tent," said Cyrus, taking charge. "Howard, you carry her."

"I thought you were coming back with me!" said Berenice, as I felt strong arms lift me into the air.

"Are you for real?" said Leo. "She's hurt, you absolute—"

"Berenice, no one's forcing you to stay," said Cyrus.

"Stop arguing!" Claudia said. "Let's go, already!"

"Where?" said Howard, shifting my position.

"Town square," said Cyrus. "Come on, we have to hurry."

The last thing I saw was Leo's concerned face, peering down at me, before everything faded away.

15

BLOOD AND OIL

The world swam in and out of focus. I heard a flurry of movement around me and realised I was lying on a hard surface. A bench. Wooden slats poked me in the back.

"What happened?" said a low, urgent voice. It sounded familiar. Then I placed it—the fortune-teller.

"Harpies attacked us in the library," said Howard.

"You were in the library again?"

"We were trying to find out about Ash's ancestry."

I heard a sharp intake of breath. Cold hands traced the burning wounds on my arms, and I moaned, though the pain lessened.

"Hang on, Ash," said Leo. "You'll be okay. They got me, too, couple of weeks back."

"That's because you punched one of them!" said Claudia. "Ash didn't do anything to provoke them. Have you any idea why they might have targeted her?"

"No," said the fortune-teller.

In spite of myself, I raised my head, dizzy, and said to Leo, "You *punched* one of them?"

"He was drunk," said Claudia, and, from her tone, I imagined her shaking her head. "First night of Freshers' week, and he had to attack a harpy."

I laughed, and it turned into a cough. But the pain was fading, and the world was coming back into focus. I moved my hands and pushed myself upright.

"Ash, are you okay?" said Leo.

The pain was almost gone now, and for the first time I could see my surroundings. I was in the fortune-teller's tent, and, above me, a cluster of starry charms glittered in the light of a hundred scented candles. Their mingling aromas didn't quite mask the bitter, sharp smell, which seemed to be coming from somewhere nearby. I looked down at my arms, and felt my pulse quicken. The cuts had completely healed, leaving only twin, faint, pinkish scars that ran the length of each arm, from wrist to elbow.

The fortune-teller surveyed me with a nod of satisfaction from between her white curtains of hair. "That should suffice. The scarring's a little more than I expected, but the Venantium will have no reason to suspect it was one of their harpies that attacked you. Can you stand?"

I nodded and slid off the bench. Evidently, someone had dragged it in from outside. My own blood splattered over the wooden panels. I couldn't believe it. I felt totally normal, almost energised, even, as though the attack had never happened.

"Why won't the Venantium know, if they see these scars?" I asked. "I mean, they're pretty noticeable. I've no idea what I'm going to tell everyone I did."

"Even if they recognised it for a harpy's mark, the Venantium control only a select number of them. Do you know much about harpies?"

"Only that I wouldn't want one as a pet."

Leo laughed. Even the fortune-teller looked amused.

"They're trained to mark intruders, so they aim to wound, not kill," she explained. "But, as with any Dark-world creatures, any sorcerer is at liberty to summon and control one. The Venantium control the harpies around this area."

"So why did they pick on me?"

"Because you're the newbie?" Berenice still hovered around, pacing by the door like she was desperate to leave.

"Brilliant," I said. Tiredness washed over me without warning, my sudden energy depleting. I swayed, unsteady from losing so much blood.

The fortune-teller said, "I'll put a cover-spell on you, so you'll be invisible to the Venantium for a few hours. That should be enough to get you safely home." She gave me one of her intense looks. "Be careful, Ashlyn. Someone is after you. That much is clear."

And, on that note of confidence, we were dismissed.

AN HOUR LATER, as I walked up the hill to the student village with Claudia, she pulled me away from contemplating the fortune-teller's words by muttering, "Maybe it wasn't a coincidence."

"Huh?" I said.

"Maybe someone took that book out on purpose."

"What, you think someone knew we were after it? How would they know?"

"I don't know. It just seems strange. Cyrus and Howard have been breaking into that place for over a year, and it's always been there. I had the impression even members of the Venantium itself didn't dare open it except in the case of an emergency."

"What exactly *is* the book?"

"It's like a giant family tree, showing the interrelations of every magic-user in existence. Without exception, all sorcerers are connected in some way. It has the details of the original Venantium members, who, odds are, are in your ancestry somewhere. They're in mine, and Cyrus', and Howard's——everyone's."

"But why's it dangerous?"

"Because it's laced with all the protective spells the original *venators* could place on it. Anyone who isn't a sorcerer would be burnt alive if they so much as touched it. It's an old curse, and no one's been able to remove it."

"That's horrible," I said with a shudder.

"Well, it's always under lock and key, anyway. Ash, why's your light on?"

We'd reached the right building, and I saw with a sinking heart that, once again, my window had been thrown open, and my light blazed onto the field in the misty night.

"I didn't leave it on," I said. "I never forget to turn it off. Someone's been in my room again."

Claudia followed me up to the window. The black marks were still there, and fresh ones overlaid the ones from before.

"Looks like tar," Claudia commented. "Or oil or something. Whose is the motorbike?"

My heart dropped. "My flatmate, David's," I said, reluctantly.

"Is he the weirdo?"

"No, that's Terrence."

"Which is *his* room?"

"Round the other side, I think."

I cast a fleeting glance at David's window as we passed it, but the curtains were tightly closed. So were Terrence's, though Claudia tried her best to peek through the slight gap at the top.

"There's a weird glow in there. I think he has a TV on," she said.

"Or he's conducting evil experiments."

Claudia looked at me. "You think that?"

"Eh? I've no idea. It's this joke my flatmates and I have, because he went out the other night saying he was going to the 'lab.'"

"Hmm. Does he have anything against you?"

"Me? No, he's rude to everyone. But he lives in the same flat as I do. He wouldn't have a reason to break in from the outside. Neither would Pete or David."

My room was, as before, just as I'd left it. Apart from the light and the window, nothing was amiss at all. *What?*

"Is there a spell that I can put on my room to stop people from breaking in?" I said as I examined every item on my desk to see if anything was out of place.

"That's what I was about to suggest," said Claudia. "Okay. You need to envision an invisible barrier surrounding the whole room. It's the kind of magic that needs more than one person to do it right. I'll stand over here"—she moved to the window—"and you stand by the door. When I tell you to, contact the Darkworld, and I'll guide you from there. Got it?"

I nodded.

"Good. Let's go. Now."

As I made contact with the Darkworld, I gasped as my arms flared with white-hot pain again, and a voice—if the sound could be called a voice—shrieked something unintelligible. A second later, the pain vanished.

"What?"

"What's wrong, Ash?"

"N-nothing." *That was weird.* "Let me try again."

This time nothing stopped me. I reached out to the Darkworld, and it sent me a shadowy cloak to drape around the room, extending to outside the window. I could see it if I concentrated hard enough, but its presence already reassured me.

"No one can break in using magic now," Claudia said. "It won't stop someone picking the lock, but these flats are designed so you can't do that anyway."

"That's good enough for me," I said, though my heart still beat erratically. *What was that scream?* I sank onto my bed, exhausted.

"Ash, you okay?"

"Tired," I mumbled. "And confused. Why does this crap keep happening?"

"Don't ask me. You can always back out of the group if you like. The others don't know how to play it safe."

I sighed, looking around my room, at the photos of Cara and me, at my books, my laptop. After the library, it seemed a different world. Student Ash and Sorceress Ash had nothing in common but their name.

"You'll get used to it," said Claudia. "Being in two worlds. I only really started dealing with it when I came here."

"Reinventing yourself at university?" I gave a weary laugh, shook my head. "Honestly, these days, I haven't a clue who I am. In the past few weeks, I've been clubbing, climbed a mountain, battled monsters, and got attacked in an underground library. It's crazy. Before university..." That life really did feel like a dream. Eighteen years of going to school, hanging out with Cara, all the times we'd talked about our futures. So many things I'd wanted to do. Get my degree. Try new hobbies. Travel. Cara and I had made plans for a round-the-world trip after we graduated. Somehow I'd lost sight of all that after the demons appeared. But I *had* been reinventing myself, hadn't I? Wasn't leaving home about trying new things, figuring out who I was?

"I'm not quitting," I said, half to myself.

"Good," said Claudia. "I'm around if you want to talk about the crazy, all right? I know it's tough. Been there, done that."

I smiled. Perhaps she was right. I could deal with this.

"Anyway, I'm shattered, and I have a seminar at nine tomorrow morning. See you at next week's meeting?"

"Sure," I said. "'Night."

Figuring out who I was. Right. To start with, I needed to figure out who was messing with me. Bonus points for answers as to why I couldn't summon fire.

I conjured up a small light and sent it buzzing around my room, admiring the glow as it reflected in the window. If I could do that, then why not fire?

The scars on my arms flared, cold rather than hot. I gasped, sitting down as a wave of dizziness came over me again. *Need to sleep it off.* I fell backwards, my eyes closed, and a piercing laugh echoed in my ears. Cold. So cold.

I couldn't speak, couldn't scream. No. Not again. *I'm awake.*

"We're coming, Ashlyn. Soon."

Who are you?

"You know, Ashlyn. We're here, always here. You're ours."

I gasped, pins and needles shooting up my arms, and the paralysis let me go. I sat up, breathing as though I'd just sprinted through the woods.

My fists clenched. *No. You can't hurt me here.*

But did I really believe that?

∾

I COULDN'T GET to sleep, partly because my nerves still buzzed, but also because I kept thinking I heard footsteps outside my door. Several times I got out of bed and peered through the spy-hole in my door, but I couldn't see anyone in the corridor. Finally, I gave up on sleep and pulled back the curtains, letting the weak, dawn light flood the room. And nearly jumped out of my skin when I saw David standing about a metre away from my window, his eyes narrowed in anger, which swiftly turned to surprise.

"David!" I said, pushing open the window with shaking hands. After last night, his appearance outside freaked me out.

"Oh, hey, Ash!" He forced his face into an unconvincing smile. "You're awake early."

"Speak for yourself! What on earth are you doing out there?"

"Someone's tampered with my bike again. It's worse this time—they've trashed it."

Even from here, I could see the bike was no longer the gleaming model it had been a couple of weeks ago. Both of the tires were punctured, and mud coated the handlebars.

"Who would do that?" I asked.

"God knows." David's eyes hardened. "I'm seriously considering leaving it at home in future."

"Maybe someone got drunk and decided to take it for a ride?"

"It was padlocked, but someone's mangled the locks. I wouldn't say anyone who was wasted would be capable of it. These locks are practically impossible to get off."

Not if they used magic. The thought crossed my mind unbidden, and a chill went through me. Was it the same person who had broken into my room?

"I'll have to take it into town later," he continued.

"God knows how. I can't ride it like this, and there's no way in hell they'd let me take it on the bus."

"I can help," I offered. "We can go into town when the shops open. I don't have any lectures 'til afternoon today. I don't mind."

David smiled at me, a genuine smile this time. "Cheers, Ash. That'd be great."

"Um, sure." I adjusted my position at the window, elbows propped on the sill.

"How was that Gaming Society thing, anyway? I saw you in town last night."

"Did you?" I decided feigning ignorance was the best move. "It was pretty good, yeah. We just went to a couple of bars."

"I saw you at the Coach and Horses. That big guy you were with looked pretty rough."

"Howard? Yeah, he's a real sore loser at Xbox." That much, at least, was true.

Once again, I was lost for anything to say. I wanted to divert the conversation away from last night, and yet... "Oh, great."

"Huh?"

I held up my arm. "What the hell's this stuff? It's all over my window!"

David shook his head, puzzled. "That's oil, isn't it?" He stared at his bike, confusion furrowing his brow.

"Why's it on my window?"

"Very good question."

Relief rushed through me. *Of course it wasn't him.*

David seemed to be coming to conclusions of his own. "I reckon it was someone in our block who trashed my bike," he said.

"But who would do that?"

"God knows." His eyes narrowed in annoyance once

again. "I'm going to see our head of college now. Their security's shit if they let stuff like this happen."

His abrupt departure took me by surprise.

"I'll see you later, okay?" I called after him, but he didn't seem to hear. With a sigh, I withdrew into my room. It looked like my pyjama sleeve would be permanently stained black. Not that it mattered. Maybe hanging out with David would take my mind off the crazy.

I went for a walk around the woodland trail for something to do and got back to the flat to see David's bike was gone. Had he left without me?

Inside, I found Alex and Sarah engaged in a heated discussion about *Paradise Lost*, today's seminar's text for discussion. "Have either of you two seen David?" I asked.

"Why?" Alex looked up from the hefty anthology she'd been perusing.

"We were supposed to be going into town, but it looks like he's gone." I joined them at the table, sitting in a vacant chair.

"You sure he's not at a lecture?"

"His bike's gone. We were supposed to be going to get it fixed."

My phone buzzed with a new message. From David. "Sorry I was a grumpy idiot. The college head is helping me get my bike sorted out, but do you want to go to the library later? I liked your study group idea. :)"

I blinked, my traitorous face flushing like a traffic light. Naturally, Alex picked that moment to glance in my direction.

"Ha!"

"What?" I said, stowing my phone in my pocket.

"You're arranging a study date with David?"

"How did you—"

"Gotcha."

"Very funny."

"Don't spare us the details." Alex raised her eyebrows at Sarah.

"There's nothing to tell," I said.

"Hello? Isn't this, like, the third time you two have made plans?"

"I wouldn't call our last trip to Redthorne a wild success," I muttered. "He showed all the life and interest of a corpse." Except when those guys appeared. But I wasn't going to mention that.

"Maybe he's a zombie," said Alex.

"Maybe he really hates shopping," Sarah suggested.

I groaned. "Please don't start with the theories, guys. We're just friends. Well, he hasn't said otherwise, anyway. I've not seen any hints."

"Maybe you keep missing them." Alex made no attempt to hide her smirk.

"Look," I said. "I've never had a boyfriend before, all right? No guy's ever so much as looked at me. Besides, when he asked me to Redthorne, we both needed to get hiking boots...stop looking at me like that."

"Seriously, girl," said Alex. "You should take the initiative. Figure out what his game is."

Easier said than done.

"All right. We're heading to the library later."

"Cosy."

"Shut up."

Perhaps she was right. Perhaps I did need to get an answer from him. But I had enough to think about already. It would help if I knew what *I* wanted.

Who had taken David's bike? Could it really have been someone in our flat? If someone had broken the locks using magic, then it couldn't have been anyone I knew— they'd all been at the library last night. Was there a rogue sorcerer at our university, or was there something Claudia and the others weren't telling me?

⟿

DAVID'S KNOCKING at my door jerked me awake. I'd gone back to my room to avoid Alex's teasing, and also because the last few days were catching up on me. Disoriented, I sat up and caught sight of my reflection in the wardrobe mirror—a mess of frizzy curls stood on end. *Great.*

David knocked again. I snatched up my hairbrush, and went for the door.

"Hi," I said. "Sorry—fell asleep."

"That's all right," he said. His smile showed none of the fury of that morning. Perhaps this time, things would go my way.

Yeah. Wishful thinking.

"Your bike's okay?"

"Yeah. Well, it's being fixed. Guess some moron has a taste for danger."

"I'm sure it'll work out," I said. "What did you want to study, anyway?"

"Milton. I can't get my head around it at all."

I groaned inwardly. Yep. Wishful thinking, Ash.

Once I'd tamed my hair—or tried to—and shoved my heavyweight textbooks into my rucksack, we set off for the library.

"You remember me saying I know *Paradise Lost* backwards," I said. "Right?"

"I forgot," he said. "Was that for your exam? We did *Macbeth.*"

"Yep," I said. "No light, only darkness visible."

Damn. Could I have picked a worse line?

David blinked at me. "Impressive." He paused. "Life's

but a walking shadow, a poor player…something something."

I grinned, resisting the urge to finish the soliloquy. That fell into the category of "lame showing off".

"I give up," he said. "I'm not good at remembering lines."

"It takes me a while," I said. "Doesn't really help in interviews either."

I thought of Alex's joking about a study date. I wasn't sure how many dates involved quoting iambic pentameter at one another, but it was possible David and I were at a different level of nerdiness. That, or it was easier than actual conversation. I didn't want to read too much into it.

Maybe I just wanted to feel like someone thought I was worth paying attention to, without the pressure of the crazy. This didn't have to turn into anything romantic. Not that I was an expert on the subject, but someone whose favourite love story was *Romeo and Juliet* might not be the best candidate. Or that might have been my inner literary nerd being picky.

Still, we both left the library with our seminar work done, which was more than I could say of the average night in Flat One. I couldn't help thinking of something Cara had said when lecturing me about my non-existent love life.

"You need someone who can keep up with you," she'd said. "That, or a laugh."

Well, David wasn't really much for joking, but we'd found common ground. My penchant for overthinking things didn't help. Plus, I jumped behind a pillar when I saw Berenice across the courtyard coming out of the library, even though she was headed the other way.

"What's up?" David asked.

"Nothing," I said. "Thought I'd forgotten one of my books."

I had an inkling that I wouldn't be able to keep deluding myself for long. Sooner or later, my two lives would smash into each other—I just hoped my newfound friendships would survive the fallout.

16

BACK INTO THE PIT

To my surprise, I lasted two weeks without any other strangeness happening. Between course work, study sessions with David and movie nights with Alex and Sarah, before I knew it, I'd been at university a whole month. So much had happened in such a short space of time that moving away from home seemed insignificant by comparison. Strange to think that I'd never been so long without seeing my parents or Cara. Cara was busy with course work, but I invited my parents up to visit one Saturday, which happened to be Halloween.

"We've missed you, Ash," said Mum, hugging me as I opened the door to the flat.

Peering into my room, Dad asked, "You've settled in okay?"

"Yeah," I said.

There was so little about my new life I could tell them. *Yeah, in my first few weeks of uni, I broke into a library and got attacked by harpies. Just your typical Fresher's experience.*

I related some amusing stories from Freshers' week instead, whilst giving them a tour of Blackstone. Still, part of me couldn't help but wonder: *can they feel this place is different?* After what Claudia had told me about the Dark-world connection being hereditary, I'd been wondering. If I'd inherited it from distant relatives, why did neither of my parents have it? I'd seen no evidence last year that they'd had the slightest inkling there was anything more sinister than exams on my mind.

You're not like them, a voice whispered in my ear. True enough, I'd always been the odd one out in the family. The first to go to university, for one thing, and neither of my parents had the slightest interest in reading. We'd never done many things together as a family, but that wasn't unusual.

Quit that, I told the voice. Anyone who looked at us could tell we were related—Dad's curly hair stood on end the same way mine did, and Mum and I had the exact same hazel eyes. Eighteen years of photo albums told the same story. Nothing weird had ever happened in my life until that day in assembly. Maybe the crazy skipped a few generations.

"Dad," I said as we sat down to a late lunch at a pub in Blackstone, "does Aunt Eve still have our family tree?"

"I think so. Why?"

"We were talking about our Victorian ancestors in last week's English seminar. I got curious."

"Well, we haven't heard from her in a while," said Mum. "When was the last time she phoned? Last Christmas?"

"Must have been." Dad frowned. "Come to think of it, she was asking about it then. Said it was missing. Don't you remember?"

"Vaguely," said Mum. "She said a few things went missing when she moved, didn't she?"

"Doesn't surprise me. Her house was bursting with old junk. Still is. She never managed to sell it."

Although I often forgot about my token crazy relative, I remembered Aunt Eve's peculiarities. Distant and reserved, she never showed up to family gatherings and had once said she'd live in her little Windermere cottage until she died. She'd surprised to all of us when she'd packed up and moved to Canada five years ago without so much as a warning. She still sent money every Christmas and on my birthday. The amethyst pendant was the only material thing she'd given me.

Wait. In the letter she'd sent with the pendant, she'd said that it had belonged to someone in the family. Maybe she knew of other heirlooms, gifts passed on through the generations. If anyone knew about magic, Aunt Eve did. She'd always loved old myths, and she used to read to me from books of fairy tales when I'd stayed with her over summer. She'd even looked a bit like a witch—albeit a kind one, not a fairytale hag. I couldn't remember her face; my memory was hazy.

I made a mental note to write back and ask her about the family tree. *I still haven't thanked her for the present. Why did I forget?* Surely *someone* would be able to give me answers. None of my grandparents were still alive, and my dad's brothers had never expressed an interest in family history. So that just left Aunt Eve.

After Mum and Dad left late afternoon, I started sorting through the jumble of letters and leaflets in my drawer, looking for the letter from Aunt Eve. I'd thrown everything in haphazardly, from bank statements to vouchers for Bargain Burgers. Eventually, after combing through all my papers and emptying out my drawer, I admitted defeat. Maybe I'd left the letter at home. I texted Mum asking her to look for it then joined my friends in getting ready for our first big night out since Freshers' Week.

Alex insisted we go to Satan's Pit's Saturday Night Extravaganza. She'd also insisted the three of us dress up as the three witches from *Macbeth*, seeing as it was Halloween. My black dress worked fine, so I didn't have to buy a costume, and I also wore my amethyst pendant again.

As it turned out, Sarah had a gift for applying face paint, and we actually looked pretty cool when we set out. She drew elaborate cobweb patterns on our faces and shadowed our eyes, so we looked like we hadn't slept in weeks. *I look almost as bad as I did this time last year.*

"Annnnnd... Satan arrives!" boomed the loudspeakers as we descended the spiral staircase into the nightclub. The customary guy in the devil costume descended via the rope from the ceiling to wild applause.

Since Satan's Pit already looked the part for Halloween, there wasn't a whole lot the decorators could do to make it creepier. They'd enhanced the cobwebs and eerie red lights, with the addition of glowing skulls hanging from the ceiling, and replaced the candle brackets with pumpkins. I readjusted the pendant around my neck as I scanned the crowd.

I caught sight of Claudia, dressed to kill in her off-the-shoulder, shimmering black dress and a pair of uncon-vincing rabbit ears. Guys surrounded her as she danced wildly amongst the flame-like strobe lights. Then I spotted David with a group of people I didn't recognise, possibly the people he'd been with at the pub the other night. I tried to catch his eye, but he wasn't looking at me. I couldn't decide whether I felt more disappointed or relieved that I didn't have to talk to him in front of all his friends. Which was irrational, but I was starting to think the rational part of my mind had long since departed.

You're being stupid, I told myself, but I couldn't help it. David had declined to come with us, pleading tiredness, yet here he was.

Coming back to the club was the worst thing I could have done, considering what had happened last time. The heat, the lights, and the pounding music made me feel dizzy. The flames on the walls and floor changed colour, pulsing from green to red to blue. My pendant glowed, and it felt cold against my chest. I watched, almost hypnotised —and then froze, mid-step.

A large and shaggy figure stole across the dance floor. Even from here, my eyes filmed by dazzling lights, I knew it was no Halloween costume but a similar creature to the one from the hike, only smaller—a shapeless mass around four feet high, with slavering jaws agape and madness in its red eyes.

And it was heading right towards Claudia, through the crowd of admiring guys, none of whom seemed to notice as it shoved them aside with its long paws.

"Claudia!" I screamed.

My cry of warning was lost in the cacophony of music and laughter, but Claudia seemed to realise the danger a split second before the creature pounced. In one fluid movement, she caught hold of the monster's shadowy fur. There was a flash, indistinguishable from the strobe lights, a squeal of pain no one but the two of us could hear, and, a second later, Claudia held the creature in a headlock.

Holy crap.

I pushed my way through the oblivious crowd, heart beating fast in my ears. *This isn't happening. Not again.* Not here, amongst all the noise and laughter and dancing. But it was. The beast squirmed in Claudia's grasp, like an over-large dog.

"Ash! Couldn't give us a hand, could you?" she gasped.

"You're joking!" I elbowed my way past a couple who danced so close together; they were tangled in one another.

"We can't let it run around in here!" said Claudia, attempting to drag the shadow-beast away from the crowd. The creature snarled, and she muttered a curse, a flame leaping from one hand. The monster let out a shrill whine and shrunk, now more dog-sized than lion-sized. But those teeth still snapped, its mad eyes rolling in its head.

This was totally surreal. *Calm down*, I told myself, as the beast snapped its teeth at me. Once again, Claudia's hand lit up, and it went limp.

I took up a position on the creature's other side, its head draped over my arm, making sure the fangs were at a distance. There really was nothing more difficult than trying to drag a great, shaggy monster out of a packed nightclub. True enough, no one gave us a second glance, but the creature kept squirming. Every time it tried to escape, Claudia's hand blazed with fire, and it howled and went limp as a sack of potatoes. But I knew she couldn't do anything too overt for fear of drawing unwelcome attention.

"Wish—Howard—were—here!" Claudia panted.

The beast had gone very still, but as we reached the top of the stairs, it lunged at me, fangs bared. I cringed, and that one movement was enough for it to break Claudia's hold.

"No!" she shouted as the creature disappeared into the crowd of Halloween revellers on the stairs. They scattered, some of them looking around, baffled. None of them could see what had pushed them.

We ran, slipping on the floor now wet with spilled drinks.

"I'm sorry," I panted.

"Don't worry about it," gasped Claudia. "No one saw. If I ever find the idiot who summoned it, I'll set his ass on fire."

We emerged from the nightclub into darkness, and it was impossible to see where the creature had gone.

"Shit," said Claudia. "Shit." She groaned. "Howard won't be happy."

"Howard?" I said, gasping for breath. "Why?"

"He's paranoid the Venantium are on the lookout for unregistered sorcerers," said Claudia, pausing to catch her breath. "And, let's face it, most of the time, they are. Every time something like this happens, the blame always lands on someone who isn't registered. And he's both unregistered and a troublemaker. Because of the mess he got into a couple of years ago, some of them are convinced he's a user of forbidden magic, and they're determined to catch him at it."

"Seriously?" I said, my heart still thumping louder than the pulse of the music behind us. "Is he even out tonight?"

"Probably, if Berenice dragged him out. Shit, this is bad."

"Should—"I peered into the darkness ahead; I didn't want any more craziness tonight—"we try to find it?"

She shook her head. "There's no chance now. The best we can hope for is that it went straight back to the Darkworld."

"Crap." I shook my head. "Who summoned it? Why did it go for us?"

"God knows. This is getting ridiculous. Last year, the only time we saw shadow-beasts was when we went after them ourselves. Now, they're targeting us. Or, more specifically, you."

"You think the person who summoned them is after me?" Though I hated to think about it, I'd had the exact same thought myself.

"Has to be. Of course, they could easily be after both of us, or any of the group, but you were the only one of us on that hike."

"Yeah, but nothing attacked me last time I came here to Redthorne. During the day."

"Really?" Claudia frowned. "Who were you with?"

"David." I swallowed.

"Hmm. Well, whoever's sending those things after you, they don't expect much of your abilities. My guess is they don't know what you're capable of."

"Neither do I," I said, voicing one of the anxieties that had plagued me ever since the beginning of term. "I didn't know I'd be able to fight that creature. I just reacted instinctively."

"That's all magic is, most of the time," she said. "The one limit is your own strength, and the only way to find that is to test it."

"Right," I said. "Well, it would help if I had more of a clue what's going on. And if I knew more about demons."

"I'll tell you more at the next meeting. Look, your friends will be wondering where you are. Go back and find them. I'll text you later, okay?" She turned back to face Satan's Pit, sighing.

"Uh, sure." True, I needed to get back to the others. Would they swallow the helping-a-drunk-girl-to-the-bus-stop story twice? I hated lying to them. I didn't want this. I didn't want secrecy and paranoia. I wanted life to go back to normal—even though a part of me wanted to explore this hidden world further. Not the chasing shadow-beasts part, mind. Was this the lure of the Darkworld? Would I be drawn in deeper and deeper, until it was impossible for me to escape?

A loud noise drew me back to the present—the roar of a motorcycle. A second later, it appeared on the road adjacent to us, leaving a trail of black oil that gleamed in the moonlight—and a dark space.

"Claudia!" I called, and she turned back.

"Holy crap." She looked at me, eyes wide, and whipped out her fan. "Stay back. I'll take care of it."

"I'm coming," I said, following her across the road. The darkness blotted out the lamplights and seemed to grow wider as we approached. I shivered as coldness bit into me.

Something crawled out of the dark space. Several small shapes. Shadow-foxes.

17

SHADOW-BEASTS

Claudia summoned fire to her palm and threw out her other hand, urging me to stay back. I counted seven shadow-foxes, slinking towards us across the pavement. They seemed to carry the darkness with them, the square shape of the Darkworld extending as they moved until it was difficult to see each creature within it.

My heart leapt into my throat, and my pulse raced.

"Back off." Claudia threw a handful of fire, briefly illuminating the darkness. A pitiful screech indicated she'd hit her target. "I. Said. Back. Off."

Fire blazed along the length of the fan, and she brought it down like a whip. Again and again. But the darkness remained, a menacing wall in front of us. My skin had gone cold as ice, and I was pretty sure it was only the spike of adrenaline that stopped my legs from collapsing underneath me.

I clamped a lid on the fear, pushing it behind the icy chill of the Darkworld that swept through me as I raised my own hands. *Come on. Fire.* But the heat from Claudia's flames burned my skin even from a distance, and I moved away.

Then a hand grabbed my ankle. I swung around, stumbling, and choked on a scream. A small human-shaped figure clung to my ankle, its body twisted and shrivelled. Its limbs were overlong, hands ending in curved claws instead of fingers. Sunken, red eyes gleamed from holes in a face that was more like a skull. They were unnaturally large in proportion to its child-sized body. I shuddered with revulsion, fear clawing at my throat.

"Let go!" I gasped, kicking. But it clung, its filthy nails digging into my bare ankle. I kicked again and again. My leg throbbed, and my mouth was dry. "Get off, get it off!" My voice rose to a high pitch. Panicking.

"Hell!" Claudia swung around. Another hideous creature clung to her back, mouth open in a gaping screech. "Ghouls! The crafty bastard's set a trap." She dropped her fan as she tried to keep the creature's claws from reaching her neck. Fire flared from her fingertips. "Ash, contact the Darkworld!"

Panic had made my connection drop, but I could still feel the piercing coldness. I reached out to the Darkworld, like I did on the mountain, to the cold that waited like an old friend. Ice sprang to my fingertips, and a feeling of certainty overrode my fear. The ice was already moving from my hands to my arms, and I directed it down my leg to the creature that clung there. With a piteous squeal, it let go, rolling over on the ground, its scabbed legs kicking.

I rushed to help Claudia, but she dislodged the other creature, kicking it with her heeled foot, now ablaze. "Any more of them?" she said, aiming another fireball at a shadow-fox which had materialized from the shadows, about to bite my ankle.

I spun on the spot, jerking away from the darkness.

Five shadow-foxes remained. *Come on! Fire!* I could summon only ice, so cold it burned. But maybe it was enough. I imagined a ball of frozen fire in my palm, and my connection to the Darkworld deepened, swirling around me, like I'd plunged into the ocean's depths.

The ice flickering over my palm moved fluidly, and I gathered a handful and threw it at the nearest shadow-fox. Without as much as a yelp, the creature broke apart, shattering like glass made of darkness. Disbelief shot through me. *Holy crap. Did I really do that?*

Claudia was preoccupied with another shadow-fox that dodged her attacks. I threw a second handful of ice-fire and hit it square on the forehead, almost as though another force directed my hands. Whirling, exhilaration filling me, I turned on the remaining shadow-foxes, which backed away. The darkness receded with them, and in one leap, they jumped into the dark space.

Panting, Claudia said, "They're all gone?"

"Looks like it," I said, but didn't take my eyes off the dark space, all the same. I'd begun to tremble all over. Now that the adrenaline started to wear off, the stark reality of the danger sank in. I instinctively raised a shaking hand and closed it around the amethyst pendant I'd forgotten I was wearing. Its smooth, cold surface countered the chill of the Darkworld, and my pulse raced against it, making it feel like the stone itself had a heartbeat.

"This is more than a regular sorcerer. This one has serious nerve. Ghouls? God. They're like a step up from shadow-beasts and freaking vicious. Ugh." She kicked off her other heel. One lay smoking on the ground. "I can only summon fire to my hands," she explained. "Otherwise I tend to set things ablaze. You need real control to do what Leo does. Ouch." She showed me her blistered foot. "Don't suppose you have any spare shoes?"

"Nope," I said. I felt a little dizzy. More than a little. I leaned on the wall with one hand.

"You manage to summon fire there? Good shot, by the way."

"Thanks," I said, though my heart beat unnaturally fast. *Not fire. Ice.*

"Well, I take back what I said about the sorcerer underestimating you. Question is, who was it? Did you see anyone?"

"Apart from that motorbike? No."

"Motorbike?" She hobbled over to the road. "Hell, you're right. There's oil all over here. You don't think…"

David's face came to mind. *No way.* "It moved too fast for me to see who rode it, but I swear that dark space wasn't there before."

"You sure?"

"Honestly?" I shook my head. "I don't know. I'm starting to question everything. It might have already been here."

Claudia limped into the road. "The bike went this way, right?"

"You're not thinking of following it?"

"I just want to see where this leads." She gestured towards the thick, glutinous oil.

"Even if it's true, wouldn't it be best to leave it up to the Venantium to catch the sorcerer? And I wouldn't stand in the road," I added.

"Right. Good point. Death by bus after killing shadow-beasts and ghouls? That'd suck." She re-joined me on the pavement. "Hmm. I guess walking into a sorcerer's lair probably isn't a good move either. But I want to *know.*"

"Me, too. But I don't think we should do anything reckless." The dizziness was getting worse. *Please don't pass out.*

"Can't hurt to look, I suppose. I've tracked shadow-beasts before," she added. "Ghouls, too. They're vicious, but stupid. This is low-level stuff."

"Don't speak too soon," I said. I breathed. In and out. Steady. "Have you ever met a demon, for real?"

"'Course not," she said. "If I had, I wouldn't be alive. I've seen them on the other side of the Barrier, but that's different."

"Pain in the ass, though," I said. "But I'd take staring eyes over ghouls and shadow-beasts."

"You're braver than I am."

"Nah."

"Trust me. I nearly passed out when I saw a demon the first time, and I was lucky I had my parents to explain what was going on. I couldn't imagine living with it like you did. I'd go mad."

"Well, I thought I *was* mad," I said. "Or that my subconscious hated me."

"You're not mad. Just… different. And who wants to be normal?" She took a few steps forward.

"Where are you going?"

"Just to take a look!" She gestured. "The trail goes in a straight line for a bit. Come on. If we can get an idea of where the sorcerer went…"

"Then what?" I hurried to catch up. She moved fast for someone with no shoes on.

"Then… I don't know."

I sighed. I couldn't let her run off alone. Besides, I vaguely knew where we were from when I'd come here with David. We stood on the main road leading into town, the location of several other bars recommended to us by the Freshers' Reps.

"Tanner's Wine Bar," she said, as we passed it. "Might pop in for a quick one on the way back."

"Shit," I said. "My friends will be leaving now."

"Text them saying you met someone."

I groaned as I saw several missed calls on my phone. "Hell. Alex'll think I'm dead."

"Really? Intuition?"

"No, she's just very dramatic. But I'd better let her know I'm alive anyway."

I sent a quick text as we passed the wine bar. The trail of oil continued along the road, growing thicker as we reached the junction where the three main streets met. Then it veered away to the right, a large pool gathering where the rider had turned a sharp corner. I started shivering again as we followed. Poor lighting accentuated the shadowed alleys between shops, and every instinct told me to turn back.

Claudia stopped dead, frowning. The trail ended at the roadside, but there was no sign of the bike.

"Come on. Let's head to the bus station," I said. "I suppose it's quicker to get it from here, now."

She didn't answer.

"We can't stand here all night." Then my chest burned. I looked down and saw the pendant *glowing*. "What the…" Fear gripped me. I knew a menacing presence watched me, calculating.

"It's been too long, Ashlyn."

I peered down the alleyway, into the violet eyes of a demon.

Claudia said, "Holy shit."

"What—what do you want?" I said, my voice shaking.

"You might find it wise to leave soon, Ashlyn. They are coming."

"Who's coming?"

Claudia grabbed my arm, pointing at the sky. "You've gotta be fucking kidding. Harpies? Now?"

"Guard your heart well, Ashlyn."

The eyes vanished.

Before I could even process the demon's words, Claudia seized my arm again and dragged me into an alleyway. "Shit," she whispered. She trembled beside me. "Shit. Oh God. If the Venantium blame us for this…"

"They won't, will they?"

"Duh, 'course they will. We're unregistered. You've got a shield on you, but they know who *I* am, because my parents worked for them. Oh, God." For the first time since I'd met her, she seemed on the verge of a breakdown. I couldn't say I blamed her.

What the hell did that demon mean?

"Ash, you are in some serious shit. That demon spoke to you!" She leaned back against the wall. "Don't scare me like that. You can't give into them, you have to ignore them."

"I know that. Why would you think I'd ever give into a demon?"

"I mean demons don't tend to give you a choice in the matter. If they have you targeted, then they're looking for a way to get through to you."

I was shivering so hard, my teeth chattered. My mind whirled. Had that demon given us a warning? No. I couldn't believe demons could ever *help* us. What about the one I'd tried to take out with a dictionary? With no features, there was no way to distinguish one demon from another. *That must get confusing.* I berated myself for even thinking that now, with us knee-deep in shit. But rational thought calmed my racing heart. Clinging to logic had been the only defence I'd had over the past year.

Breathe in. Breathe out. Don't look up. Don't engage. I glanced at Claudia beside me. Her hands had clenched into fists, and she, too, looked like she was concentrating on steadying her breathing. Her eyes opened, and she moved to the alleyway's entrance, peeking out to see if the coast was clear.

"No harpies," she whispered. "Come on. To the bus station."

Thankfully, the bus depot was only a short walk away, and I thought Claudia might cry with relief at the sight of a bus already at the station. I paid for both of us and dragged her to the back.

She collapsed into a seat, groaning. "Never. Again."

I rested my head on the seat opposite and closed my eyes. My heart raced and tremors still rocked me.

"Okay," she breathed. "I'm okay. You?"

"Never better," I said. I felt cold sweat on my back and my forehead. Brushing my hair out of my eyes, my hand caught on the pendant around my neck. It no longer shone, but I remembered the way it glowed just before I saw the demon. And in Satan's Pit, too. But I was too tired to think on that now.

"I reckon the Venantium will have caught the guy," she said, a touch of her old confidence back in her voice. "He won't get away."

I didn't want to contradict her, so I nodded.

The drive to campus passed in no time, and I'd never felt more relieved to see the comforting lights of the student village.

"I'm going to sleep for a year and a half," said Claudia, using her fob to open the door to House 12. "Nah. I won't sleep after that." She shuddered. "I'm gonna have to be boring and say don't go out for a while, 'kay?"

"Like I planned to after that," I said, stepping into the building.

"See you soon, anyway. I'll text you if anything comes up. Or if you wanna talk nightmares." She gave a brittle laugh.

"Sure," I said as we parted ways inside the block, Claudia heading upstairs to her own flat.

"By the way, you were totally awesome back there," she called down the stairs.

"Same to you," I said. "'Night." *More like morning, really.*

Back in my room, I sighed, kicking off my shoes. Too much to think about right now. Too much for my mind to cope with. Before I pulled my curtains shut, I looked at the field. No sign of David's motorbike outside. *Could it have been his? Maybe he just took it home, like he said he would.*

My head spun. I fell forward onto my bed and let the dreams take me.

18

THERE ARE NO ANGELS

T he one thought that dominated my thoughts over the following week was that at this rate, I'd be lucky to survive my first term at university. Since I was terrible at hiding my feelings, Alex and Sarah knew there was something on my mind, and, in the absence of any other evidence, they latched onto what they thought was the only possible cause.

"Just talk to him!" Alex yelled at me.

I jumped, having been contemplating the patch of grass beneath our kitchen window for the past few minutes. "Huh?"

"David! Stop your bloody moping and ask him whether he's going to ask you out or not."

"I'm not moping," I insisted. "I'm just tired. And I'd ask, if I ever saw him."

"You live in the same flat. It's not hard to knock on his door."

"He's never in."

Alex rolled her eyes.

I said nothing. If letting them think me a love-struck

moron would divert attention from the real cause of my problems, then, like it or not, I'd have to endure it. At least it'd stop them telling me off for ditching them on Halloween. Not that I particularly wanted to discuss David at the moment. It was true—I hadn't seen him in the flat since the night before Halloween. Either we kept missing each other, or he was sleeping in the library to get his essay finished. But that explanation didn't fit right, seeing as up until recently, we'd been going there together. I'd have thought he'd at least ask me if I wanted to join him.

"Speaking of people not being in, have either of you seen Terrence lately?" I said.

Sarah shook her head. "Not for a while."

"I have," said Alex. "He was sneaking off to the 'lab' again last night. If you ask me, he's conducting Frankenstein-style experiments in there. If we get attacked by animated corpses, we'll know who's to blame."

"You never know," I said. "I saw a weird glow coming from his window the other day."

"Maybe he's an alien!" said Alex. "And when he's ranting on Skype, he's actually communicating with his mother ship. That's why there are so many weird noises coming from his room."

I laughed. It wasn't hard to send Alex off on a complete tangent.

"As for Pete," she said, "*he's* going to end up with a restraining order on him if he's not careful. He won't leave Danielle alone. He keeps ambushing her as she leaves her flat."

"Seriously?" I said. "Doesn't she mind that he's stalking her?"

"She seems to find it funny," said Sarah. "She and her friends were laughing about it the last time I saw her."

"Yeah," said Alex. "To be honest, none of them seem

that bright. They probably consider it an honour to have a stalker."

We discussed Pete's stalkerish tendencies and Terrence's possible extra-terrestrial origins for a while, but of course I couldn't expect them to forget about David.

"Really, Ash," said Alex. "It'd be better if David was stalking you. At least then you'd know."

"I don't want a stalker," I said. "Hell, I don't even want a boyfriend. I just want him to be straight with me. I don't get why he keeps saying one thing and doing another—like saying he was tired, and then showing up at Satan's Pit. And then disappearing off the face of the earth."

"I'll ask, then," said Alex. She stood up and made for the door.

"What are you doing?"

"Doing you a favour." She knocked on David's door with both hands. "Open up, David! We want to talk to you!"

"Stop doing that!"

But there was no reply, to my relief. "He must be out."

"I'm going to pounce on him when he comes back."

"*That's* a bit stalkerish, to be honest," I said.

"No, it isn't!" She hesitated. "Actually, it kinda is."

And we left the subject of David behind. But, even as we planned a film night for that evening, I couldn't help but think Alex had a point—at least with a stalker, I would know where I stood. And that was, generally, as far away as possible from the person in question. Where I was now with David, God only knew.

And that pretty much applied to the rest of my life. After Halloween, the weekly meetings with the Circle of Sinners always ended in arguments about conspiracy theories. I still didn't feel entirely at ease around the rest of the group. Howard was always liable to snap at someone or throw something, and Berenice still regarded me as if I was some kind of novelty the others had dragged in for her entertainment. To no one's surprise, Howard took the view that the Venantium had been behind the shadow-beasts that had attacked Claudia and me.

"Maybe they're trying to provoke you into using magic, so they'll have an excuse to arrest you," he said at one meeting.

"The Venantium would never summon shadow-creatures, Howard," said Claudia, who sounded weary of the topic by now. At least Claudia hadn't told anyone the demon speaking to me.

"They use harpies," said Howard. "They're shadow-creatures. Hypocrites, the lot of them."

"Yeah, but there's a limit. Harpies are easy to control. Shadow-beasts and ghouls, though? They wouldn't go so far against their own principles."

"*You* would say that. Just 'cause your parents used to work for them."

"Howard, for God's sake! You just want to blame them for everything."

"Shut the hell up," snapped Howard.

"Chill out," said Leo, who looked rather bored by the whole thing. He lounged on the sofa, more absorbed in the Xbox than in the conversation. Once again, he and Howard battled it out on some fighting game.

"Yes, please!" said an irate Cyrus from the corner, who'd brought his work along to the meeting and now looked as though he regretted it.

"I think the newbie's attracting the demons' attentions," said Berenice, glancing up from her copy of *Cosmopolitan*. "They're drawn to her like mosquitoes."

"Lovely image," I said, though part of me feared she

was right. "So, what is it I'm doing to attract their attention?"

"Don't ask me. Subliminally telling them to follow you?"

"You can't use subliminal magic on a demon, Berenice," said Cyrus. "You know that."

Berenice shrugged. "Whatever. There's something not right about the newbie, anyway."

"Excuse me?" I said. "I'm right here, in case you hadn't noticed, and I do have a name."

"Fine." Berenice rolled her eyes. "There's something not right about *Ash*."

"Stop being bitchy," said Claudia, who'd started skimming through a large, leather-bound book that looked as if it had come from the Venantium's library.

"I just don't want any of us to get killed on *her* account!" Bernice continued.

"I'm not trying to get you killed," I said.

"That's not what Claudia tells me."

I turned to face Claudia, hurt and surprised.

"I didn't say that," said Claudia. "I just said it's weird that you're always there when the creatures appear. That seems to suggest whoever's summoning them is after you—like I said."

"But *is* it my fault?" I said. "What if I *am* drawing their attention?"

"Demons are attracted to overt use of magic," said Claudia. "And you haven't used any before now, have you?"

"No. The demons were always there anyway."

At that moment, Howard and Leo's heated game-related discussion reached its peak. I didn't hear what Leo said, but it must have been rude, because Howard threw down his Xbox controller and stormed out of the room.

Berenice sighed, looking at the door as it slammed. Then she put down her magazine and took his place as Leo threw his own controller down, shaking his head.

"He needs to watch it," said Claudia.

"Why do you bother playing with him if you know he's going to overreact?" I asked Leo.

He shrugged. "Cy's not much of a challenge."

"Hey!" said Cyrus. "At least I didn't break your copy of *Grand Theft Auto*. Which was originally mine, by the way."

"Yeah, I know, I know."

"Brothers," said Claudia. "Can all of you chill out, please?"

Leo raised his eyebrows at her. "Thought about taking your own advice?"

"Don't push me," she said. "Ash and I had a seriously close call on Halloween, and bickering about irrelevant crap is *not* helping. Something out there's working against us. *All* of us. And it's not just the Venantium."

"I know," said Leo. "But unless you want to go snooping around Redthorne looking for trouble, there's not much we can do. Whoever it was got away, right?"

"Yeah. We never saw them," I said.

Except for the motorbike. But that would send me down a road I really didn't want to take. Besides, David had been in Satan's Pit. Which left the other possibility. The sorcerer had taken his bike.

I sighed. "I'm sick of suspecting everyone. Isn't the Venantium supposed to deal with rogues, or whoever attacked us?"

"Yeah," said Claudia. "But it was Halloween. Aka, the most common day for idiots to attempt to summon demons."

"Mostly false alarms," said Leo. "Melmoth, my guardian, said there wasn't anything serious."

"Hmm," said Claudia, biting her lip.

"Isn't anyone going to come and play this crappy game?" Berenice demanded from the sofa.

"Hey, don't trash WWE," said Leo. "Ash?"

"I'll kick your ass, newbie," said Berenice.

"All right," I said, taking the controller from Leo. "Might as well. My flatmates think I'm at the Gaming Society meeting anyway. And I plan to keep them out of the loop on demons, and shadow-beast attacks, and harpies, and whatever the hell this crazy universe throws at me next."

"Good plan," said Leo. "I forget how mental this must be for you. I'm used to balancing life with the weird shit, but I guess you must be going through some tough times now, right?"

"What, apart from being attacked?" I shook my head. "Honestly, after seeing demons for a year and not knowing what they were, it'll take a lot to beat that in the trauma-tising factor."

"Told you she's braver than me," said Claudia to Leo.

"More like all talk," said Berenice. "All right, newbie. Let's do this."

She beat me at the game in two minutes flat, but I didn't care. I was aware of Leo watching me, and Claudia's comment on my so-called bravery made me feel strange, like I'd stolen someone else's position. Old Ash would never have fitted into this world.

"Ash?" said Claudia. "Would you say the creature that attacked you on the mountain looked like this?"

She held open her book. A picture of a ferocious-looking black shadowy mass stared at me from the pages. The photo alone brought out chills, conjuring an image of a desolate landscape, a snowdrift, a monster bearing down on me.

"Yeah, that's the one. Like the one in Satan's Pit, except bigger," I replied.

"How big? Six feet or taller?"

"I don't know. Probably. I was up to my neck in snow at the time. Does it matter?"

"Not really," said Claudia. "A standard shadow-beast, by the sound of things. They're dangerous whatever form they take. Even shadow-foxes can take a bite out of you."

"I was wondering," I said. "Can shadow-beasts possess you, like demons?"

Claudia shook his head. "No, they can't. They might be able to cause physical damage, but they have none of the advantages a true demon has. They're fairly stupid, whereas demons are at least as intelligent as people are——more so than most."

"Not that shadow-beasts are harmless," Cyrus added. He'd taken a neutral position during our debate and refused to take sides with or against Howard—in a quiet, calm way that somehow managed not to aggravate anyone. Kind of impressive. "They take on different forms, but they all share the trait of being semi-corporeal. In other words, they can walk between this world and the Darkworld, taking on a partially physical shape in our world. They're easy to summon and control, which is why they're a favourite with so many rogue sorcerers. It's like having a troop of well-trained dogs."

"Can they kill you? Is it different than a real dog biting you?" I asked.

"It's like being mauled to death by a lion," said Leo.

"Lovely."

"It also makes them easier to kill and not necessarily by using fire," said Claudia. "That's how you did it, right?"

"Actually," I said, remembering the rush of icy flames from my hands, "it's more like I used their own strength against them. On the mountain, it was freezing, so I couldn't imagine fire. I swear it was ice that hit it. I did it to those shadow-foxes, too."

"Liar," said Berenice. "That kind of magic is beyond you. Only the higher-ups in the Venantium learn how to do that."

"I'm not lying." I found it more difficult than ever to not slap her smirking face. Even the bitchiest girls at my school hadn't been that obnoxious.

"She's not lying," said Claudia. "I thought those flames didn't look quite right when you stopped that shadow-fox. Ice-fire?"

"Maybe," I said. "Stranger things have happened to me."

"Whatever," said Berenice, unimpressed. "You might have got all this lot under your little spell, but I'm not so naïve. And I'll be damned if you're going to put anyone else in danger."

"That's very noble of you." said Leo. "But you're damned anyway, so it makes no difference. Same as the rest of us."

"What, you really think we're going to Hell?" said Cyrus.

"No, I don't believe in Hell. But you know what the original Venantium used to say about magic-users. They think we get our power from the Devil."

"That's ridiculous," said Claudia. "They used magic themselves. They couldn't have created the Barrier without it."

"They say using magic to defend humanity against the demons of the Darkworld doesn't count," said Cyrus. "I don't agree with it either; it's the most hypocritical attitude you can have. Thankfully, these days, the Venantium are more open-minded."

"You'd say that," said Berenice. "What about Howard?"

"I'm not saying I agree with their policies, but what they do is necessary," said Cyrus. "If it wasn't for them, we'd be screwed. The demons would use our world as their playground. That's why they want every sorcerer on their side, to make sure they have maximum support."

"Even if they break their own rules," said Berenice. "Look at the harpies."

"I have a question," I interrupted her, addressing Cyrus. "How can a demon be killed with fire if they're not physically here? Shouldn't it go right through them?"

"Technically, it should," said Cyrus. "But, when a demon enters this world, it can't stay unless it has an anchor. This means they attach themselves to a person by means of possession, but to hang on longer than a few seconds, they need a talisman. Precious stones are a favourite amongst rogue sorcerers. Charge one with enough magic energy, and it becomes a stone of power. The demon can't resist the lure of the magic and latches onto it, feeding on the energy, until the stone becomes one with itself. That's how you can tell when someone's possessed. The stone fixates here." He tapped the centre of his forehead. "Like a third eye. They call it the demon's heart. As long as there's energy there, the demon stays in control. Even if the sorcerer dies."

"So the sorcerer willingly gives up their body?" I said, my insides contracting at the thought.

"Yeah," said Cyrus. "They get the demon's power, the demon gets free rein for a bit. The perfect trade. Except the demon always takes over. That's why the Venantium have this hang-up against rogues, sorcerers who haven't had access to the same knowledge they have. Ignorance is dangerous, and new kids with a Darkworld connection are the perfect target for demons looking for a bit of freedom. They tell them lies, tell them anything that'll make the sorcerer summon them. Of course, soon as the demon's loose, the sorcerer realises they've been lied to—but it's too late." He shook his head.

"And to send a demon back to the Darkworld," said Leo, "you need to cut off the anchor. Demons are creatures of darkness. Light and fire are their enemies. But fire has more effect than that—magical fire burns away a demon's energy supply."

"But that doesn't kill it?" I asked.

"You can't kill a demon," said Berenice, in the tones of one explaining to a five-year-old that the Earth was round.

"True," said Claudia. "But you can send them back to the Darkworld powerless, and that's all you want. The Barrier stops them from getting back through."

"Can I have a look at that?" I asked, indicating her book. It was the first one I'd picked at random from the library: *The Seven Princes of the Darkworld: A General Guide to Demons*.

"Sure. I wouldn't look too closely at the pictures, though."

I could see why. Images of demons and shadow-beasts, so realistic they could have been painted from real life, sent a deep chill through me. The hideous ghouls sat side-by-side with harpies, their almost-human faces the creepiest to look at.

I skimmed through the book, which was divided into two parts: *Shadow-Beasts and Other Lesser Demons* and *True Demons*. Within the latter section, I flipped open the book onto a later chapter entitled "Higher Demons."

"Are some demons more powerful than others, then?" I asked.

"Yeah, they have a hierarchy within the Darkworld,"

said Cyrus. "But no one really understands it, not even the Venantium's Demon Researchers. They say the highest demons have the ability to make the human they possess live forever, as they do, but there's no proof of this."

"So, some sorcerers summon as many demons as possible in an attempt to gain enough power to contact these so-called higher demons," said Leo. "It's a waste of time. Read that book. It says the higher demons appear in this world only when they want to. They can't be controlled. They walk around in a human-like form, so no one can track them in either world."

"What about angels?" I asked, looking at the pictures of twisted creatures and thinking of Dante, of Milton, of all the poets who summoned up a vision not only of Hell but also its opposite, Heaven, a supposed antithesis to the place of evil. "The fortune-teller told me they don't exist, but how do we know for sure? In all the myths about demons I've read, angels always appear as the opposite."

"That's where people get the wrong end of the stick," said Cyrus. "They think demons are pure evil in themselves, but they're not, not as evil as some of the sorcerers who conjure them. The problem with demons is that people have this image of them as servants of Satan, but all they're doing is acting in their own self-interest. Which is pretty human, in my opinion."

"Or you could look at it like this," said Berenice. "People made up the myth of Heaven to escape from the fear of the reality of Hell. But there are no angels. No one can save you." She wore a twisted smile, but the look in her eyes was more like rage. Then she blinked, and I wondered if I'd imagined it.

"Which is why beer exists," said Leo, opening a can.

"Enough!" said Claudia. "Not every sorcerer believes we're all doomed. Demons are like the ultimate temptation, with a hell of a sting in the tail. Doesn't mean they're going to kill all of us. Some people just have an incredibly pessimistic worldview." She gave Berenice a meaningful look. "And I for one am sick of sitting around being miserable. Anyone want to come to the bar tonight?"

"Can't. I've got to finish my seminar work," said Cyrus. "Next week, definitely."

"I'll come," said Leo. "How about you, Ash?"

"Er… I shouldn't. I have work to do," I said, aware of how lame I sounded. Well, there was only so much of the crazy I could take.

"Come on, Ash," said Leo. "Just come for one drink. No crazy stuff. Promise."

"Well…" *Come on.* This was campus. Definitely no demons here. Plus, if I went back to my flat, I'd get an interrogation about why I hadn't talked to David yet.

"Well, okay, then. But I'm not going back to Satan's Pit!"

19

COLD WITHIN

I felt a tad guilty for neglecting my friends as I left the flat that evening for the bar. I'd make it up to them at some point. *When all this is over.* Whenever that might be.

"Hey," said Leo, who waited outside the bar. "I thought you might have had second thoughts. The others are already in there."

"Second thoughts?" In spite of everything, I laughed at that. "What, is it worse than breaking into a library? Like a hard-core induction into your secret society?"

"Nope, just a harmless game of pool with a group of lunatics."

"Do you count me as a lunatic?" The question slipped out before I could reel it in.

"You're hanging out with us," he reminded me.

"Touché." Maybe I could get to like Leo.

The Common Room was packed out, totally different from earlier. Cyrus waved at me from by the pool table where Berenice sat on Howard's lap in the only available seat, and Claudia leaned against the wall, playing a game on her phone.

"Hey," said Cyrus, handing me a pool cue. "We're taking it in turns. You're up."

"Uh… right." Conscious of everyone watching me, I fumbled the cue and almost took out some poor girl's eye.

"Sorry," I said as Berenice laughed.

"Quit that," Leo said to her. "You did the same thing ten minutes ago."

"There's no room to move here," I added, wondering if it would be such a bad idea to take a swing at her. She was asking for it.

"Yeah," said Leo. "Your turn," he added to Berenice. "Show us your skills, O great one. I bow down to your superior talent."

He sounded so ridiculous, I snorted.

Berenice's face could have made water freeze. She took the cue and hit the white ball with such force, it went flying off the table and rolled out of sight.

"Such brilliance!" Leo declared.

Grinning, I went to find the ball, since I was closest— and walked smack into someone. David.

"Oh," I said, panicking slightly. "Hi."

"Could I talk to you a second?" he said.

My heart plummeted. This couldn't be good. "Sure," I said, trying to keep my tone steady.

"It's nothing, only… well, let's go outside."

Now is not the time. But I didn't want to drag him over to the others, and it was kind of hard to hear ourselves think in here. "Okay. But only for a second, I gotta get back over there." I waved vaguely in the direction of the pool tables.

"Where?"

"I'm with some… people, friends."

"It'll only be a minute."

Relenting, I followed him outside.

"My bike was taken again," he said. "I found it halfway across the field last night, like someone dumped it there. Bastards are playing a game with me. I still don't know how the hell they're breaking the locks. I've talked to everyone else, and they don't know. I wondered if you'd seen anything odd."

I shook my head. "Me? No."

"Right." He pressed his lips into a slight frown.

Did he not believe me? "Won't the security cameras have picked it up?" I said, my heart sinking as I remembered the bike in Redthorne and the trail of oil.

"Angela, the college secretary, checked them. Someone's tampered with the footage from the last few weeks. It keeps going blank, like the screen's been obscured. Haven't you seen all the posters around campus asking for information?"

I shook my head.

"Well, anyway, are you sure you don't know anything?"

I nodded. "Of course."

"See you later, then."

He walked away, leaving me outside the common room, totally confused.

Although I managed to shake off the others' questions by saying I had to speak to my flatmate, I couldn't get back into the mood, even though Leo had us in stitches doing a word-for-word impersonation of the *Family Guy* episode on the TV. But then a group of football fanatics took over to watch the match, and the mood deteriorated. Claudia and Leo were happy to take shots of Jäger until the sun rose, but I made an excuse and went back to the flat early.

Now, there was another mystery. All the evidence suggested there was someone at the university—most likely within the student village—who was a magic-user.

But was this the same person who was summoning the shadow-beasts? I didn't know, but I couldn't fight the growing feeling that there was something very wrong.

The next day, however, drove all thought of foul play from my mind. As we waited for Sarah and Alex to come out of their rooms ready to go to the afternoon's lecture, David asked me, "Do you want to come and hang out with me tonight?"

His words didn't register at first. When they did finally hit home, I'm pretty sure he could read the total shock written all over my face.

"Um, sure," I said. "With your friends?"

"No, I don't think they'll be around. I've been invited to a party, but I'm not really feeling it. I'll let you know later, okay?"

Before I could gather my thoughts into a coherent reply, Alex came out of her room. "Ready for another thrilling lecture?"

"I don't mind Payne's lectures," said David.

"Are you kidding me? Payne's a psycho. I think he wants us all to fail."

I let them carry on about the bad-tempered professor without joining in. My thoughts spun out of control. Was this it? Had David just asked me out?

God, I needed to get a grip. I didn't quite trust David not to disappear again.

∼

BUT HE DIDN'T. He knocked on my door at seven, and my heart flipped over as I went to answer. *Talk to him. Ask him why he's been avoiding you.*

"Hey," he said. "I was thinking, it's been a while since we talked. Want to come to the burger bar?"

Not exactly a five-star restaurant, but if it meant I got to ask what his game was, I was more than happy to go along with it.

"Sure thing," I said, locking my door behind me. "I've barely seen you the last couple of weeks."

"Yeah, things have been kind of manic. I went home for a few days over reading week."

So that's why he hasn't been in the flat.

"Okay. Just wondered, because we haven't been to the library in ages."

"Yeah, I miss our study sessions." He smiled at me, kind of shyly.

My face heated up. "Uh, me too."

Come on. Common sense.

"I saw you on Halloween," I began.

"Oh, sorry about that," he said quickly. "I got this last-minute invite. I should have texted you or something."

"No worries," I said. "I was just surprised."

"Yeah. Alex and Sarah said you disappeared that night."

My heart sank. "Uh. Yeah. This girl was totally wasted and went wandering off into town."

"That's not good," he said. Damn. Why did he have to look at me so intently? It scrambled my thoughts.

"It was okay," I said. "Nothing to worry about. Alex just won't let anything drop."

"Yeah, she's a bit dramatic," he said. "That's kind of why I've been hanging out with people from my politics class. I mean, no offence to your friends, but we don't have that much in common."

"I guess not."

"Hey, I still want to hang out with *you*, but I don't want to sit in the flat all day."

"Sure."

Well, this is awkward. David seemed to realise, as he changed the subject, and we talked course work all the way to Bargain Burgers. It was easier to talk when we were in a crowd, and I found myself relaxing around him for the first time in weeks. He hadn't been avoiding me. And he'd left Redthorne on Halloween at the same time as my friends, so there was no way he could have been the person on the motorbike. Not that I wanted to bring that up—just for one night, I wanted to forget about the crazy.

Another case of wishful thinking, as it turned out. When we went to the bar for a drink, Claudia, Berenice, and a few people I didn't recognise sat at a table right by the entrance. I couldn't avoid them.

I tried not to catch Claudia's eye, but Berenice spotted me anyway, and called out, "Hey, Ash!" like she was pleased to see me. But her smile was more like a smirk.

I ignored her and walked with David to the bar, but he'd already seen. "Who was that?"

"Someone from GameSoc," I said. "The Gaming Society are kind of weird."

"Right. I'll get the drinks. You can go sit with your friends, if you like." His voice took on an irritable tone, like the presence of the others annoyed him.

"No, it's fine. I'll come too," I said, wanting to get out of Berenice's sight. She looked at me as if daring me to come and speak to her. What was *with* her?

David fidgeted, constantly checking his phone whilst we waited at the bar. He kept looking around, and his eyes lingered on the table where Berenice and the others sat. I saw him catch Claudia's eye, and a strange expression crossed his face. Like recognition.

Finally at the front of the queue, David starting lining up shots of tequila on the counter. I said, confused, "I don't like tequila."

"I know, they're for me."

I watched with raised eyebrows as he started downing them. "Holy cow. I thought you just wanted to come for one drink?"

"I'm going to a party," he said shortly. "You remember?"

"I thought you weren't going."

"It's my mate's birthday. I can't not go."

That's not what you said earlier, I thought, but I was too aware of Berenice's gaze on my back to argue. "Oh, right."

"Sorry," he said, not meeting my eyes. "You can come if you like." But what I heard was *go away.*

I didn't make it back to the flat before the tears came. Of course, Alex and Sarah accosted me as soon as I opened the door.

"You went on a *date* with David, and you didn't tell us?" said Alex. "I'm ashamed of you."

"How was it?" said Sarah.

I was too choked up to speak.

"What's wrong?"

"It wasn't a *date*, and he doesn't even like me anyway." The tears came thick and fast now. "He totally spurned me."

Alex hugged me. "What a prick. Tell us all about it."

"I don't know what happened. We were getting on fine, then we got to the bar and he suddenly said he had to go to this party and ditched me. He'd already told me he wasn't going. It was like he just changed his mind. Again."

"Maybe he's bipolar," said Alex. "Asshole. Don't bother with him."

"But…I don't get it," I said, cheeks burning with humiliation.

"It *is* pretty weird," said Sarah. "You didn't say or do anything that might have upset him?"

"Not that I know of," I said, reluctant to bring up the fact that Berenice and Claudia had been there—damn, I should have spoken to them, and I would have done, if I hadn't been on the verge of tears. I'd let Berenice have it at the next meeting.

"Dickweasel," said Alex. "He's not worth your time. Honest."

It was all very well for her to say that, but his abrupt personality change was more than upsetting—it was frightening. Had Berenice had something to do with it? Things had been fine until she'd spoken to me.

"Dickweasel?" said Sarah, stifling a giggle. "That's pretty much the best insult ever."

"I do my best," said Alex, with a mock bow. "Right. I'm voting for a Disney night, to cheer you up, missy."

"But…" In truth, I just wanted to go to sleep. But my dreams weren't playing nice, and my thoughts were all tangled up in confusion and hurt.

"No buts." She more or less hauled me to her room, where she set the TV up with *Beauty and the Beast* in the disc drive.

"How'd you know that's my favourite?" I asked, wiping my eyes.

"I know you better than that asswrangler does," said Alex.

I didn't know whether to snort with laughter or sob, so the sound that came out was a mixture of both. Attractive.

It wasn't much of a restful night. But an amusing one. Except for Terrence, who started hammering on the wall around midnight, presumably in protest.

"Oh, who gives a shit?" said Alex.

"Hope David can hear," I said, and then wished I hadn't thought of him again.

"Hey," said Alex. "It's okay. We've all made mistakes. At least you found out before he took advantage."

"I don't think that was his plan," I said. God, it was too confusing. I hadn't even decided whether I liked him in that way in the first place, but being spurned stung regardless.

"Something similar happened to me," said Sarah. "Before I met Liam. It sucks, but you know better now."

"Sucks donkey balls," Alex added.

I laughed feebly.

Then two people came into the flat, a guy and a girl. Before my brain caught up with me, I'd shot to the door to peek out the spyhole, ashamed at my pathetic behaviour when I recognised the guy as David. I couldn't see the girl—she was just out of view—but I felt colder than I had on that mountain. David wouldn't—would he? I pressed my face against the door, but, short of opening it, there was no way of telling what was happening. David and the girl talked in low voices, too quiet for me to catch the words. Then I heard his door close.

It felt as if a dark space was opening up inside me, like I'd been sucker-punched in the chest.

"What's going on?" said Alex.

"David's out there. With another girl."

"*What?*"

"What a dick," said Alex and made to open the door.

"Wait!" I said. "Don't. Just leave it. He clearly never liked me anyway. It doesn't matter."

"Oh, *Ash*, don't be so melodramatic!"

But the mood was spoiled. And it was four in the morning. Saying goodnight to the others—and making Alex promise not to kick down David's door—I went back to my room and fell into bed, not to sleep but to recuperate. It didn't last long. Restlessness soon seized me, and I leapt up to pace the room. I noticed in a detached way that ice crystals were forming on my palms. *Does magic react to strong emotions?*

To test this theory, I imagined my hurt and anger to be like a fireball inside me. I tried to coax the Darkworld into responding, but the coldness dominated, and I ended up lowering the temperature in the room so much that icicles formed on the windowsill. Not for the first time, I wondered about the extent of my abilities. Was there a limit to what I could do?

I watched as ice crept over my hands. Admiring the way the gleaming transparency covered my hands, I imagined slamming my fists into David's and the anonymous girl's faces. *Better control that urge.* I knew I had no right to be angry, that I'd never had a claim to him anyway, but I felt wrong-footed and confused by the way he'd taken off. I wanted answers, and I resolved to confront him in the morning, whether he had another girl with him or not.

I wish I'd kept my mouth shut. The truth is, I wouldn't have got so carried away if people hadn't kept asking me about him.

I let the ice on my hands melt, dripping onto the carpet fire. Why couldn't I summon fire? That element was supposed to be the simplest kind of magic, yet I hadn't even come close to it. If I could do so much with ice, then why was this sort of magic beyond me?

Drained, I collapsed back on my bed and fell asleep this time.

I dreamt I was in the library in Blackstone. Numerous labyrinthine pathways ran between rows of endless bookshelves, and, when I turned around, I found I wasn't by the entrance but in the middle. I could no more discern the way I'd come in than I could the way out. But one particular passage seemed to call to me, like it wanted me to go down there. By dream-logic, I didn't question it. I took a step forwards into the maze.

Instantly, all the candles went out, plunging the tunnel into darkness. For a second, I panicked, then I remembered I needed only to contact the Darkworld to conjure a light of my own. Holding the light above my head like a strange, wobbling piece of torchlight, I began to walk.

After only a short time, I heard footsteps behind me. I spun round, heart in my mouth, but there was no one there. Every few minutes or so, I heard another noise, yet every time I turned around, I saw nothing but shadows. I felt a sense of urgency building up inside me. I needed to find what I was looking for fast, before it was too late. What *too late* meant, I didn't know. But I had to get there soon.

Then I rounded a corner and saw a pedestal at the end of the path, and, on top of it, a book. I couldn't make out any details from here, but there was no doubt in my mind that this was what I was looking for.

I walked faster. Footsteps echoed behind me and seemed to quicken, too, but I was too intent on my goal to pay attention—until a pair of hands clasped around my neck. I gasped, panic blossoming. It felt like I was drowning, as cold hands squeezed my throat, cutting off my air supply. I writhed, my vision going blue around the edges, a roaring in my ears, a bleeping sound, like an alarm.

I jolted awake. For one heart-stopping second, I thought there really was a stranger's arm wrapped around my neck, then I realised it was my own. I'd been sleeping on it, and my entire arm had gone numb. I sat up, flexing my arm to get feeling back into it, and looked at the clock. *Oh, crap.* I'd forgotten to reset my alarm, and now had only fifteen minutes to get to campus.

I jumped out of bed and started feverishly pulling on my clothes. One glance in the mirror to check I was decent, then I grabbed my bag and left my room.

I stopped dead. David stood outside. And he wasn't alone. To her credit, the girl looked ashamed. She glanced at me, biting her lip, not meeting my eyes.

It was Claudia.

20

BETRAYAL

I stared at her. The choking feeling from my dream rose within me again, like the breath had been knocked from my chest.

"Hey, Ash," Claudia mumbled. I'd never seen her so uncomfortable. "Um, you've got a lecture now, right? I'll catch you later, okay?"

I stood, numb, and watched her leave—until I noticed David was half-out the flat door. I crossed the corridor and blocked his way.

"What?" he said.

"What do you mean, *what*? What the hell was that? What was she doing here?"

"It's none of your business who I talk to," he said, pushing past me and striding off across the courtyard.

"Hey!" I followed him, having to speed-walk to keep up. "Why did you take off on me yesterday?"

David turned to face me, and the hostility in his expression rooted me to the spot. "I'd have thought that was obvious." His voice was cold. He hitched his bag back onto his shoulder and walked away.

"What," said Alex, from behind me, "the hell was that about?"

I shook my head. "I've no idea. I didn't say anything. I don't know what's with him. First he acts like I insulted him, then he hooks up with——" I couldn't go on. Tears stung my eyes. I'd thought Claudia was my friend. And I'd thought David was… damn. He'd been an asshat from the start. Alex was right.

Alex gave me a hug. "Don't let him get to you."

"We're going to be late," said Sarah. "We'd better move."

"I just wanted to talk to him," I said as we trudged uphill towards campus.

"Corner him after the lecture," said Alex. "It's in a public place. He won't be able to make a scene. And, if he's a twat, I'm happy to kick him in the balls for you."

I managed a feeble smile. "Thanks."

I'd never concentrated less in a lecture than my life. I couldn't believe how fast things had gone downhill. David had treated me like shit, but that was nothing compared to the pain of Claudia's betrayal. I hadn't told her what was going on with him, true, because I hadn't known myself. But surely he'd seen us together, had known she was my friend. I couldn't understand his complete personality change. I'd thought he was *nice*.

My attempt to corner him failed. He'd taken a seat right at the back of the lecture theatre, so I'd struggled to keep an eye on him and take notes at the same time. He must have slipped out of the room early. When I'd looked for him, he simply wasn't there.

Not that I was about to give up so easily. I knocked on his door as soon as I got back to the flat, but got no answer. Alex joined me in hammering away at his door.

"Stop it, Alex," I said. "He's going to complain that we're harassing him. Leave it."

I jumped as the door opened. David glared at me. "What's your problem?"

"I'm not the one with the problem," I said. "I think you owe me an explanation."

"For what?"

"Don't play dumb," said Alex. "I don't think sleeping with someone's so-called friend is a nice thing to do."

"It's none of your business who I sleep with."

"It's not that," I said. "I want to know why you ditched me last night. I deserve to know why you were a complete dick, because to be honest, I'm sick of whatever game you're playing. It's not funny." I breathed heavily, and to my horror, felt the touch of the Darkworld creep to my fingertips. I put my hands behind my back.

He hesitated, biting his lip. "Look, Ash, I don't know how to say this, but I don't think we should be friends any more. I don't think you should talk to me."

"But, why?"

"Trust me, it's for the best. I have my friends. You have yours. That's okay."

"What about that other girl?" Alex cut in. Right then, I wished she wasn't there. It made this even more difficult. "She's Ash's friend. Well, she *was*."

"Look," he began then shook his head. "Whatever. Sorry. I'll leave you alone now. Just don't talk to me anymore, okay?" He shut the door. I heard the bolt click and knew he'd knocked it from the inside.

"What," said Alex, "is his problem?"

I had only one answer—*me*. Somehow, I'd made an enemy of him. Why, I didn't know. But if he wanted to ignore me, then I wasn't going to act like a pathetic stalker and hang around outside his door. However much it might hurt, if he wanted me to be invisible to him, then I would be.

That didn't stop me from Skyping Cara and ranting for a good hour about what a douchebag he was. Cara agreed with my plans to pretend he didn't exist, though at first I had to convince her that coming up to campus and drop-kicking him in the face wouldn't help matters much. However entertaining this might be to watch.

Next time I saw Claudia, though, I was going to let her have it.

ALEX AND SARAH, to my relief, didn't say a word about David the following morning. As it was Saturday, Alex said we ought to go shopping. I agreed, partly because it would get me out the flat, away from David. Although I didn't have much money, it was still fun trying on crazy outfits, before I walked out of H&M—and right into a dark space.

I felt the odd sensation of seeing two worlds at once, one a bright high street, one a dark tunnel, before I passed through the space and saw a pair of violet eyes watching me from an alleyway. Alex and Sarah, having disappeared into the next shop, didn't notice me halt.

"What do you want?" I hissed, after checking no one was near enough to hear me. I had a sense of déjà vu from the last time I'd been here with Claudia. Was it the same demon? I felt all the anger and frustration I'd been suppressing well up inside me. I clenched my fists, my fingertips growing numb.

"We want you." The voice was ice-cold, a whisper in my ear. I shivered, even though I knew the creature couldn't harm me.

"Why? What do you want from me?"

"Your heart."

I blinked, uncomprehending. "What do you mean?"

"You will know, if you can find it. But you'd better be quick."

"What's that supposed to mean?"

The demon grinned. *"It's in your interests to come to us, before we come to you. Bring us your heart, Ashlyn, before others take it away from you."*

"You could take lessons from the fortune-teller," I muttered. "What does any of that mean?"

The demon just grinned at me. Then, like a light fading out, the patch of darkness vanished.

Well, that did it. I was sick of living a double life. From now on, I'd concentrate on what mattered—my degree and my friends—and ignore the demons the way I used to. No more sneaking around libraries, no more secret meetings. I wasn't getting anything out of them anyway, apart from an increasing sense of frustration. Once I'd confronted Claudia, I was done. I could figure out my problems on my own.

When I got back to campus that night, after watching the fireworks in Blackstone with my friends, I noticed with a sinking heart that my window was ajar, my light on. Who had got past the protection on my room?

I rushed back into the flat, finding my door unlocked and cracked open. Someone had wedged a book in the doorway. And my room had been trashed.

All my belongings were strewn everywhere. Clothes and books littered the floor, lecture notes had been ripped from their bindings, and my jewellery box was upturned. Black marks stained the windowsill on both the inside and outside, though it was closed. The intruder had done nothing to hide his trail. The protective shield around the room must have been broken.

But if they'd got in through the window and my door

was open, then that meant they'd come into the flat—they might be here right now.

My mind made the logical, if irrational, connection, and, before I knew what I was doing, my feet had taken me to David's door. I knocked loud enough to wake the dead.

"What the hell were you doing in my room?" I demanded, as he appeared at the gap in the door, looking slightly alarmed.

"Huh?"

"Look, I know you don't like me, but it's no reason to destroy my things. What the hell were you even looking for?"

"I don't know what you mean."

"Don't lie." I hissed and cold anger swept through me, so sudden and intense that it took my breath away. I realised I'd stepped right up to the threshold of his room, and ice was forming at my fingertips, and I had no control over it. He let out a faint noise of surprise as ice began to form on his hands too, spreading up his arms and across his torso. Ice flowed like water, encasing him entirely from head to toe.

I watched, half detached, half in fearful anticipation, as David turned to ice before me, still wearing an expression of surprise. Then the spell broke. I dropped to my knees, a sob rising in my chest. What had I done? *How* had I done it? David was a living ice statue. I had to find a way to free him, but it was too late. He'd seen me use magic.

Whatever Claudia had done, Leo and the others didn't deserve any more trouble from the Venantium. How could I ensure he kept quiet? He hated me. *Oh, God.*

As I hovered in indecision, I heard a knocking from within his room. Claudia was knocking on the window. I knew from her face she'd seen it all.

21

POWER SOURCE

I got to my feet and went over to the window. It took me several attempts to open it.

"Ash," she whispered. "What have you done?"

"What does it look like?" My voice wobbled, and I braced my hands against the window, willing myself to stop shaking.

Claudia wore a pained expression. "Ash, I'm really sorry. The other night, it wasn't what it looked like."

"It looked like you slept with my flatmate," I said. "Pray tell me how I could have misinterpreted that?"

"Look, please let me in. I can put him right, erase his memory and everything."

"Good for you." *Don't cry. Don't let her see.* But I was hopeless at hiding my feelings.

"Seriously, Ash! Look, I didn't sleep with him. I was interrogating him. I told you I was going to investigate your flatmates."

There was an awkward silence.

"I thought you meant Terrence," I said.

"Him, too, but this guy confused me. I thought I'd seen him before, and I was right. Can you let me in?"

"Oh, sure, whatever." I ran to the door and out into the foyer. She met me there, having let herself back into the building.

David still stood frozen in the corridor. Not a drop of the ice had melted. Whatever spell I'd put on him, it was good.

"You don't do things by halves," she said. "Why didn't you just ask me about it?"

"That's not why I did it," I said. "He trashed my room."

"What? No, that can't be right."

"Come and see."

Claudia swore when she saw the mess in my room. "Who did that?"

"David," I said. "It couldn't be anyone else."

"That's illegal, though! The Venantium *never* break into someone's property uninvited unless they suspect them of consorting with demons."

"What makes you think it was—" Then it hit me what she'd said. I stared, my heartbeat loud in the silence.

Claudia took a deep breath. "David's one of them. He's an agent of the Venantium," she said.

I said nothing, numb again. Couldn't find the words. I'd known there was *something* off about his behaviour, but never had it crossed my mind …

Except when he'd run away from those guys in blue. Who else could they have been? *I'm such an idiot.*

"I'm sorry," she said again. "I thought you should know. I think he was supposed to be investigating you, but he got cold feet about bringing you in for questioning. At the bar the other night, there was another agent supposed to be showing up, but he sent you away. I think that was why."

I swallowed. Had to say something. "How?" I croaked. "How did you know he was one of them?"

"He talks to the harpies. I've seen him, leaning out of his window, sending messages. I didn't realise you were friends, but I thought it would be quicker to get it over with. I told him to leave you alone. I think he was glad to do that. I imagine he was stuck in a moral dilemma for a bit."

"So, is he going to report me?" *God, no.* He might be a liar, might have spurned me, but surely he wouldn't. Images of being dragged away by masked figures filled my head. I wrapped my arms around myself, feeling goose bumps spring up.

"He *wasn't.* He might change his mind after this. I'll use a subliminal magic trick, make him forget he saw you tonight. God, I hate Influence, but we can't risk it."

"What about this?" I indicated my strewn possessions.

She shook her head. "I have no idea. Is anything missing?"

"I haven't checked."

"Do that. This whole thing seems like a set-up. I'll unfreeze that guy."

I followed her out of my room to where David stood, unmoving, in the middle of the corridor. She contemplated him. "How'd you even do that?"

"I've no idea." The chill beneath my skin grew more pronounced. The paradoxical burning cold that came from the Darkworld. I'd drawn on it somehow, and it felt both wrong and, yet somehow, *right.*

"Okay." Fire sprang from her palms, and shadows spread along the corridor, gathering around Claudia as I watched. She touched the fire to David. Nothing happened. "Maybe you have to take it off yourself."

My heart sank. "Really?" Right now, I preferred him like this. At least he couldn't cause me any more grief as an ice statue. I gave a weak laugh. The whole situation was ridiculous.

"Yep. No getting around this one. Come on, Ash. You faced down shadow-beasts."

"Right." I placed my hands on David's forehead, feeling uncomfortable, like I was taking advantage of him. I reached for my connection to the Darkworld and tried to direct it to undo the spell. Shadows gathered around my hands, and the ice seemed to evaporate before my eyes, turning to smoke that dissipated almost instantly.

"Wow," I said then jumped back as David blinked at me. *Oh shit. He really will think I was assaulting him.*

"Ash?"

"Quick question, *venator*," said Claudia. "How much do you value your memory?"

"Huh?"

"We could do this the easy or the hard way. If you play nice and don't report us, I'll leave you untouched. If you can't promise that, I'll remove all your memories of the last twenty-four hours. You'll still walk away unscathed. I'm feeling generous."

His face paled. "Remove my memories?"

"Yeah. You *venators* love Influence, don't you?"

"You're not registered! It's illegal."

"Oh, cry me a river. You won't remember it anyway."

"Look," he said, his hands shaking. "I won't say a word, but they might read it from me anyway. You don't lie to them and expect no repercussions."

"Coward. All right, then. Ash, help me." She drew the

shadows around her once again, and the cold feeling rushed through my body.

Suddenly, a series of images played before my eyes, David talking to me, ice forming over his body. Not images. Memories.

Claudia's voice spoke from somewhere nearby. "Just the recent ones."

"How——" But some strange sixth sense guided me. The closest comparison I could think of was using a computer mouse or game controller to guide the actions of an on-screen character. I was both here and not here, holding the images in my hands and scattering the ones that showed past events. Me turning him to ice, our argument, Claudia following him into his room.

A pang went through me at the sight of David and me sitting at the bar. Would I have to erase that one, too? "Stop." The images faded away, and, with them, the shadows creeping in around my vision. The fluorescent lights of the flat corridor seemed unnaturally bright after the fog of memory.

"I thought you'd be a natural," said Claudia. She leant on the wall, panting as though she'd run a long distance. "Right. You, go back to bed." She kicked open David's door and pushed him inside. His mouth was half-open, and his eyes glazed. "It'll take him a few minutes to come to his senses, but he won't remember any of it."

"Mind telling me how I did that?"

"We broke into his mind through the Darkworld." She sank to the floor. "Holy hell. You know, it's only the second time I've done it. The last job took four of us. Leo's overly-curious flatmate saw us using magic," she added. "This guy was tougher, being a magic-user. Did you see the shadows?"

"Um." My mind struggled to process what she said. "Did you say we *broke into his mind?*"

"Yeah. So?"

"Isn't that what you said demons do?"

"No! Well, I guess. It's the same principle, but we couldn't go any deeper in than that. Demons go right through, see every thought and memory of your entire life at a glimpse. They have total domination. Magic-users can manipulate memory and sometimes dreams, but no more than that."

"Dreams," I said. "Sometimes I'd swear someone was manipulating mine."

"Maybe they are," she said. "The Barriers are strong here, but low-level mind manipulation like this still works here. And dream manipulation, I guess. It's where the idea of nightmares come from."

"And sleep paralysis?"

"I've no idea. Look, the fortune-teller's an expert on that kind of thing—well, all sorts of magic, really. She's the person to ask."

THE NEXT DAY, after a sleepless night spent returning my room to its former state, I went into town with Claudia and, for some reason, Leo, who turned up outside our block saying he was bored.

"*Paradise Lost* isn't interesting enough," he said. "It gets boring after the part with the Devil. Milton was blatantly Satan's bitch. You read it?"

Claudia interrupted before I had the chance to reply. "When you've finished your intellectual discussion, we should get a move on."

"Why? Do you think the *venator* will come and arrest us for talking outside the flat?"

"It's not *funny*, Leo."

I said nothing. My insides plummeted as it hit me that everyone thought David was the enemy. Whatever he'd done, I didn't think he was a bad guy. But maybe I was just blind.

Blind and stupid.

The market wasn't on in town, but the fortune-teller's tent was still there, tucked away in a corner of the square near the entrance to the cemetery. The tent, this time, appeared smaller, folded in upon itself, and no one else seemed to acknowledge it, leading me to conclude it was hidden to everyone except us. The three of us approached casually, and, without bothering to ask for admittance, Leo slipped through the front gap.

Madam Persephone sat behind the table as if she waited for us.

"You again," she said to Leo. "To what do I owe the pleasure, Master Blake?"

"It's Ash who needs to talk to you," said Claudia. "There's a spy for the Venantium in her flat, and we think he broke into her room."

The fortune-teller looked at her sharply. "Broke into her room?"

I nodded. "My room was totally ransacked. I don't think he took anything, but he didn't even bother to cover up his tracks."

"Are you sure the intruder took nothing?"

"I think so. Nothing important."

"Check again. Make sure." She seemed more troubled about the possibility of a thief than that one of my flat-mates was a spy. "As for the *venator*, I'd advise you not to do anything rash. Do you have any proof he was the thief?"

"Well, no," I said. "But I don't know anyone else who would do something like that. Besides, only a magic-user could have got past the spell Claudia put on my room."

"And only demonic magic could have undone those bindings," said the fortune-teller, "which leads me to conclude that either this young man is a traitor, or there is another magic-user at your university, one who's dabbling in demonology."

"And they're summoning the shadow-beasts?"

"That is most likely."

"A demon did give me a warning yesterday," I said. "In town."

"A warning?" Madame Persephone's eyes flashed.

"Well, I think it might have been a warning. It was pretty vague." I repeated the demon's words, as well as I could remember.

"They're after your heart?" said Claudia. "What the hell does that mean?"

"Who knows?" said the fortune-teller. "It is not uncommon for demons to fabricate, to beguile and deceive you. I would not dwell on it. Now, you should leave."

Taken aback by this abrupt dismissal, I said, "But what about David? I can't let him get away with breaking into my room."

"Do you have a shield?"

"Yes, but it didn't work. The intruder got in through my flat. That's why it must have been David. He lives down the corridor."

"If that's the case, just make sure you always lock your door."

"No shit," I said, frustration making me snappish—ordinarily, I'd never have spoken to an adult like that. "I did lock it, I'm sure of it. And I always put the bolt on the inside when I'm sleeping."

"I see." She frowned. "Did the shield cover the door?"

"Oh, crap," said Claudia. "That must be it. We only put it on the room. The outside of the door wasn't affected."

"An easy mistake to make," said the fortune-teller.

Claudia groaned, slapping her forehead. "I'm an idiot for not thinking of it. Sorry, Ash."

"It's no problem. Guess I should have looked up magic shields."

"So," said Claudia, addressing the fortune-teller again. "back to the demons. Do you think they're after something from Ash?"

"Demons prize magic above all else. They target those with strong magical potential who can see them. But this is an enigma." There was an emotion in her eyes I couldn't place, like sadness or regret. Was she telling me the full truth? What were the demons after? Did I have some power they desired? I still had no idea of my own strength, and it disturbed me to think of what I'd done to David. I had to learn to keep my powers under control. But how could I do that when the only advice the fortune-teller gave was cryptic nonsense?

THE FLAME-LIKE LIGHTS of Satan's Pit spun around me as a stranger approached across the dance floor, masked. He took my hand, and I accepted, in the hazy logic of dreams. As he twirled me around, I said, "Take off the mask, I want to see your face."

He obliged, and I froze as I looked into the blank, violet eyes of a demon. A third eye winked at me from the centre of his forehead, this one ice-white and gleaming, like a single star in the night's sky.

I backed into the crowd of other masked figures. One put his hands on my shoulders. I wriggled away, twisting to find myself faced with another demon. This one's eyes burned with a fevered light, and the third eye—the demon's heart—gleamed vivid blue, like lapis lazuli. Beside him, another figure removed its mask to reveal purple eyes, and its gleaming hematite heart.

One by one, the figures unmasked and revealed their true eyes, gleaming in the darkness, demon hearts glittering like a constellation of stars.

"Give us your heart, Ashlyn," the demons whispered.

And I knew. I knew what they meant.

I lifted the amethyst pendant over my head and held it so the stone was positioned in the centre of my forehead. I saw myself reflected in the eyes of the demon closest to me, and I saw, with a thrill of horror, my own eyes burning violet, like those of the other demons.

I snapped awake and lay in the darkness, waves of horror coursing through me. Sweat stuck the back of my head to the pillow, and my breath came out in frantic gasps. *You're okay. You're awake.*

But not entirely human. *I am one of them. I am partly a demon.* Had I known it all along? It had been right in front of me. The dreams. Being cold all the time. The demon in Redthorne. As if terrifying demons would give a warning to a human sorcerer. They wanted my heart. They wanted *me.*

That was why I couldn't summon fire. That was why they were so fascinated by me. That was why shadow-beasts stood no chance. I could summon up ice on instinct —or, part of me could.

And that was why someone wanted me dead.

Did David know? Was that why he'd ransacked my room?

I leapt out of bed in an instant. I'd assumed nothing had been taken, but now I thought about it, I didn't recall seeing my necklace. I rummaged through my jewellery box, panic rising with every second.

No. It was gone.

"No," I whispered. "Oh, God, no."

What was it Claudia had said—a demon's heart attracted other demons because it was a potent source of magic? David had seen me wearing it plenty of times.

Aunt Eve, I thought. She'd sent me the pendant; she must have known what it was. Now I thought about it, that letter she'd sent with the necklace had sounded a little odd. I couldn't remember the wording, but I was almost positive I'd read the words "guard your heart well." But the letter was gone, too. Had the same thief taken it? How could anyone else possibly have known about it?

Without even beginning to formulate a plan, I left my room. I stood in the middle of the corridor, my heart beating fast, indecision rooting me to the spot.

A male voice spoke behind me without warning, a familiar one. "Be grateful I didn't kill you."

I turned around.

"It would have been much easier, but I need you alive. You shouldn't have interfered."

The world was beginning to blur before my eyes, and it felt as though someone sifted through my mind, scattering memories like scraps of paper.

"Why?" was the only word I managed to say before everything went black.

THE NEXT THING I was aware of was someone yelling, "Ash? Ash? Are you okay?"

"Of course she's not okay. She's passed out on the floor!" said Alex to Sarah. The two bent over me, concern etched on their faces.

"I'm fine," I mumbled. The glare of the fluorescent light hurt my eyes. I felt dizzy, and my head throbbed. Had I really passed out in the hallway?

"Jesus. Were you drinking last night?" said Alex.

"No," I said, though, truth be told, my memories were a little hazy. I remembered something about a night-club, but I hadn't gone out. I'd gone straight to bed, right? "I must have been really tired. Guess I've been overworking." I got to my feet, trying to gather my dignity.

"You're telling me," said Alex. "I haven't even started that bloody essay yet."

Relieved at having diverted attention from my mysterious appearance in the hallway, I joined in with bemoaning the difficulty of referencing, whilst wondering what the hell happened last night. Something was missing, but my head hurt when I tried to think back to the last part I remembered: I'd spent the evening with my friends after the last cryptic conversation with the fortune-teller, then got an early night. I remembered drawing the curtains and falling into bed...

And that was it. Had I sleepwalked into the corridor? Unease crept along my skin, and I felt like I was missing a vital clue. I trusted my own memory, right? I must have come here myself and fallen asleep on the floor. No other explanation made sense. I hadn't seen anyone when I'd come into the flat. I thought I remembered getting into bed, but not getting up again. But maybe I wouldn't, if I'd been asleep.

Again, my head swam with half-thoughts, like something important was missing. So now I had memory loss to add to the list of weirdness happening around me. I wondered what Claudia would say to that.

Claudia. How could I have forgotten? She'd told me to be careful, and I'd gone and fallen asleep on the floor. David could have done anything to me while I was lying there. Even knowing he'd faced some moral conflict over whether to report me to his bosses, I knew I could never trust him again. He'd lied to me. There was no getting around it.

For now, I'd just avoid him.

22

FORTUNE FLEES

"If you ask me," Claudia said at the next meeting, "you had a lucky escape. *Venators* always cheat on you in the end. Well, that's what I've heard."

"Did Howard tell you that, by any chance?" I said. For the first time, the two of us had shown up early, so we were alone in the Games Room.

"Maybe." She shrugged. "My motto is: don't get involved with sorcerers."

"What about Cyrus? And Leo?"

"Nah. They're not my type. Cyrus is leaving this year, anyway, and Leo... I don't know. He's a bit too arrogant for me. And childish. You know, he and Howard thought it would be funny to try and shoot down a few harpies the other day in the middle of the courtyard. I mean, not to be a killjoy, but it was right out in the open!"

"Hmm," I said. "They aren't worried about being caught by the Venantium? David must have figured out I was a sorcerer, somehow. Unless I was really obvious."

"You didn't have a shield on at first, don't forget."

"I guess." But I didn't remember him acting oddly in

the first week, not until our first trip to Redthorne. Not that I could ever know for certain. "God, I'm such a moron."

"Don't worry about it," said Claudia. "Everyone's done stupid things for the sake of love."

"That's just it. I don't even think I liked him in that way. He was the first guy to pay me a compliment, and I know that sounds like the lamest thing ever, but it's true. Plus my flatmates jumped to conclusions."

"People do that," said Claudia. "Best thing to do is ignore what everyone thinks. Best life advice, really. Also, perspective. You've loads of time to think, to live life. Nothing is ever set in stone. You don't get only one chance."

She had a point. I'd been feeling I had to choose, one life or the other. But maybe there could be a compromise. Maybe that was what had brought me back to the meeting room, even after everything had gone wrong, like I couldn't let go of the notion that there were answers. An explanation.

Also, of course, staying at the flat risked running into David again. Considering we lived two doors away from one another, though, we'd done a pretty impressive job of avoiding each other in the days since the incident.

What a mess. If I admitted it, I missed our brief study sessions, but my memories were tainted by the fact that the whole time I'd known him, he'd been spying on me.

Since I'd frozen David, though, I'd also stopped using magic. Not out of fear, but because I just… couldn't. Magic wasn't working for me the way it used to, compared to a few weeks ago, when it always hovered underneath the surface. I could still lower the temperature, still summon ice to my fingertips, but the response from the Darkworld always felt oddly muted. I couldn't fathom why.

"Do you think I over-used magic when I froze David?"

I asked Claudia. "I can't even summon up a light anymore."

"That's odd," she said. "Not at all?"

"Nope."

"Maybe it'll work when you're angry."

"Hmm. Maybe Berenice'll wind me up again." If there was anyone who deserved to be frozen into a block of ice for a while, it was Berenice. But she'd never triggered a reaction in me the way David had.

"Or self-defence? I was thinking of taking classes next term."

"Um…no. Believe me. I tried karate once, and hit myself in the face. Don't ask how, I've no idea."

"Wow. And you can fight shadow-beasts like it's no problem."

"Tell me about it. It's weird."

I got that odd, dizzy sensation again, like I was trying to recall a distant memory. I shook my head to clear it.

"We can talk to the fortune-teller again, if you like."

I nodded. She was the one person who might have answers.

Naturally, the universe had other plans. The next day, when we arrived at the stall-packed town square, we found her tent absent.

"That's odd," Cyrus remarked. "She's always here, even when the other stalls aren't around."

We searched high and low, but there was no sign of the black tent. Leo disappeared for a few minutes, and, when he emerged from the alleyway between the cathedral and the museum, he clutched a piece of paper.

"This was on the Blackstone Memorial," he said. "Not exactly respecting the dead." He held up the paper. The handwriting was so looped and elaborate that I had difficulty making out the words.

"Travelling, by the looks of it," said Cyrus.

"Seems random," said Leo.

"Maybe she's gone away for the holidays?" Cyrus said, frowning. "Never happened before, though."

"Maybe the Venantium were on to her, and she had to scarper," said Howard.

"You would bring them into it," said Leo.

"Well, maybe it's true," said Berenice.

I rolled my eyes. *Here we go again.*

"Come along, children," said Cyrus. "I'm freezing. Let's go back."

The fortune-teller's absence made me uneasy, though I didn't know why. No shadow-beast had attacked any of us since the incident at Satan's Pit, and no demons had spoken to me, either. They were still there; I saw them every time I went outside the area, lurking. But I no longer felt their eyes on me. Why *that* should feel unsettling, I had no idea. I'd hated the feeling of a thousand penetrating eyes studying me all the time, but, in its absence, I felt oddly exposed.

The fear that I'd get attacked again never quite left my mind, but I refused to stay confined to campus. I even signed up to a hike in late November with Alex and Sarah. Nothing would take my mind off stress quite like scaling a colossal mountain in below-freezing temperatures while trying to keep up with our far-too-enthusiastic leaders.

At the next meeting, Claudia planted a book on me. It was the *Seven Princes* book. It seemed I was right in thinking that Howard had liberated it from the Venantium's library.

"See what you find in there," said Claudia. "It has a bit about magic blocking, like mental blocks and whatever. Maybe that's what's up."

I nodded, taking a seat and flipping to the first page. The old-fashioned language was a little confusing, but I was an English Literature student for a reason. The book intrigued me. I wanted to learn more about magic, of course, but I couldn't deny demons fascinated me, and I seized the chance to study them. I wanted to make sense of their behaviour around me. Surely this comprehensive guide to demons would have answers?

A good third of the book was devoted to these, so-called, "Seven Princes." According to popular belief, there were seven demons more powerful than any others, who had abilities beyond any other magic-user, demon or human. Able to take on human form, they were blamed for the rise of forbidden magic users, since it was believed that, whilst disguised in human form, they could mate with humans.

The legend said that whenever a demon took a human lover, the demon entrusted the lover with its heart, which was held by the family and passed down through the generations, serving as the repository of the family's stored magic. Abilities would pass to their offspring, and these children were unique, part-human, part-demon. They were more human than demon, but they tended to have an affinity for demonic magic.

Something told me this ought to be resonating with me, but why, I didn't know. I often skimmed through the book when I was bored, or when I couldn't sleep. I learned about the other demonic creatures, incubi, and succubae, now mostly eradicated. Both were able to take on human form for a short time in order to seduce humans, both male and female. The Seven Princes were the same, though they hadn't come to this world in hundreds of years.

Through all the text and the information, the one thing about this book that did stand out to me was that unlike many of the other books, it wasn't biased in favour of the

Venantium. They distrusted anyone who wasn't related to a *venator*, even if they intended no harm, but some independent sorcerers did live in an uneasy truce with them.

"Like the fortune-teller," said Claudia, when she explained this to me at one meeting. "She's not allied to anyone we know of. The Venantium let her run her little stall in exchange for her silence. Sometimes, even they need to ask her advice. To tell you the truth, I thought it was part of the deal that she could never leave Blackstone."

"I think the Venantium might have something to do with her disappearance," said Howard. "And I'm not saying that because I hate the bastards," he added as Leo started to interrupt. "The *venators* are far more paranoid than usual. I saw hundreds of harpies flying over Blackstone the other day."

"Maybe you're right," said Claudia. "But we can't prove anything."

Leo kept shooting looks at me, like he was trying to figure something out. When I left the meeting, bored with the arguments, he offered to walk me back to my flat. I agreed more out of politeness than anything, weary with the roundabout conversations which never ended in any conclusion.

"You know you can tell me if anything's up?" he said as we walked through the student village. "Really. I'm not going to tell the whole world. Or, well, Berenice and Howard. If you don't want me to."

Maybe I should confide in someone. But I wouldn't even know where to begin. It was like there was a gaping hole in my mind where my magic used to be, and the absence bothered me more than I thought possible, considering I'd once thought of my connection to the Darkworld as a nuisance. But now, whenever I tried to think hard about it, a weird buzzing sensation would rise in my head, and I wouldn't be able to focus for long.

"I'm good," I said, the lie tasting bitter. "Really. Maybe it's a phase. I started being able to use magic out of nowhere, right? Maybe I'm just different."

"Sure you are," said Leo. "But this feels off. You know what I mean?"

I nodded. I didn't want to bring it up with the others, but the fortune-teller's absence bothered me, too. I felt like I needed to talk to her, but when I thought about why, my reasons slipped away. This happened a lot, in fact. Sometimes, I'd wake up in the night from dreams of being chased and swear there was something I needed to do. Maybe it was stress. But the dream suggested something was wrong.

Every night, it was the same: I walked through Blackstone in the dead of night, the cobbled streets deserted and the windows in the houses dark. No harpies swooped overhead, and the starless sky looked like an empty void. Always, just ahead of me, there was a figure, tall and black-cloaked. But they disappeared into smoke, and then I'd wake up in a cold sweat, my thoughts roiling and the scars from the harpy attack on fire.

I tried everything—sleeping pills, napping, pulling an all-nighter. Nothing worked. The night before the Big Hike, which I'd almost forgotten about, Alex insisted that I go to bed early so I'd be up on time.

I groaned. "It's insomnia, Alex."

"Yes, and you're not missing the hike," she said.

"Why did I sign up for it?" Sarah asked, indicating the frost creeping over the windows. "It's supposed to snow tonight."

"All the better," said Alex. "Come on, you two. It's the end of term, lighten up."

I rolled my eyes, but agreed on the early night plan. To my own surprise, I blacked out almost as soon as I fell into bed.

That night, the dream was different. I followed a path I could walk blindfolded now, through the hidden alleyway, into the cemetery. I followed the shadowy figure past the weather-beaten, lichen-splattered tombstones. Every time I rounded a corner, I saw the cloak whip out of sight. I reached the low stone wall at the back of the cemetery, and climbed over. The woods were as silent as the town. Not so much as a single night creature stirred, and even my own footsteps were muted. In no time at all, I passed through the trees and emerged onto the cliff top.

Waves lashed against the cliff's edge, throwing salt spray into the air. The figure stood, overlooking the sea, silver-fair hair streaming out, a long black dress billowing. The fortune-teller turned to me and cried out a warning I couldn't hear. Then the waves rose up to engulf her, and, when they fell with a deafening crash, she was gone.

I stood rigid, drenched in seawater, so cold—and awoke, once again, to sleep paralysis and the sound of my alarm clock.

23

SNOWBOUND

W hen I'd coaxed my limbs into moving, I drew back the curtains to be greeted by the beautiful sight of the first snow of winter. The field was a glittering white carpet, and frost coated the edges of the window, outlining the view like a scene from a Christmas card.

Too bad I had to go hiking in it. Looking at the foot-deep snow piled against the building, I could already tell it wasn't going to be fun.

Alex kept up a pep talk all the way out the flat, but as we climbed aboard the minibus, my heart sank. Of course David had signed up, too.

I took a deep breath. It was okay. I didn't have to talk to him. I rarely had the energy to communicate on hikes, anyway. Besides, he was a spy—and a coward, at that. Try as I might to forget, just a glimpse of him reminded me of how angry I was at being taken in.

The sky was clear when we reached our destination, the winter sun harsh, blinding. We walked past a lake, its smooth, oval surface like silken cloth, reflecting the snow-covered ridges and peaks surrounding it. It was beautiful, but I soon had to put my camera away, needing both hands to keep my balance as we crossed frozen rivers, skirted icy rocks, and climbed a slope that steepened until it was almost vertical. Recent snow coated the path, often masking ice beneath. Almost everyone fell over at least once. Melting snow soaked through my clothes to the skin.

A blizzard started as we neared the summit. A curtain of powdery flakes swept over us, and soon, we could see nothing but whiteness. Even the leaders looked worried—never a good sign.

"We'll have to get down soon," one of them said.

But the path, we were meant to be following, had disappeared in the whirling maelstrom. Sure enough, an hour later, the leader shouted at us that we were lost. Everything looked the same coated in white, so this didn't surprise me.

"If we die up here, I'm blaming you, Alex!" said Sarah.

"We're not going to die!" Alex insisted, though her bravado had slipped somewhat over the past hour. Snow clung to our hair and melted. I shuddered as it trickled down my back.

On the descent, my torchlight flickered and died, leaving me in semi-darkness, penetrated only by an endless swirl of snowflakes. I struggled on, not knowing if we were even following a path anymore. I'd faced death so many times lately, it seemed absurd that it might be the elements that killed me after all.

It was so cold; the breath felt frozen in my lungs. Incoherent shouts from up ahead came through the blizzard, and I distinctly heard Alex cry out, "Landmark!"

In minutes, we were within sight of the small village where we'd parked the minibus. Gasping, and dragging my numb feet, I found my way back to Sarah and Alex.

Sarah was almost sobbing. "Never again," she said.

We piled back into the minibus, too exhausted to speak. Icy mud coated my hiking boots, and snow had piled up inside my hood. I just wanted to take a hot shower and fall into bed.

Half an hour's drive later, through winding country roads buried under snow, the minibus started to slow. When we reached a particularly steep hill, the tyres lost all grip. The bus slid downhill and backed with a groan into a wall of packed snow. Again and again, the driver struggled to guide the minibus up the hill. Eventually, someone told us to all get out and push—which we did, forcing our protesting limbs into action. But even the combined strength of the entire group couldn't shift the vehicle. We were stuck.

As I sank against a snowdrift, my Darkworld connection flared up without warning. I found myself standing up and moving closer to look at a dark patch of trees just off the path.

Someone was standing in the shadows.

I walked towards the figure, almost against my will. I couldn't see his face, but he looked familiar. A guy with dark hair. *David?* Pulled by some instinct, even though a voice in my head screamed at me that I was stupid, I followed him. Melted snow penetrated every inch of my clothing, soaking into my skin. But another kind of coldness drew me, one that writhed in my veins like slow poison, drawing me into the forest, even as instinct told me to flee.

I walked on, stumbling over the snow-covered undergrowth. Not a pinprick of light penetrated the thick canopy above. These were unfamiliar paths, not like the woodland trail on campus. The trees were gnarled, hostile figures, clustered around me like conspirators drawing me into a sinister trap.

Get out of here! my subconscious screamed. But still I walked.

I had no control over my legs, and I felt more terrified than I'd ever been in my life. It was like I was possessed. I couldn't turn back, not even to look at the path behind. Something was controlling me. *Subliminal magic?*

One step after another, we walked until the trees thinned out, revealing a run-down, overgrown cottage. Flurries of snow danced around us, like spectres. The figure stopped. He turned to look at me. Not David. Of course he wasn't.

Terrence grinned at me, holding up my amethyst pendant. A wild light shone in his grey eyes, and I could see that in the centre of his forehead, another stone winked at me, white as the snow around us. The heart of a demon had melded into his skin.

It happened in a lightning flash of clarity. I remembered it all: I was part-demon. The crystal was my demon heart. And he had it. He had control over my every move.

"What the hell did you do to me?" I whispered. Because it was obvious. So obvious, he had to have blinded me to it. The same thing I'd done to David. "You're a sorcerer."

A powerful one, if he could mess with my memory.

Terrence's smile widened, stretching his face, unnatural. "Yes, Ashlyn," he said. It was like being addressed by a machine. "You and your friends aren't the only ones who can do magic. And now I'm more powerful than any of you." The demon heart between his eyes gleamed.

"You have something of mine," I croaked, indicating the necklace. *Idiot. Way to state the obvious.*

"I know," said Terrence. "Well, technically, it's your

family's treasure, but it's yours by right of birth. This must have the combined strength of ten generations, at least. And only you can control it. Which is why you're going to help me."

His smile widened. It looked almost inhuman now. I couldn't remember ever seeing him smile before——or say so much at once. It was like he'd been saving his words for this moment.

My limbs weakened, like the weight of the Darkworld itself was pressing down on me. "I——I don't understand," I said, playing for time.

"It's quite simple. I have your heart, your power, in my hands. Now I have a demon on my side, too. You're part-human. You're inferior. But only you can help me take the power of your demon heart."

A shadow flitted across his face, and, for a second, his outline blurred, showing something else beneath. A dark space.

Numbness penetrated every inch of me. I couldn't take my eyes off the swinging pendant. Part of me. How could I have let him take it?

"I knew you were something different. I knew you were like me. But I never guessed you were part-demon. Now we're more alike than ever." He laughed, and the sound echoed around the open space. "Doesn't it bore you, having to pretend to be like them? To be normal?"

I didn't answer. The words "like me" echoed around my mind, bringing images, one after another. Cyrus telling me people with Darkworld connections were unstable. The fortune-teller's warning. The dreams. Almost like I was watching a memory reel, like when I'd broken into David's memory. Was this what it felt like to watch your own life flash before your eyes?

I'm going to die. That thought pushed all the others aside.

I'd never see my friends or family again, never make it out of the cold. I'd die out here alone.

So cold, so tired. Like the chill was inside me, deep in my bones, numbing all sensation. As his grip tightened on my pendant—my heart—I gasped aloud. Pain radiated from somewhere deep within me, a part without a name. I couldn't even scream, but at the same time, another voice cried out in the back of my mind, a horrible, wrenching howl. The demon. *My* demon.

The world swam before my eyes.

"I tested you, y'know." Terrence's voice passed over me, thick and slow, pulling me back. He grinned, as if he knew exactly what he was doing. Like he *enjoyed* it.

"I wanted to see what you were capable of," he continued. "But I didn't believe it until I saw what you did to that shadow-beast on the mountain. Only another demon could have left marks that distinct. But you *looked* human. I knew you must have another power source somewhere. And I was right."

He waved the necklace, and its purple glint flashed in his eyes for an instant.

"So, I need you to do something for me. I can't access all this power myself. I need you to unlock it. Contact the Darkworld."

I shook my head. "No way."

"You don't have a choice." The words came out as if he was in pain. "If you don't let me take your power, I'm going to kill you, Ashlyn." The shadow flitted across his face again.

I felt the demon before I saw it. My spine prickled, and a familiar fear chilled my blood. Terrence grinned. His eyes glowed violet. The third eye shone out from the centre of his forehead, pure white in colour with a red outline where it had pierced the skin.

This was what I'd always feared. The monster in the dark. The eyes, watching, always watching me.

"I know what you are." It wasn't Terrence who spoke. I knew because the voice was inflectionless, emotionless, ageless. I heard it echo in my ears, and I knew it was too late, far too late, to save him. *"Come with me, Ashlyn."*

24

THE DEMON'S HEART

The demon watched me with unfathomable eyes. I looked away into the dark forest, clinging to the last remnant of hope that one of the others—Claudia, Leo, or Howard—might appear to join me, that I wouldn't have to face this battle alone.

No such luck.

I met the creature's eyes again. In silence, we stared each other out. One heartbeat followed another. Like a ticking clock. Each waiting for the other to make the first move. The snow turned to ice as it made contact with my skin, coating my hands in gloves solid as steel. The Darkworld responded to my call, giving me strength, preparing me for the blow.

The demon leapt.

Ice curled around my fingers, forming a set of icicle-like claws. The demon yelled, arms poised to wrap around me, and I ran the claws across his face, tearing through skin with an ease that filled me with revulsion. Blood splattered the snow, but its grin remained in place. The demon was entirely unaffected.

"You have to do better than that, Ashlyn." Its grin widened. There was no sign of the boy behind the demon's mask, not anymore.

"He was just like you, Ashlyn," the demon whispered. *"Alone. Afraid. You could have talked to him, preventing him from falling in with the wrong crowd."*

The demon's presence pushed against my mind, and images flashed before my eyes, again—Terrence, sitting in a room full of people, an ancient book opened on his lap. Voices around him, sounding fuzzy, like a radio with bad reception. The word *demon*, repeated. Terrence arriving at campus, standing in the middle of his room, talking to something that wasn't there.

"I came to him when he called," the demon whispered. *"His connection was particularly strong. Too strong. We broke his mind."*

The images faded, and my own sensations came back in a rush. Terrence's face still grinned at me, and I backed up. I couldn't feel sorry for him. Not now. But what could I do? How could I beat a true demon? Even if I killed Terrence—and there was no way I could do that—the creature would make for the next available target: me.

Veins pulsed all over its face. It looked as though Terrence was locked in a battle of wills with the demon, making a tremendous effort not to surrender complete control. But, from what Claudia had told me, the instant he'd let a demon into his mind, he was already dead.

He still held the amethyst pendant. I took a deep breath. This was my only chance. Maybe several generations' worth of magic would be enough to beat the demon.

"Join me, Ashlyn. No one else need suffer."

"Give that back!" I yelled as I threw myself at him. My hands scraped against his knuckles, and we both fell backwards into a heap of snow.

Terrence's body writhed on the ground beneath me,

yelling in pain, both human and inhuman hissing breaking through. The demon wasn't fully in control yet.

"This is mine!" Terrence roared, his face contorted in agony – he must have pushed the demon back. "I need it. I need your power. Give it to me! Then all demons will obey me, and me alone!"

He's mad. To think we used to joke about him being crazy, when all the time he was summoning shadow-beasts.

He pushed me back with a sudden burst of strength, hands shooting out and locking around my throat. I choked, the nightmare sensation of drowning overwhelming me, like my lungs had given up.

No. Don't give up!

"You'll never control it," I gasped, each word like glass in my throat. "He's lying to you. Demons don't share power with anyone." Black dots crossed my vision.

"What do you know about it? You might possess this power, but you're weak. Gullible. Human. Tricking you was too easy. Let me take your power, and I might ask the demon to spare you."

His grip tightened. The world went blue around the edges, and I could hear a roaring in my ears.

"Your choice!" Terrence screamed. Blood ran down his face in rivulets. "Contact the Darkworld—or die."

"I'd rather die," I whispered. His face flickered in and out of view as the darkness threatened to claim me. I sucked in a last breath of freezing air, knowing I was about to die.

Cold. So very cold.

All I could see was a black void. The chill of the Darkworld penetrated every inch of me. My skin buzzed with it. If I was dying, then why did I feel so much more alive than ever before?

Terrence cried out. His grip loosened, and I gasped for air.

The demon said, *"Give her the heart."*

"No!" Terrence gasped. "I have control over you! Possess her! Take her power and give it to me!"

I was paralysed, outside and in, but my veins tingled with power. I felt a presence touch my mind, something vast, something powerful. My head throbbed. A sharp pain burst behind my eyes, and for a second, the black void flashed purple.

I was looking through a demon's eyes. *My* demon. The voice that had cried out in pain, the presence bound to the pendant. Part of me. This was the presence that summoned ice. The part of me that was eternally lured to the Darkworld.

I heard Terrence's demon's voice like a whisper in my ear. *"Set me free. I cannot possess you any more than I could possess another of my kind. He does not know that. He is merely an ignorant human sorcerer. He enslaved me, but you can set me free."*

The world pulsed black. Then it came back into focus through my eyes. Not my demon's. But I still *felt* it, that presence, alien and familiar, cold as ice.

"You are one of us. You must understand," Terrence's demon whispered. *"Mortal things are ephemeral. Embrace what you really are."*

"I'm not," I croaked. "I'm not one of you. I'm human."

The demon's cold laughter pierced the air. Terrence's grip on my neck loosened even more. Now I could see his face—he looked terrified, and his eyes had gone back to their normal grey. But beside him was a maelstrom of black smoke, from which a dark shape grinned.

"You may have the blood of a human, but your heart belongs to

demonkind. Take it from him. Take your heritage," whispered the demon. *"Take it, and set me free."*

The pendant. It hung loose in Terrence's grip, as though he had forgotten he held it.

"You have power," it continued. *"Use it. I cannot claim the power of one of my own. It is yours. I am not your enemy."*

I made my decision and reached for the pendant. As my hand closed around it, I felt a surge of coldness so strong it burned my palm. It jolted me back to full awareness with a gasp.

Terrence's demon still grinned at me.

I hovered on the brink, indecisive. Terrence, not the demon, was my enemy. But I knew the demon wouldn't hesitate to kill any other human it encountered. I couldn't set it free.

The presence of the Darkworld whispered at me, and I wondered how I'd ever lived without it there, close as a breath, cold, and deadly, and full of power. Power that was... mine.

I'd never done this before, but I knew the theory. I reached out to the Darkworld, to my demon, and felt the vast stores of magic flow through me, bringing icy fire to my fingertips. I shaped it with my thoughts, guiding the ice into the form I wanted—a jagged blade, dazzling white like starlight. I raised the weapon of pure frozen fire, and stabbed the glittering white stone in the centre of Terrence's forehead—the demon heart.

A piercing cry rent the air. The smoke dissipated, and for a second, all I could see was the endless black hole of the Darkworld. Then the blackness was gone.

I dropped back to my knees, still clutching the pendant. Someone was on the ground beside me. Terrence. He lay face-down in the snow. I ran to him and turned him over, my heart a frantic drumbeat in my ears. There was no pulse, no whisper of life. The demon had killed him. *Like a light switch, it can switch off your life.* A sob rose in my chest.

I don't know how long I knelt there, numb, but I became aware of another sound. Hurried footsteps. I looked up. The fortune-teller ran towards me, gasping as though she'd run for miles.

"Ashlyn," she whispered. "Thank God. I felt a demon here, and I thought I was too late."

"How——how…" I couldn't get the words out.

"Come with me. In here."

I stood up, shaking, and saw she pointed to the run-down cottage at the edge of the clearing. I let her drag me through the front door.

"Come on. Tell me everything," she said once I'd sank into an armchair.

Huddled in front of a fire, she rekindled it using magic, and I told her everything——including what I was. I told her how it had been Terrence who'd been practising demon magic, that he'd sent all the shadow-beasts after me, intending to test me, and finally stolen my demon heart. Then I told her what had happened out there in the snow. How the demon must have tricked Terrence, convinced him to lure me there. Terrence had been a young sorcerer, the perfect target. He'd thought he was in control of the demon, and that he'd be able to take my power, too. But the demon had really wanted me to set it free, turn it loose in the world. And I'd killed it. At what cost to me, I didn't know. For a minute out there, something had taken hold of me. I had this whole other part of me, which I hadn't even begun to understand. Thanks to Terrence messing with my memory, the past couple of weeks were scattered in my mind.

"What if he did permanent damage to my memory?" I said, swallowing.

"It's not possible," said the fortune-teller. "He had no idea what your demon heart truly was. I think the demon told him very little. If I had known he was a sorcerer, I could have helped him."

"I didn't know, either." I swallowed again. "He lived in my flat, but never came out, never wanted to talk to us. Maybe if I'd tried harder, I could have helped."

"He doesn't sound like the type of person who would listen to reason." The fortune-teller's brow was furrowed. "Don't blame yourself for his mistake, Ashlyn. Guilt can take you over." She paused. "I expected to have more time to prepare you for this. I was almost too late."

"Prepare me?" I echoed. "What do you have to do with it?"

"Everything." She sighed again. "I've not been straight with you, but there's a reason for it. Every second we spend in each other's company puts the both of us in unimaginable danger. You see—" She took a deep breath—"I sent you the pendant. I knew the time had come for it to pass on to you."

"*You*? But I thought my Aunt Eve—"

She shook her head and regarded me with eyes full of a deep sadness. "I'm sorry, Ashlyn. I'm sorry for lying to you." Her outline blurred before my eyes. I half-leapt to my feet, expecting to see another demon—but instead found myself looking at my Aunt Eve.

"I learnt long ago how to change my appearance at will using magic," she said. "It's something very few people can do. It wouldn't surprise me if I was the last remaining person with the skill."

I gaped at her. Words failed. This was too much. "So —" I said. "you're not my actual aunt?"

She shook her head. "Your Aunt Eve is just one of the identities I have constructed over the years."

"I—what?" My mind spun. It made no sense. "You disguised yourself as my aunt?"

She nodded, her own appearance coming back like a camera focus adjusting. "It was necessary. I had to be close to you."

I thought about Aunt Eve, *really* thought about her. It was as though a veil lifted from my mind, like when my memories came back. "You told me stories. You told me about how you travelled around the world. But Mum and Dad never talked about you at all. It was like you existed only when you rang us or when we came to visit you. Was that a subliminal mind trick?"

"It was necessary."

"You lied to us!" I was aware that I was shouting, like a child in a tantrum. But, the words poured out in a rush. "Now I get why you said messing with memories doesn't do permanent damage. You did it to me, you did it to my family. What gives you the right? How do I know you're not doing it right now?"

"Believe me," she said. "I did no more than necessary. I didn't want to interfere with your lives. I hated to fool your parents, but the only way to get close to you was to trick them into thinking I was a relation."

"Who are you, then? Part of the Venantium's Family Demon Heart division? Is it your job to screw up people's lives?"

"No." She shook her head. "I told you—I have no allegiance to anyone, least of all the Venantium. My aim is to ensure no one can use your heart for evil."

"So, do you have a lot of them?" I said, imagining hundreds of people like me, part-human, part-demon. I couldn't decide if the idea made me feel comforted or scared.

"No. I am certain of it—you are the only living sorceress with demonic heritage."

"Do my parents know anything about this? I thought this—" I held up the pendant—"was a family heirloom."

"It is, in part, but its power skips generations sometimes. No one has had the connection to the Darkworld in your family for over a hundred years."

"You seem to know a lot about it—about me. Why did you have it?"

"I'm an expert in family histories. It's an obsession of mine. But I also want to help magic-users who desire to remain independent of the Venantium. So, I make a point of tracking potential magic-users."

"Who gave you the necklace?"

"It is, as you say, a family heirloom. It was always meant for you. Your ancestors' powers dwell within it. I could look after it only until I knew you were ready, to prevent those who would use it for evil from claiming it."

"Demon magic." I shook my head. My breathing had calmed now, although my anger hadn't quite abated. "I don't understand how I can be part-demon. I mean, they're spirits, aren't they?"

"I thought you'd have read that book. It tells you all about higher demons. Shapeshifters. The Seven Princes."

"I thought it was just legend. That's what the book says. I mean, how can they know someone's part-demon? How's it different to being possessed?"

"There's no doubt. The Seven Princes exist, although none currently walk among us. One of them is your ancestor. That makes you demon in part, but only as far as your magic is concerned. You're human in every other way. And you're in control. Unlike possession, the demon is a part of you, not a separate entity."

"That's… bizarre." I shook my head again. "What now, then? I suppose the Venantium will want me dead?"

"No!" I jumped at her sharp tone. "No one will harm you," she said, her words softer now. "Not as long as I am here. Even when my own life was in danger, and I was forced to drop the mask of your Aunt Eve and fake emigration, I stayed here. This house may be abandoned, but I still use it as a place of safety. If your life is ever in danger, you will be safe here."

I looked around. Underneath all the dust, I recognised the room we were in—the sitting room of Aunt Eve's lakeside cottage.

"How…"

"This is the place where your heart has the most power. Terrence was drawn to it, even though he didn't know why."

I shook my head. Nothing made sense any more. "But, how did you know I was part-demon? You never said anything to me about magic, not when you were Aunt Eve."

"I knew. I always knew. I intended to stay here, but when circumstances conspired against me, I sent you the necklace at the first opportunity."

"Seems awfully risky, sending it in the post."

She gave me a slight smile at that. "Magical protection. It's one of my talents. You might say it's the reason I'm still alive after spending so much time around fugitives and covert sorcerers."

She kept silent, whilst I tried to sift through the questions jostling around in my head.

"You said you were an expert in family trees," I said. "And 'Aunt Eve' had a copy of my family tree. Would it tell me who the demon was?"

I was still having trouble believing I was talking to Aunt

Eve. True, the memory was hazy, but I'd never placed the fortune-teller's mannerisms as my aunt's. How could I? It was absurd even to think of.

"The tree was a fake," she said. "A necessary decep-tion." She paused. "I think there's someone outside."

I turned to peer out the dust-encrusted window. She was right. Someone walked towards the house.

"Friend or enemy?" I said, as she made for the door.

She stood in the hallway, indicating I should go out first. "You decide," she said.

I squinted as the person wandered close enough for me to make out his features. It was David.

25

DARKNESS SUPERIOR

I slipped the pendant into my pocket as I walked out into the clearing. I didn't want anyone else to know about it yet, if ever. As far as David was concerned, I was just another unregistered sorcerer.

"David," I said. We looked at each other, as if in a staring contest. He broke away first.

"Where have you been, Ash?" he said. "Everyone's looking for you."

"Don't play dumb with me," I said. "Didn't you know what Terrence was?"

"Terrence? He——" His eyes widened as I pointed to Terrence's crumpled body. "You killed him?"

"Of course not! A demon did that. The same demon who tried to possess me. Isn't that your job, tracking down rogue sorcerers?"

"I'm more in the Admin division." David shifted, embarrassed. "I'm not high up enough for that yet. Jesus. All along, there was one right in front of us."

"Maybe you'd have spotted him sooner if you hadn't been so busy spying on me."

Perhaps I was being unfair, but I'd had enough. I was bone-tired, freezing, and sick of all the lies.

"Look," he said, with another helpless glance at Terrence. "I'm sorry about what happened. I really do like you. But——"

"But we can't be friends. I know. Well, good for you. Didn't you say when we first met that to judge people was sad?"

He started to reply, then shook his head. I seemed to have cowed him into silence.

The fortune-teller spoke—I still couldn't think of her as Aunt Eve, which wasn't even her real name. "I'll deal with him, The Venantium need not know, if that's what you wish, Ashlyn."

I nodded, my mouth dry. They couldn't find out about how I'd beaten the demon, otherwise they'd find out what I was. And then I'd most likely be arrested. *Shit, my life's a complicated mess.* It had been easier living with gaping holes in my memory.

"I won't say anything," David gabbled. He seemed terrified of the fortune-teller. I suppose she did look quite intimidating, back in her familiar guise with her fair hair flying and her knowing eyes piercing. Even though I suspected that this body was another disguise.

"Good," said the fortune-teller. "Now that's cleared up. I'll escort the two of you back to your group. And David?"

David gulped. "Yeah?"

"Tell Ashlyn why you didn't report her to your superiors."

David blinked at her.

"You *know* what I'm talking about."

Not looking at me, David mumbled, "I ran a scan on your magic to make sure you weren't working against us. I had to. I did it in the first week of term, in your room."

"So you *did* break into my room?" Anger swelled within me, but exhaustion dragged me down. I didn't want to fight with him anymore.

"Sorry, I had to check. It's part of my duty to monitor magic-users."

"Well, it's none of your business. That's why you made friends with me, too, right?"

"No." He shook his head. "Honestly, I liked you."

"Well, you know what, David?" I said. "I really *hate* guys like you."

I turned to follow the fortune-teller back through the woods, towards my friends.

"How about this one?" Cara asked.

I rolled my eyes as she presented me with Dress Number Forty Five, a poofy, pink-sleeved number. Like the others, I'd never be seen dead in it in a million years. "No. Absolutely not."

"Come on, Ash. You can't own just *one* dress." Cara rolled her eyes.

"Why not? I like it."

"You need a new one. This is a *ball* we're talking about."

"It's a fancy name for a Christmas night out. That's all." After hearing we could invite outside guests to the Winter Ball, I'd asked Cara if she still wanted to come and visit. Her initial huffiness at my having unintentionally ignored her for the last few weeks vanished at the prospect of a good night out, and she invited herself to come and stay a few days early, so she could drag me shopping in Redthorne. Term for her had ended a week ago. The timing worked out pretty well.

I'd used the workload and the problem with David as an excuse for why I'd not been in contact, and, to my relief, she didn't ask too many questions. I'd had enough of that from Claudia and the others. I was sure they knew there was something I wasn't telling them, especially Leo, who'd asked me to confide in him, after all. They meant well, but I couldn't tell them the full story. Not yet. They might claim to be non-judgemental, but after David—well, it was out of cowardice that I kept silent. After that, I'd needed to do something normal. Even dress shopping.

Eventually, I caved and bought a cheapish blue dress. I drew the line at new shoes, though. By now, nearly all my money was gone. A good thing it was the end of term.

I saw a few dark spaces in town that day, but I didn't acknowledge them. Like it or not, I knew it was only a matter of time before someone noticed the demons bowed their heads to me. Regarding me not as an enemy, but as one of their own. As their *superior*.

I still felt horrified, sometimes, to think I had demon magic. The one comforting thought was that the blood in my veins was purely human—demons didn't have blood, after all. I'd read every page of the *Seven Princes* book now, goaded by nightmares of never growing old, of simply enduring as demons did. But the book assured me, almost as if the author knew what was on my mind, that people like me—part-human, part-demon—weren't immortal. Other than the pendant I now wore everywhere, and kept close to my heart, I was human in every way.

Thank God. Who wants to live forever?

As for Terrence, Claudia had ransacked his room and found all kinds of occult stuff in there, some of it real, some of it fake. He'd been messing about with magic all term, and somehow a demon had gotten through to him and persuaded him to steal my demon heart. Though his fate still gave me nightmares, I couldn't deny he'd brought it on himself. Thanks to the fortune-teller, no one, aside from a select few of us, knew what had happened. As far as the university was concerned, he'd never existed in the first place. I wasn't sure if anyone would move into his empty room.

A few days after the hike, Alex told me David had requested to be moved to a different flat. I felt nothing but relief at that. I wouldn't have to watch my back any longer. I was free.

The Winter Ball might have been taking place in a rented room in a hotel in town, but it was still great fun. The bar was decked out in silver and blue, with Christmas trees and mistletoe everywhere. Cheesy Christmas music blared from the speakers, and a troupe of Santas led a conga-line around the dance floor.

"Hey, there's Pete!" said Alex, and we all tried not to laugh as we watched him pursue Danielle with a clump of mistletoe, dodging in and out of the crowd and face-planting in the middle of the dance floor.

"Take a bath, you loser!" Danielle yelled at him.

"That's told him," said Alex, giggling.

I *did* see Claudia and the others later, but they weren't huddled in a corner like conspirators. That must mean nothing was wrong, no shadow-beasts out there this time. Berenice and Howard were lip-locked in the corner. Claudia commandeered the dance floor, surrounded by a throng of admirers, and Cyrus stood at the bar with some other people I didn't recognise.

"Hi, Ash." I turned to see Leo behind me. To my surprise, he actually wore a tuxedo, and the dark colours made his dark eyes stand out. He looked totally different—less scruffy, for one thing.

"Hey, Leo," I said. "How's it going?"

"Not too bad. I told them to leave you alone tonight," he added, indicating Claudia and the others. "Figured you could use a break from the questions."

"Thanks," I said and meant it.

"Um." He hovered, looking for the first time like words were a struggle. "I just wanted to say, well, congratulations on beating the demon."

"Not dying's always a good thing," I said, smiling in spite of myself.

"Also, you look really pretty." He said this in a rush, his face reddening.

I looked at him, narrowing my eyes. "Are you drunk?"

He blinked. "No. Well, not yet, anyway."

"Um, thanks, then," I said, my cheeks warming. *Great response.*

"Well, I'll see you later, Ash." He'd gone before I could say anything more.

Cara came over. "Who was that guy?"

"No one. Just a friend from GameSoc. Don't you even *think* about it," I added, as much to Alex as to her. I could see Alex whispering to Sarah, wearing her most mischievous expression. I refused to think about what Leo had said. I didn't need this crap complicating my life again. *It's not worth making a fuss over.* Hell, demons were complicated enough.

I was going to miss the student life over the holidays, even though, by now, most of my depleted student loan was gone. I also desperately needed to do laundry, and my sleeping pattern had reversed, thanks to deadlines and late nights. But I'd miss living with my friends, the strange conversations in the early hours of the morning, and the even stranger sights I often saw on campus. After witnessing a group of people dressed as lions enter the on-campus shop to buy a crate of beer, I suspected life at home would seem unbearably dull by comparison.

But maybe I needed that. Maybe I needed two lives in order to keep both in perspective. I might have some power inside me that even I didn't understand, but, tonight, as I danced to Christmas hits with my friends, I could ignore it.

ABOUT THE AUTHOR

Emma is the New York Times and USA Today Bestselling author of the Changeling Chronicles urban fantasy series.

Emma spent her childhood creating imaginary worlds to compensate for a disappointingly average reality, so it was probably inevitable that she ended up writing fantasy novels. When she's not immersed in her own fictional universes, Emma can be found with her head in a book or wandering around the world in search of adventure.

Find out more about Emma's books at www.emmaladams.com.